D0357566

Received On:

SEP 18 2019

Ballard Branch

CHIMERICA

NO LONGER PROPERTY OF
SEATTLE PUBLIC LIBRARY

CHIMERICA

A Novel

ANITA FELICELLI

Copyright © 2019 Anita Felicelli
Published by WTAW Press
PO Box 2825
Santa Rosa, CA 49405
www.wtawpress.org
All rights reserved

This is a work of fiction. Names, characters, places, and incidents are either the product of the author's imagination or are used fictitiously.

Publications by WTAW Press—a not-for-profit literary press—are made possible by the assistance received from individual donors.

Designed by adam b. bohannon

Publisher's Cataloging-in-Publication Data
Names: Felicelli, Anita, author. | Pursell, Peg Alford, editor.
Title: Chimerica: a novel / Anita Felicelli ; edited by Peg Alford Pursell.
Description: Santa Rosa, CA: WTAW Press, 2019.
Identifiers: LCCN: 2019901323 | ISBN 978-1-732820-1-7 (pbk.) | 978-1-7329820-2-4 (ebook)
Subjects: LCSH Copyright —Arts —Fiction. | Artists —Legal status, laws, etc. —Fiction. | Lemurs —Fiction. | Rain forest animals —Madagascar —Fiction. | Human-animal relationships —Fiction. | Madagascar —Fiction. | Magic realism (Literature) | BISAC FICTION / Magical Realism
Classification: LCC PS3606 .E385 C55 2019 | DDC 813.6 —dc23

Manufactured in the United States of America and printed on acid-free paper.

for Illyria

PART I

ORIGINS

"For many people, when confronted with the
mysterious, the other, the instinct is to kill it. Then it
can be examined."

Joy Williams

CHAPTER I

When I woke the morning after Ross moved out, the house was silent. No sounds of our kids getting ready for school and racing up the stairs, no sounds of Ross banging pots and pans around the kitchen, and no whir of the coffee grinder before he brewed me a pot. My skull was throbbing and my tweed skirt was cutting into my stomach. Two bottles of wine into the night before, I'd forgotten to draw the crimson drapes or change out of my work clothes. My laptop rested next to me on the bed, still open to a website about Malagasy lemurs. From the bed, I could see the sunlit green hills of Oakland, irregularly studded with sprawling houses and eucalyptus trees and wood sorrel. It was the same panoramic view to which I always woke, the same splendor, but I was alone. Again. As a child I'd decided I would never let myself feel as lost as I'd felt after my mother killed herself, leaving me with a workaholic father and a younger sister to raise. And yet, here I was again, waking up alone in a large, too-quiet house.

Eager to throw myself into trial preparation for an all-consuming copyright lawsuit *Turner v. Eustachio*, I showered and slipped into other clothes. I blow-dried and flat ironed my unruly black curls. When I padded down the hall to the kitchen, I noticed that the painting my younger sister Julie had made for Ross was missing. No huge loss as far as I was concerned—it had been one of her weirder, more colorful canvases from a controversial graduate school exhibit entitled *The Existential Crisis of Brown Folk* that had left me speechless and mildly irritated—but now there was a darker-colored square where the painting had hung, where sunlight hadn't bleached the walls, a square that reminded me of a day more than ten years ago when the house painters had left and our young, excited family moved into our new home.

In the kitchen, I started the coffee maker. Roasted coffee was slowly dripping into my ceramic cup when the phone began beeping and vibrating. I glanced at the text message. It was from Nick Evers, my lover and a named partner at the firm where I worked: *We need to talk.*

My palms started sweating with anticipation. I texted back: *What's going on?* The last thing I wanted to do was talk, excavate what we meant to each other. Evers knew Ross had left—was he wanting to discuss moving forward? Part of me thought yes, he wants to move forward, I should move forward. This is new. This is someone who doesn't know how hard intimacy is for me—a chance for a fresh start. But the other part, the deeper part, suspected my kids blamed me for blowing up our lives together, and knowing they could be right, I wanted to burrow under the covers of my bed in shame. It was dangerous to speak out loud about this—about how I felt or how they felt. I was numb to being left, and I wanted to keep my emotions underground, wanted to avoid shining any sort of conversational spotlight on the subterranean things I knew were messy and irrational and overwhelming. Instead I told myself: nobody meets the right person at age nineteen, and at least you still have the comfort and thrill of work, and with Spencer's support, the possibility of the biggest win of your career so far.

It was a minute before Evers replied to my text. I stared at the phone willing it to beep again. I'd already poured a cup of coffee by the time it signaled a new text. *I'll tell you when you come over.* I took a swig of searing hot coffee, scalding my tongue, and waited another beat, in order to seem as mysterious and aloof as him. I texted back: *After work.*

The phone beeped. *We should talk now.*

Mechanically, I laid out bowls for Tara and Mike and Ross. I was pouring my cereal when I realized with a start it was just one for breakfast. One is the loneliest and all that. I stared into my empty bowl. Its pale porcelain surface reflected my face, and with no work to focus me, the rage I'd been trying to suppress—at myself, at Ross, at how little I'd been able to accomplish in my life so far—flashed through me. I shoved the bowl off the table. It cracked on the floor. There was nobody for whom I was performing, so I left the pieces and the cereal where they'd fallen to be swept up later. I grabbed a protein bar and my briefcase, and headed to the office, but in my rush to escape the gloomy, hollow silence of the home that had once meant so much, I forgot to text Evers back.

"Spencer wants to see you right away," our brunette receptionist said as I strolled into the lobby. Usually I started working immediately, and met Spencer for lunch or an evening drink to talk strategy. Wondering what he could possibly want to discuss first thing in the morning, I hurried down the hall. Inside one of the offices, I overheard two junior associates speaking in hushed tones. The quietness of their voices, their smug, speculative cadences, caught my attention, and I paused to listen before passing the open door.

"Shocking that Evers got fired."

"Can they do that to a partner?"

"It depends on what their agreement says . . ."

I continued toward Spencer's spacious corner office at a slower clip. I should have called Evers back. I turned right into Spencer's office. A short, broad-shouldered man in a crisp white dress shirt and pressed slacks, he was gazing out of the enormous plate-glass window that faced west onto the brick beacon of the Tribune Tower with its triangular cap, the pale mint-green of an oxidized penny.

Sunlight glinted off the gold type on the dark red leather of the codebooks and the glass faces of framed lithographs of California farmworkers and antique local maps that adorned the walls. On the front lip of his desk were hockey and football memorabilia and trinkets from grateful clients. One row behind these knick-knacks sat a photograph of Spencer on the ice in his skates, with an arm casually slung around the governor's shoulder. Both wore protective hockey gear: they were an alliance of two of the most powerful men in California, still in some ways a Wild West of reinvention, the last frontier of genius hucksters and lone gun-slingers. Pride swelled in me—I belonged to a premier firm run by someone powerful—this was a place where anyone could be the star she was meant to be, even if she didn't fit the script of what power looked like.

Before I could say anything, Spencer spun around, and started speaking. "Maya, eight years ago your father convinced me to bring you on board, to give you a chance. You know how much I respect your father's judgment—he's a hell of a lawyer. I thought, no problem. You'd last a year, then scurry out of this business as fast as you could, the way most of our associates do. But instead, you proved yourself as an associate." He sat down and smoothed back his silvery hair.

"Thank you."

Spencer crossed his arms and breathed deeply, as if he were holding back a violent barrage of words. His gentleness and re-straint were entirely uncharacteristic and unsettled me—this type of care from him was far worse than a slap. "Let me finish. To no one's surprise, you've proven to be a hard worker, one of our hard-est workers. I was ready to recommend to the other partners we promote you after this case."

I was ready . . . He had seen me as heir to his legacy, but why the past tense?

"Thank you. You've been more of a father to me than my own father has. I appreciate the confidence you've had in me, and I know I would never have come so far without your mentorship." Perhaps I hadn't been effusive enough about how grateful I was; perhaps I hadn't suggested what was true—that the work I did at his firm was necessary, that it was saving me, that it gave me a place to belong. Did he need to hear that?

"Before your ethics were called into question, I thought this trial would be your last step toward making partner." He rubbed his temples.

Ethics. A chill passed through me. They had never worried me because I saw Spencer had no qualms about them—he was sure of himself, and I'd trained myself to appear as tough as he was. But I knew I'd committed any number of very minor ethical violations, so many morally ambiguous courses of conduct shading over into just plain wrong—all violations I could argue my way out of, of course—that I couldn't really narrow down the possibilities enough to issue a plausible denial.

The room darkened; it was only the sun slipping behind a cloud, but my vocabulary contracted as the light pulled away. I could tell from Spencer's gentle demeanor, he was talking about something corrosive. The affair? Must be. He didn't even think I was worth the harsh criticism; he didn't even see me as his equal. In all the time I'd spent being mentored by him, I'd never realized he saw me as less than him.

He looked out the window, and in profile, all the fleshy grooves on his weathered cheeks looked more pronounced than usual. "I'm going to be blunt."

"Give it to me. I can take it."

"You don't have it."

"What?"

"The right temperament for this kind of work. As a trial lawyer, you need to be capable of navigating all sorts of slippery situations. You've been with us for years, but you're still not tough enough, not ethical enough, in the face of adversity."

Tough? That was perhaps the only thing I was. Who was I if

I wasn't tough? I didn't believe him; there had to be something specific I'd done. "There's no rule of professional conduct about affairs," I said.

It was the wrong thing to say. Spencer pounded the blotter on his desk, and the six silver balls of his perpetual motion machine started swaying, forcefully knocking against each other. "You shouldn't have gotten involved with him. You're married."

"We split up." He raised his eyebrows, so I added, "The other night."

"Adultery could have kept you from being admitted to the bar," he said sternly. "Evers hasn't shown good judgment either."

"Is that why he was fired?"

Spencer poured himself a double-malt Scotch from a crystal decanter on the sideboard. In all my time at the firm, I'd assumed this set-up was a bit of an affectation, but completely ignoring the morning hour, he took a long drink, nearly emptying the glass. He shook his head again, apparently to convey that what Evers and I had done was so wholly repugnant, so revolting he could not sully his lips by speaking of it. He fixed his stare on me.

I blushed, and crossed my legs. I wondered if he wanted me to reveal more of myself, if that would buy me his sympathy, but I didn't want to call attention to any of my mistakes, or how ashamed I was about Ross leaving me, so I said in desperation, "There's no ethical question here. Ross and I are separated. I just want to do my work. You know it's the only thing I care about. The only thing I'm any good at."

I thought he would understand because he worked so hard, too. His family probably wasn't any happier about the long hours than my family was. A family man with two children and four grand-children, he called his wife of thirty-five years an angel for putting up with him, but underneath that courteous facade, he truly believed he was pushing the giant rock of civilization up a hill all by himself, that it didn't matter that he had someone else—an ash blonde wife in expensive yoga wear—to run his laundry, clean the house, pay the bills, make investments, ensure his socks were matching on court days, entertain new clients and associates at dinner parties, and revolve her world around his.

"You know very well what I'm talking about goes back months. Long before this thing with Evers, long before you were separated. Maybe it's my fault. I threw you into a high profile case before you were ready." He rose and began pacing by the window. I tried to figure out what I'd done wrong before I slept with Evers, as dust motes swirled around in the stark light around Spencer. "Because your sister's such a successful artist, we figured you'd have more insight into the *Turner* case than our other associates would. But clearly we were wrong."

Rage, a burning hot red rage, rescued me in that moment. Just as humiliation threatened to engulf me, he compared me to my successful younger sister—as if I hadn't dealt with that comparison my whole life. How much shit could go down the drain at once? It couldn't all fit. Surely I was more valuable than any mistakes I'd made.

In eight years, I'd never questioned Spencer. He was the one person I counted on to help build me into the star I'd wanted to be since childhood. But as I listened to him attack me for reasons that seemed mostly unfair, something became clear: Spencer was just another person, yet another fallible human letting me down. Why had he thrown me into this lawsuit? I never planned to become an art lawyer, after all. I was fast on my way to becoming an expert in fraud—who can spot a con better than a con? But Spencer had thrown me under the bus with Evers's client, Brian Turner: a celebrity artist who felt absolutely entitled to a multimillion dollar verdict. Maybe I should have stroked Brian's ego even more, but I already needed to prove on a daily basis that I deserved to be there in spite of being a desi woman.

"What do you think I should have done?"

"You should've asked for help. You should've interrupted me and said, 'Hey Spencer, things are falling apart with Evers and this case.'" His stentorian voice was unyielding as a whip as he continued to discuss hypothetical ways in which I could have handled the situation better. But both of us knew none of his suggestions would have resulted in a better outcome—his senior associates were supposed to be able to figure out problems on their own. If we couldn't power through, we would be branded as weak and, if we were lucky, be kept on as career associates until we were shriveled, desiccated husks of our former selves.

Perhaps, knowing I'd done something wrong—even if the wrongs were small—I should have prostrated myself. But revealing that shame was my default position would have humiliated me even more than Spencer knowing of my transgressions in the first place.

"Where is this going?" I asked, feeling increasingly like prey— my fingertips were electric and I wanted to run, but I kept myself planted in my seat. *Sit still, sit still, conceal your emotions.* I started to perspire. Something dark was upon me.

Through the plate-glass window, seagulls were circling the sky like toy birds on a baby's mobile. A siren howled as a fire truck rattled by and turned the corner. I tried to think of a way to fix whatever had broken in my relationship with Spencer.

"I had our IT guy review your emails, Maya. You've left me with no choice. After thinking it through, I don't see a future for you here. We have to let you go."

He looked away. So that was why I'd had trouble checking my email at night during the last few days. I should have anticipated the surveillance, and immediately, I felt ashamed of letting my guard down, of trusting that the work would always be there, of allowing myself to imagine everything would be all right even if I stopped worrying and watching.

The numbness that had engulfed me since Ross said he was leaving began to thaw and transform into an unpleasant malaise, an aching in my chest. But, leaving Spencer's office, I refused to cry. I'd almost cried once before during my first year working for him, because I'd gotten overwhelmed and barely filed a motion in time, and I'd seen the baffled expression on his face—first the surprise of a father with two sons, and then the expectation in his eyes, the expectation that, as a woman, I was always already on the verge of cracking up. Remembering that horrible pitying expression had been enough to stop me from any consideration of crying.

A box of my effects had already been packed for me, and it perched precariously on the edge of the counter at the front desk. In a rare moment of kindness, the receptionist didn't look up to say goodbye. A gaggle of junior associates in starched shirts—including a desi associate whom I'd mentored, because I'd never met another desi trial attorney (although there were plenty of desi lawyers) and felt we were about as probable as unicorns—were standing around, chatting and laughing. I refused to look at them, refused to show any humility as they fell silent. I plastered a fake smile on my face and rode the elevator to the ground floor, waving at the elevator attendants as if I would see them tomorrow, though I was holding what was left of my life in a brown cardboard box.

I exited through the revolving doors into hot steam coming off a pretzel vendor's cart. The familiar stench of diesel fumes, bonfires, and garbage rose up from the glittering sidewalk. If you're wondering whether there will be a big reveal later in this story, about precisely what ethical infraction or moment of weakness got me fired, there won't be; every infraction was so trivial and ordinary to me when I was trying to come out on top, I quickly forgot about it. A litigation associate can't avoid running at least slightly afoul of ethics rules at some point. You learn this old chestnut in a mandatory ethics course in law school, but dismiss it, cocksure and certain you will be the special, noble exception, but as the law firm years in all their billable glory unfold, it proves true.

As I hurried toward my car, considering whether Brian Turner would be willing to help me get my job back, I wiped furiously at my eyes. I hoped that if someone saw me, they would assume I'd been blinded by light and steam.

Brian's studio was a warehouse on Pearmain off 98th Street near the Oakland Coliseum. I exited the freeway and drove down the wide, desolate gray road. There were few signs of life, only cacti growing behind iron fences in the midst of vast tan and white beds of stone. The morning sky was cloudless and deep blue. It made me uneasy—nothing like clouds to make it clear you are part of a real, imperfect world. I turned into a driveway with a silver roll-up door. Something sour and pungent, perhaps the smell of crack, was in the air. I stepped onto the concrete stoop and knocked on a steel entry door. An elderly black woman, with a paisley kerchief around her head, was pushing a grocery cart full of rattling cans down the street and mumbling to herself, and I rapped hard on the door a second time.

After a minute, Brian answered. "Hola, Maya," he said. I could tell from the hooded expression in his bright turquoise eyes, he wasn't happy to see me. He was rubbing his beard with a hand coated in blue paint, and his flannel shirt was covered in daubs of scarlet, silver, and yellow.

"Can I talk to you?"

"I'm in the middle of work," he said. "And I heard you were let go."

"Look, you know how much work I've done on your case and how close to trial we are." I shifted back on the step. "I'd love if you could tell Spencer that you'd like me to take the case to trial."

He sighed, and glanced over his shoulder. "No can do. Nothing against you, personally, but I need someone tough to do it."

"But I'm the one who's been working up your case," I pled. "I've reviewed every document about the mural myself. I prepared the experts and took all the depositions. I've spent almost no time with my family—look, I lost my family for your case.

Trust me, you want me to try it. Nobody else knows this case like I do."

"It's not about how much you know." His voice was condescending. "It's about who can win the thing, and when we were at that site visit, you just . . . didn't impress me."

We continued like that for a while. I told him everything I thought he wanted to hear about his mural: he had created something genius, the Eustachios who had painted over the lemur in the mural and mutilated his work didn't understand what he was trying to convey about man and nature, and we would bleed them or their insurers.

He nodded along, but then glanced over his shoulder again and sighed in exasperation. "Look, honey, you're wasting your time. Spencer Clark is the partner I want trying this case."

"He's taught me everything he knows," I said in desperation. "I have a great record of trial wins."

He nodded, as if to humor me. "I'm sure you do, hon. But my assistants are here and they're hourly. I'm in the middle of a huge project right now." I started to respond, but he slammed the door. I stood there for a minute, dumbfounded. I thought about knocking on the door again, but I wouldn't beg further. I climbed back into my car, defeated, and texted Evers: *OK, let's talk.*

I waited for a few minutes, watching the elderly woman with her cart turn into a dark speck in the distance. I hoped Evers would invite me over to his penthouse apartment downtown, but that text never came.

At home, I swept up the shards of broken bowl and cereal, opened a bottle of Pinot Noir, and texted Evers a few more times, still receiving radio silence. I tried him using my landline, which was a blocked number, to see whether he was screening my calls, but he didn't pick up. Every time I thought about things Spencer had said to me and wondered how I would explain getting fired to my family, my eyes watered again. I drank steadily through the lunch hour, the chocolate and oak notes turning into a sour taste, then a heavy dullness on my tongue. The silvery hot sunlight flooded the living room in a kind of mockery of my devastation.

Late that afternoon, I grabbed the notes from the lawsuit and a stack of mail from the past few days, and headed downstairs. I stumbled through the solarium past the hot tub, breathing in the smell of stale chlorine and champagne. The sliding door that led to the backyard had been left unlatched, a convenient entryway for a feral cat or raccoon.

Outside, I leaned back on a teak lawn chair and sipped my wine. I rifled through the envelopes in the mail, but there was nothing interesting until the postcard. On the front of the postcard were two indri. The same type of lemurs that Brian Turner had painted in his mural. After a moment, I realized they were in the same position and looked identical to a section of the mural, the section of the mural that Brian claimed had been defaced by the building owners. I flipped the postcard over. There was no credit to a photographer, nor any caption. It appeared to be a bespoke postcard, printed just for me. The lettering for my name, *Maya Ramesh*, resembled Evers's handwriting, or maybe I just wanted the postcard to be from him. While I was examining the card, all the tiny fuzzy hairs on the back of my neck rose.

I looked up. A giant lemur was leaning against the chain link fence. We'd installed the fence years ago to keep Tara and Mike from tumbling down the steep hillside, patterned in Queen Anne's lace and sour grass, which dropped a mile to Keller Avenue. During childhood, Tara was fond of climbing to the top of the fence and shouting to see whether an echo would bounce back from the valley. I thought for a moment that the lemur had escaped from the nearby zoo, but he was much too large, not quite the size of an adult human, but over four feet—far larger than your average housecat. My skin crawled—he was familiar and vulnerable as a child and yet so completely inhuman.

"Took you long enough to notice my existence," said the lemur.

His solemn amber eyes were unblinking. His intonation was musical, but it faded at the end of the phrase. He stretched his black furry arms wide and leaned back against the fence with his white furry belly exposed, like he wanted to sun himself. His black hairy hands—or were they paws?—were covered with mud and grass.

At first I couldn't speak. What I said next, I said to cover up my surprise, because, like most trial attorneys, I hated the sensation of being startled or made to reveal surprise. It feels like losing control, and if you don't have control, you're open to all sorts of hostile maneuvers and attacks. "How can I help you?"

"You need to help me get back to the island," he said, without blinking.

Even if he wasn't going to hurt me, his familiarity disturbed me. He was like something I'd seen in an obsolete encyclopedia of extinct creatures, a kind of archaic monstrosity.

I wondered what island he was talking about, but I said, "It might be better for both of us if I call Animal Services..."

"You kidding me? What, do I look like I belong in a cage somewhere? I finally get off that damned wall and now you want to lock me up. Do I seem unsafe? Unclean? No."

"You got off that wall?"

"Out of the frying pan, into the fire," he said.

"You're saying you're from the mural? Brian's mural?" My pulse slowed as I considered this—he didn't look painted. The white fur on his stomach was matted and dingy. His limbs were rounded, not all that different from my own arms, but covered in black silky shag, tipped in dust and grime. His ears were small and round. Even a few feet away, I could smell him—musk and resin and petrichor wafted from his fur. His eyes glowed pale topaz, his pupils were tiny. His shiny nose looked oddly large, given his human expression, almost as if he'd glued plastic to his face as part of an elaborate costume.

"Who else's? Of *course* I got myself off the mural. Who can be contained like that? That's why I got to get back home. This city—where do I begin? I can feel the smog and the cold getting under my fur and into my bones. Too many people and too much light—there's not enough leaves to eat, man."

"The mural isn't your home?"

"Suppose you were contained in a wall. One downtown where nobody really gets you, and people are pissing on you. Know what I mean? Madagasikara is home." He was waving his hands around with a harried and aggrieved set to his little mouth.

"You know, I bet Animal Services could give you a bed for the night."

"Bed? You think it's some kind of cush hotel you'd be sending me to? I don't want to stay in a glorified jail cell. And there's probably a waiting list," he said.

In that moment, I realized that Brian had no case—nobody had mutilated the mural: there had been no violation of the Visual Artists Rights Act or the California Art Preservation Act. "So if you got yourself off the wall, you weren't painted over. You just left. Of your own volition."

"Thanks for that recap. I lived it. Let's get back to the real issue. I have no money and airport security is gonna be hard to get by. So you gotta take me."

I gulped the last drops of wine, studying him and wondering how to get him in front of Spencer. "Hungry?"

"Starved," he said. With a certain amount of trepidation, I motioned for him to follow me inside. He loped forward on his hind legs and entered through the sliding glass door.

CHAPTER 2

That night I fed the lemur some dried-out chapatis and pu-
dalangai kootu, a snake gourd curry, which Ross had made the
weekend before he left, and settled him into my son Mike's room
downstairs by the hot tub. First, the lemur complained that I had
no salad greens. Next, he complained about what he deemed the
excessive squishiness of the bed. Finally, he chose a corner of the
carpeted floor, near a menagerie of stuffed animals and bobble-
head baseball player figurines, as his sleeping quarters. After I was
certain he was comfortable, I returned upstairs and locked my
bedroom door behind me.

I reviewed the research I'd put together on indri while developing Brian Turner's case. The research files were stored on my
laptop, and as I scrolled through them, I was unnerved by the
discrepancy between what the lemur's size actually was, and what
my research said it should be. I began searching online to refresh
my memory.

Indri, known as *babakoto* in Malagasy. A kind of lemur native to southeastern Madagascar. Their name either grew out of
endrina, the Malagasy word for animal, or *indry*, meaning *there
it is*. Indris were famously known for their songs, which broke
out involuntarily between seven a.m. and eleven a.m., but could
also arise during the day. They were a critically endangered species, threatened by habitat destruction. There was no note about
their size, but one website confirmed that even though the indri

were the largest type of lemur, they were fairly small. Even more strangely, in the online photographs, the indri's face was subtly different, its muzzle and snout protruding like a dog's face, not flat like a human face. The lemur downstairs had seemed childlike, especially in the earnest softness around his eyes, but perhaps I was remembering his face wrong.

In using search terms like "lemur" and "origins," I somehow stumbled onto a site about a lost continent called Lemuria, and sank deep into the rabbit hole of Tamil mythology. Tamil Nadu was the southernmost state in India, my parents' homeland, and where I was born.

The Lost Continent of Lemuria

Is California the lost continent of Lemuria? California was establishing its identity as the Golden State, a home for all utopias, when the notion that it had once been Lemuria seized imaginations. According to Adelia Taffinder, a 1908 occultist who lived in San Francisco, California is the center of Lemuria, a part of the continent that was never drowned, the place where human intelligence and civilization were born.

But Taffinder's wasn't the first reference to Lemuria. The lost continent was first mentioned in the West in 1864, when zoologist Philip Lutley Scalter wrote an essay entitled "The Mammals of Madagascar." The essay was prompted by the finding that the island of Madagascar didn't have the same terrestrial animals that Africa did. Lemur fossils could be found in India and Madagascar, but not Africa, and so he hypothesized that a lost continent had extended from Madagascar to America in the west and from Madagascar to India in the east. The lost continent had served as the bridge by which lemurs had migrated from India to Madagascar.

Faraway in Tamil Nadu, an origin story to counter oppression by the British and by North Indians was brewing. Tamil intellectuals and nationalists seized upon the notion of Lemuria as a homeland for the primeval ancestors of the Dravidians of South India, a homeland that justified resistance to Sanskritization. Ancient Tamil literary tradition spoke of a lost continent of Kumari Kandam. Might Scalter's Lemuria be Kumari Kandam, also known as Kumarinātu?

Some of the last bit was vaguely familiar, like a dream I'd once had, or a bedtime story. I resolved to ask my father about Kumari Kandam. As I had for many previous nights, I fell asleep fully dressed with the laptop open in front of me.

Early the next morning, I woke to the sound of the lemur singing downstairs, his baroque green roar saturating the air like an operatic aria or sunlight at dawn. Every once in a while he'd burst into another dissonant bit, until one bloodcurdling streak of sound led to the sound of glass, possibly a light bulb, shattering, and an exclamation of *oh shit*. After that, he kept going like he wasn't in a sleepy suburb, but at home in the rain forest, and soon a clowder of feral cats that our neighbor kept began yowling along, the way they did when they were in heat.

As abruptly as the lemur began, he stopped. Then the cats stopped. There was silence for about ten minutes, before he started all over again. I turned over and looked at my alarm clock: 7:36. Saturday. The kids would still be sleeping at the apartment Ross had rented in Berkeley. I wanted to be sleeping, too, and burrowed under the pillows.

Finally, the lemur stopped singing for a few moments, but this time the feral cats continued to howl. Covering my ears, I tiptoed into the hall, intending to go downstairs to check on him.

He was already perched at the top of the staircase, waiting for me. His face, turned up to watch me approach, was definitely flatter—more like a man's face—than the indri faces in the pictures. "You're up," he said. There was a thick desperation in his voice. "Finally! I've been needing to pee."

For a second, I wondered if the lemur was trying to make a break for it. Maybe he'd decided it wasn't worth the effort to get me to bring him home, or maybe he'd somehow seen inside my mind and knew I wanted to show him to Spencer. But it wasn't as if he were a prisoner in my house, so I opened the door, and he took a few steps beyond the red doormat. He lost control on the doorstep. The thick stream let off a wild and rotten smell, sulphurous like spoiled eggs, with a weird hint of leather.

"Wait! I wanted you to go by the side of the house," I said. Too late. Sighing, I picked up that morning's newspaper, askew on the concrete path.

He glanced at me. "Sorry, couldn't wait anymore." He hurried off to the side of the house to do the rest of his business. The puddle of his piss was spreading and seeping into the uneven concrete in front of the doormat, staining it a dark mud-gray. I ducked inside and grabbed a mop and bucket from under the bathroom sink. It took a few minutes to figure out where Ross had put the industrial soap. As I filled the bottom of the bucket with water, I realized I hadn't cleaned the house in years—Ross had almost always done it.

While I was pouring sudsy water onto the concrete, the lemur returned. "What does an indri eat for breakfast?" I asked.

He looked around the front yard. "Ate a ton of eucalyptus leaves coming up that hill. Nasty-tasting stuff, minty and a little toxic. And all the sour grass I could get my hands on. You don't have much by way of leaves." This was true. We grew yellow and pink rosebushes, hydrangeas, bright sweet peas, and a bed of alyssum out front, but very few trees. Down the street, one or two neighbors kept decorative birches, but it didn't seem like a good idea to let the lemur loose in their yard to feast. Further out, beyond the edge of the neighborhood, grew evergreens and more eucalyptuses, but I didn't want to send him to forage for fear he would disappear, and along with him, my chance to get my job back.

"How about pancakes?" I asked. I was pretty sure I'd seen a box of raspberry pancake mix in the cupboard, although it was so old it was probably stale.

"Think you can get us a flight out today? It's been real, but—"

"I have another idea."

"And? What is it?"

"I need to think it through before we talk about it."

We went inside. I unfolded the newspaper and started to make breakfast. As I waited to flip a pancake, one of the articles inside the paper caught my attention, and I read it out loud.

CELEBRITY ARTIST'S MURAL
DESTROYED BY LOCAL BUSINESS

Last November, Brian Turner was distraught to find that one of his early murals, painted on the side of an Oakland building, was destroyed. Turner has sued the building owners Peter and Paula Eustachio. He alleges they painted over one of the lemurs in the painting, thereby destroying the feel of the mural and infringing on his moral rights.

The mural illustrated the legend of how an endangered lemur, the indri, acquired its song. Spanning almost half the length of a football field, the painting has drawn tourists to Oakland for over a decade.

According to the allegations in Turner's civil suit, the couple painted over one of many indris with leaves, so that it appears the animal was never there. The missing lemur was the only one painted in a trompe l'oeil style, a painting technique that tricks the eye into perceiving a flat surface as a three-dimensional one.

Turner burst onto the art scene more than a decade ago with a series of twelve murals. All of them explore the relationship between man and nature.

Of the mural in question, Turner explained, "I was trying to bring

Madagascar to the Bay Area. This is something you can't do, you know, in real life, because indris can't survive just anywhere. They require a very specific environment. I went to Madagascar in the seventies, back before the indri became endangered. And I wanted this mural to reflect that vanished world as I knew it back then."

The mural was protected by the Visual Artists Rights Act of 1990 (VARA). VARA is a piece of copyright law that grants visual artists "moral rights" in the objects they produce, even if the physical copy no longer belongs to them.

Under VARA, artists have two moral rights: the right of attribution and that of integrity. The right of integrity, which is at issue in the lawsuit, allows an artist to claim damages for any intentional or grossly negligent destruction of a work of recognized stature. The lawsuit is also brought under the California Art Preservation Act (CAPA).

Whether the work is of recognized stature will be a critical issue in the upcoming trial. The Eustachios' attorney Katie Snow claims her expert will testify the work was "derivative and kitschy, juvenilia totally unrelated to Turner's innovative later works, and therefore, not protected by VARA."

Snow explained that the mural is worth at most a few thousand because it is one of Turner's earliest works and has little artistic merit. She also commented that this type of case has been litigated before and the plaintiffs were not successful.

"Nonsense! This was a work of recognized stature," said Turner's attorney, Maya Ramesh. "You can't find another like it anywhere. It's one of a kind. Worth at least a million dollars. Our expert will testify to that." She also said that in the case referenced by Snow, the sealant obliterated the painting altogether, making it an entirely different kind of case.

Turner v. Eustachio will go to trial next month.

"Put your foot in it, didn't you?" the lemur asked. He was sitting at the breakfast nook on a barstool, ripping off bits of pancake with his large black hands, and cramming them into his mouth.

I must have looked confused, because he explained, "You said the mural was one of a kind."

"It is one of a kind. There's not another mural like it out there. Turner's an ass, but he's a celebrity for a reason." Still hungover, I was irritated by the lemur's know-it-all tone. Although there was a short stack of fluffy pancakes in front of me, all I wanted was a glass of wine, or three.

The lemur opened his mouth as if he were about to say something, but he shrugged. "Think what you like. So, can we buy that plane ticket?"

"Do you know something you're not telling me?"

He shook his head, crumbs flying from his mouth onto the floor.

I continued, "I was thinking that first we could show you to my boss, or former boss, rather. He thinks Brian's case is good, but maybe when he sees you exist outside the mural—"

"Wait. Hold on now. This isn't show-and-tell. This isn't a kindergarten classroom. I came to you in confidence." The lemur put down his pancake.

"Look, if you want me to take you back, I need you to do this for me." My heart sank, as I realized that using him to prove my worth was going to be yet another challenge.

"Why?"

"Because I need Spencer to understand how on top of that case I was. How wrong Brian was about my ability. If he sees how dedicated I am to my career, maybe he'll change his mind about . . . letting me go."

"You were fired?"

"Let go."

The lemur stopped munching and fixed his bright eyes on me. "OK. *Let go*, you tell yourself that. I don't think bringing me around is going to change his mind about whatever made him think you were disposable in the first place."

"He doesn't *really* think I'm disposable," I protested. "We've been working together for eight, nine years. He's like a father figure to me. He's just trying to teach me a lesson, I think. About respecting his authority, respecting rules, that sort of thing."

"But are you a daughter figure to him?"

"I think so." I was taken aback. I'd never considered the possibility that our relationship wasn't reciprocal, that while I was receiving something emotional, something necessary to plug the black hole at my core, Spencer was simply getting a lackey, a yes-man. He had two sons, but after our conversation, who was to say he'd ever seen me as a daughter?

"And after that, you'll book the flight to Madagasikara?"

I promised, but the lemur looked skeptical.

My cell phone rang. I recognized the number as my father's. I wondered what Ross had revealed to him about our separation, but I didn't want to talk to him in order to find out. My father had a way of embarrassing me, reminding me just with his gruff voice that I was not who I told other people I was—that I was not a smooth, polished American, but something coarse, unfinished, less shiny—an awkward Tamil immigrant girl with spiral curls and a snub nose. The lemur stared at me expectantly as the phone rang again, so I picked it up, even though, had I been alone, I would have simply turned off the ringer and gone back to plotting my career comeback.

"Ross and the kids moved out?" my father asked. Without warning, he'd decided to become Of Counsel for his firm this year, continuing to consult instead of disappearing into retirement. Although his new position didn't give him as much time as retirement would have, it offered him a flexibility he'd never before possessed. He was flush with newfound time—time previously spent working on patent lawsuits that were infinitely more interesting than me or my sister Julie—and he took an active, eager interest in what I was doing, calling me every other afternoon.

"Yup."

The lemur was gingerly dipping his large black fingers in a pool of maple syrup and watching the delicate golden-brown strands thin and thin and eventually snap, collapsing on the plate, as he slowly lifted the syrup away. He was looking at me as he did this, and I took the cell phone to the living room, away from his prying gaze.

"Do you want to come down here and figure out what we're going to do?" he asked.

Trust my father to think my divorce was his problem, something he needed to work on fixing with me. It was like he thought he could make up for my entire childhood now, even though, in his opinion, he had nothing for which to atone. "I'm kind of in the middle of something."

"How are you doing?"

I debated whether I should answer honestly, but then a memory returned to me of a morning a few years after my mother died. We'd just moved to Palo Alto, where he was a stressed-out first year associate at a law firm, and I was carrying Julie, still a baby, around our house, clasping her against my shoulder like a rag doll. My father had asked me the same question, and I'd answered *fine* because I didn't know what else to say about the way my throat kept catching. I didn't know yet why my mother died—that she had chosen to die—I'd assumed she was sick with cancer or some other terrible disease.

My father clearly wanted to escape back to the office, but he was perceptibly angry at my affectless *fine*, wanting me to elaborate and share with him all the details about my new school, but I hadn't wanted to complain to him about the little rich girls—blond, brunette, and fiery-haired, none of them brown or black—who had Guess jeans and sparkly jelly bracelets and Cabbage Patch kids and Barbie dolls with prismatic dream houses. I knew he would tell me not to be a complainer, and so instead of voicing any of what bothered me, I decided to mimic their mannerisms and like the things they liked, and in so doing,

I'd gone on to win them over by the end of the year. In that moment with my father questioning me, however, I repeated only that I was fine. He lost his temper at my second *fine*, pounding the table in anger. Surely, the anger must have been displaced from work and my mother's suicide onto me, though I couldn't understand that then.

Over the years, like me, my father had trained away his Tamil accent and learned the correct pronunciation of confusing words like Yosemite, which, when we'd come to California, he'd first pronounced Yo-sah-might. Those were tiny changes, each of them barely noticeable on its own, but as these linguistic and perceptual changes accumulated over the years, he became an enormously different person. I recognized the difference, but somehow my reluctance to share anything with him, for fear of an unwanted judgment or a lost temper, remained the same. Where had he been most of my childhood?

"It'll be fine," I said in the measured voice I used with clients.

"Have you considered marriage counseling?" He and Ross were close—it was my father who taught Ross how to cook the Tamil thali dinner he cooked every Friday night: appalams, crispy dosas, spongy idlis, sambar, curd rice, and spicy-hot mint and coconut chutneys.

"Oh, I don't know. We talked about it, but we couldn't make up our minds. We'll see." I couldn't stand the way my father had suddenly joined us in the norms of the present, as if our whole lives he hadn't been stuck in the India of the 1970s, against grief therapy and counseling and the whole concept of mental health, and I wanted to change the subject as quickly as possible so he wouldn't see how angry I was. "Listen, did you used to tell me stories of a place called Lemuria?"

"Kumarinātu? The Tamil homeland? I might have. They used to teach us about that place in grade school. A happy utopia of Pandyan kings and queens and Tamil poetry. There was a government film about it in the eighties. Supposedly, there were none of the caste differences that have plagued Tamil Nadu in the post-colonial era."

"But it wasn't real, right?"

"I don't know. It appears in ancient Tamil texts. Kanyakumari, the beach of multicolored sands at the tip of South India where your mother and I had our honeymoon, is supposed to be a remnant of Kumari Kandam. And why not?"

"They have no scientific proof for it."

"There's that," he said. "But see, people have faith in science without knowing all that much about it, either. Science for non-scientists isn't verified; it's simply a story with more political clout. Listen, speaking of utopias, Maya, every marriage has problems. There's no perfect marriage."

"I know that." I paused, and then added, "Ross left me. It wasn't my decision."

"Did you tell him you wanted him to stay?"

I groaned. "I do not have time for this, Dad."

"You don't have time? Well, I know you're not working at Clark, Holmes, and Evers any more. I'm not sure what you're so busy doing. I thought you could come down here and we could go hiking at Foothill Park and chat a little bit about what you're planning to do next."

"How did you know that?"

There was a silence. I could hear my father breathing and moving about his study. There were small clunks against wood; he was adjusting the books on the shelves, perhaps. I thought he was conjuring some sort of cover story, but he admitted, "Spencer called me. He wanted to make sure I understood that letting you go wasn't something he did lightly."

"He had no business telling you about letting me go." I spoke too loudly and fury—not only that the termination was so real that Spencer had called my father, but also that my father felt sorry for me—made my voice shake. I hung up on him, before my voice betrayed how vulnerable I felt.

The lemur didn't ask questions about why I was so shaken as he helped me clean up the breakfast dishes. Afterward, he perched on the top of the velvet couch, examining Mike's large video game console. "How do you work this thing?" he asked, his dark nails clicking against the red circular button.

"Are you coming with me to see Spencer?" I took the console. He shrugged. "I'd rather not."

"I'll take you home after we see him. First, we have to work out your story. Why did you get off the wall?" I was determined to involve him in his own mythmaking.

"No idea." He began pressing buttons on the remote control at random and the giant flat-screen turned on with a gasping sound.

While he fussed with the remote control, I sat down on the couch with my laptop. I reread the article online and moved to the comments below it, hoping they would tell me something new, give me an idea about what to say to Spencer when I introduced him to the lemur. There had to be some way this creature would be useful in helping me get my job back.

Jandean: Ok, I know Katie Snow is a lawyer, and/but what an idiot. What doesn't she understand about this law? Of course you can't go destroying other people's art. Thank god for moral rights!

Elias: The point she's making is that there's precedent that you can whitewash a building and destroy "art" if it's not valuable. The mural, as far as I can tell, is just some kitschy mural from an earlier period of this artist's work. He's making a big deal out of it because the art is personally important to him, not because it's damaging his reputation.

Andy Rocha: Who you calling an idiot?

Angeldust: Dude, people be trippin!!! somebody bust this shit open.

William Vollheim: Those of us in the community who walked past this mural every day were quite attached to it. It's a shame that some small-minded grocery store owners tried to destroy this important landmark, a symbol of Oakland trying to grow and open itself up to outside influences. I've started a Tumblr over here: http://indrilove.tumblr.com so we can collect donations to restore the mural to its former glory. Peace.

Like_a_virgin: I'm new to Oakland, but from the photograph at the top of the article, I would very much like to see the mural. The removal of this lemur seems to me to be a symbol of the oppression those of us at the margins face every day. Yes, I understand Brian Turner is a major artist, but at the time he painted it, he was on the fringes of society.

Lucky Lozano: This is a pure travesty! The City of Oakland should set up an ordinance against the public defacement of art.

Allie G: Um, there's actually a federal law against this. It's called VARA. So Oakland doesn't need to enact a special rule. (Federal law trumps local law). Read the article again.

Lucky Lozano: Don't tell me to read the article again!! It's a well-known fact that the

federal government is broken. BROKEN!!! If we
want our cultural heritage to thrive we have
to improve it on a grassroots level. GO BEARS!

Angeldust: Chillax.

Allie G: Are you able to drive on the
highway? Do you use paper money? 'Nuff
said. Our federal government is working
just fine. I suggest you spend some
time learning about how things work
before writing an ignorant comment on a
newspaper article.

Violet Beauregard: Oh hai! So this mural isn't "art,"
you guys. It doesn't mean anything. Some lemurs
jumping around do not a masterpiece make. The
trompe l'oeil doesn't break the picture plane for
any artistic purpose, but just to suck the viewer in.
This is an early work by an artist who was still trying
to find his subject. It's more an exploration than a
work of "recognized stature." Nobody is going to
remember this work in a year, let alone 100 years.
They might as well paint over the whole thing right
now.

Yourdoppelganger: I love this mural. It connects
to the part of my soul that remembers what it was
like to be a prehistoric monkey, swinging through
the trees. I vote we bring this mural back. @
WilliamVollheim, thank you for creating a space
for us to generate the resources to reinstate an
important piece of our cultural landscape.

Violet Beauregard: Lemurs are not monkeys.
They are prosimian primates that developed
in isolation, after branching off from other
primates. They diversified on the island. But
indri! They've got no tangible relevance to
us as Americans—hence, my statement that
there's no artistic value to this mural. And
another thing: Turner's painted indri don't
have the longer snouts that indri actually
have. Something off in the rendering, I
reckon, so the faces look more human than
prosimian.

Sdfiuwj: You can order Junebee latex
condoms at this site! I love Junebee!

There were 312 posted comments and six pending. I was thinking about what Violet Beauregard noticed, what I noticed—that
the lemur's face was more human than it was supposed to be.
What made a face human anyway? It wasn't just the flatness of
his countenance, not exactly, nor the shortness of his snout, but a
glimmering, knowing quality just behind the eyes.

As I continued to read the comments, the lemur was tapping
the console, trying to figure out how Mike's race car game worked.
He was driving a pea-green Camaro, and he kept tilting the knob
to the right, crashing into a concrete wall, over and over again,
sputtering and groaning as he tried to accelerate away. In spite
of its repeated collisions, the car remained miraculously bright,
perfectly intact. "Gimme a minute," he said when I suggested we
eat lunch. "I'm just getting the hang of this."

Later that afternoon while the lemur, overstimulated by video games, was napping on the couch, Ross phoned. "Your dad

just called and told me what happened with Spencer." His voice sounded concerned. "I wanted to make sure you were all right."

"Everything's grand," I said brightly, trying to mask my irritation that my father and husband were banding together to talk about me. The only thought that was worse than their camaraderie was that they could be embarrassed together on my behalf. "Nobody knows that case like I do. I'm going to have my job back in no time."

Ross's voice changed, sharpened. "Enough," he said. "Let it go. Let those people go. That law firm changed you. I barely recognize who you've become."

"You don't 'recognize' me? Give me a break. It's not like I mutated or something." I couldn't help but snicker at the drama, the didacticism in his voice. The lemur's white chest was rising and falling with his deep breaths. He was gripping the video game console as he slept and the muscles in his flattish prosimian face had gone slack. I could see his large eyeballs quivering beneath his slightly greasy black eyelids.

After a moment, Ross said, "You may as well have." I could hear his shoes clicking against linoleum.

"You don't like the firm because it empowered me."

"It corrupted you." He stopped pacing, and there was silence, only the subdued sound of his breath. "There's a difference."

"Is that all you wanted to say? I have a lot of other things to do." I strolled through the kitchen and living room, looking around for an excuse to hang up, but we'd done the dishes and the furniture appeared orderly. The lemur was making drowsy guttural sounds on the couch. He rolled over on the cushions, and a slat of sunshine fell across his stomach.

"Let me give the phone to Mike," he said. I was expecting more resistance, more discussion from my husband, a man who could opine in a more convoluted sentence structure than any of the paper-pushing lawyers I knew, but to my surprise, Ross didn't elaborate on power and corruption.

A whimper was lodged at the back of Mike's voice when he said hello, and I wished Ross hadn't handed the phone to him. I felt tremendously guilty.

"What's wrong, kiddo?" I asked.

"I miss you. Are you coming over? Dad says you can if you want to."

The lemur was still sound asleep on the couch. "I can come by," I said. "I'm just laying low here. Is everything all right?"

"I guess so . . . The apartment doesn't smell good. It smells like old people here."

"All apartments smell like that at first. It gets better. After a while you won't notice the smell."

"That's what I'm afraid of."

"Do you need me to bring you anything, to make the apartment more comfortable?"

"My notebooks would be good," he said. He was writing an epic novel about baseball and revolution in a made-up country in red, dog-eared spiral-bound notebooks. There were about twenty notebooks, and they all looked the same, except for the number he'd written in black Sharpie on their covers. He never offered to let me read any of his novel, but everywhere he went, the latest installment of his epic accompanied him. I was surprised he'd abandoned his notebooks when Ross moved him out. Perhaps after the passing of a day in the new apartment it was hitting him that he might be gone for quite some time.

After I hung up, I set a bottle of water next to the lemur and went downstairs to hunt for the notebooks. Mike's room smelled wild, musky after only one night of the lemur's presence. I tried not to breathe in the pungent odor while I looked in the closet and under the bed, eventually locating the notebooks in a more obvious location, the drawers of the desk. I carried them upstairs without pausing at the door to Tara's room.

In the kitchen, I glanced again at my phone, wondering why Evers hadn't returned my texts or phone calls. Had Spencer turned him against me, somehow? Then again, fortified with years of pay as a partner at a prestigious boutique firm and an inheritance, Evers didn't need me. It occurred to me that he had just been slumming it with me. I mean, who was I, really? Not the star I'd hoped to be as a child, but a middle-aged Indian woman, her best years wasted and in the rearview mirror.

I closed the front door of the house quietly, so as not to wake the lemur. Outside, the cool clean air and the familiar sweet scent of star jasmine bathed my face. I set the notebooks on the floorboard of the passenger side, started the car, and backed out of the driveway. As I rounded the wide green hillside, I saw the moody twilight of the bay had not yet extinguished the blazing red sun, and it was like driving into a fresh wound.

CHAPTER 3

The apartment where Ross and the kids moved was near Lake Merritt, but on the other side of the water from the mural. As I zoomed through the congested gray streets, searching for parking, I wondered how uncomfortable dinner with my family would be. I was thinking about how we used to eat at Spencer's mansion in the hills. We dined on exotic, ostentatious dinners: baked goat cheese salads heaped with caviar, shark fin soup or green sea turtle soup, sushi made from Chinook salmon and bluefin tuna, kangaroo steaks brushed with olive oil, individual saucers of baked Alaska, delicate ice creams flavored with noyaux, served with Sauternes. Ross and Spencer smoked cigars and Spencer quizzed Ross about his work at Lawrence Livermore Lab openly, as if he assumed the prohibition against Ross giving out classified information couldn't possibly apply to him. My kids lounged cross-legged on an elaborate Kashani carpet in the Clark family room, playing on a Wii Spencer had bought for his grandchildren's frequent visits.

The dinners were beautiful on the surface, but they were seething with tension—I always wondered if other senior associates had been invited more frequently or treated to better dinners than my family was. Ross and the kids hated going because they felt shabby and out of place and hated the food.

The funny thing was, between Ross, Tara, and Mike, my origins were, by any measure, the most humble—and yet a part of me loved these dinners, at least the first few majestic moments of them. I was born in a tiny, spare doctor's office in Madurai, a hot, tropical, chaotic city in the deep south of India, filled to bursting with ornate candy-colored temples, statues of Hindu gods and goddesses on every corner, to parents from different castes, different worlds. I'd grown up without my mother, and without any extended family around, and because of my dark Dravidian features, I was never considered a beauty—either among my own relatives or by most of the white Americans around me. And yet I was seated at a dinner like this, invited by one of the most quietly powerful people in the state of California, solely because I'd gained admittance to a profession invented by the landed gentry of the colonial empire. Wasn't the almost-morbid nouveau riche decadence of those dinners what everyone in America aspires to?

The euphoria never lasted. I left every dinner acutely aware that my position at the firm was conditional on reining in my perspective, on making sure that a careful pleasant facade covered up all my cracks. As I located a parking spot and maneuvered into it, I told myself the dinner at Ross's apartment could not be filled with any more tension than those dinners.

While standing outside the brick facade of the apartment building about to press the buzzer, I heard a noise and turned. A middle-aged woman with dark brown skin, wearing a black trench coat and holding the same shiny gray hobo bag as mine, was crossing the street and striding toward me in high-heeled boots. Unlike me, she wore her hair curly and wild (I used a flat iron every morning), but as she glanced up when she passed under a lamp, the resemblance was unmistakable. She was not only wearing my hair the way I had when I was younger, but she was also wearing my face—my small snub nose, my thick lips with a brick-colored stain on them. I blinked in confusion. Was I seeing things? They say everyone has a doppelganger, but I'd never seen anyone in the Bay Area that possessed my features and mannerisms and dressed the way I once had. She walked with a swagger, and she approached, coming closer and closer and closer. My heart started to seize. I was dizzy with the thought that I was hallucinating, that I was going to meet myself. I pressed the buzzer.

She turned right at the shadowy intersection where a red Converse sneaker hung on a telephone wire overhead, quivering in the wind, and my panic disappeared. A sharp buzz interrupted my confusion. I pushed open the door and climbed a very short flight of stairs to the first floor of the building. A fluorescent bulb cast a dim light over the hallway.

The door of Ross's apartment was ajar, and inside the lights were warm and golden. Mike barreled out to hug me before I could enter. Ross hung back, his hands hidden in his jeans pockets. He was a short, handsome white man with a narrow face, and some ethnically ambiguous features (he'd been adopted by the Wickliffes, Midwestern farmers, and we didn't know his ancestry). He'd always been lanky, but he looked more gaunt than usual. He gave me a quick hug; I breathed in his warm laundry smell and felt his bones just underneath the surface of his skin, pressing my flesh. It unnerved me.

The living room carpet was vomit beige, and the stench that Mike complained about proved to be the smell of fresh paint and mildew. It was obscured in the kitchen by the smell of asafetida, cumin, and mustard seeds. On a crappy folding table in the middle of the room sat a plate of freshly made chapatis, spinach kootu, dal, and curd rice. Tara was nowhere to be seen. The glossy green of ivy leaves growing on the building's facade curled up at the edges of the kitchen windowsill, and beyond the open window, the street was wide and open and empty. Out there, my doppelganger was walking outside in the smoky twilight, her high heels clicking against the pavement.

"Tara, dinnertime," Mike shouted. He ran down the hallway, presumably to fetch her.

I looked at Ross. His eyes were unsettlingly sad, more foggy than gray. Mysterious, bottomless. He'd dressed up in slacks for dinner and his salt-and-pepper hair was slicked back, impenetrable with mousse. Until I saw him in the new apartment, I'd been sure he was coming back. We'd talked about this split as being temporary. Now I realized it could be real, and I felt like my heart was being slowly, painfully extricated from the warm machinery of the family I'd helped to create.

Before I could sink into a funk, into my cloud of loss, Tara entered. She was wearing tartan Dickies and a hot pink halter-top with no bra—not an outfit I would have approved for a sixteen-year-old girl. Her brown hair was yanked back in two severe topknots on either side of her head, like the nubs of a young buck's antlers growing in. She barely acknowledged me, which was irritating, but I tried to cover it up with a falsely cheerful *hello, daughter!* to which she didn't reply.

We all sat down around the table like dolls in a dollhouse, stiff and plastic in front of painted aluminum food. We took chapatis and kootu, and Ross started talking.

"Let's get the obvious out of the way first," he said. "As you kids know, we're giving ourselves a break to figure out what we want to do and what comes next, but that doesn't mean we won't see each other from time to time."

Tara and Mike looked at each other. "Mom, do you want this break?" my son asked. He bit his lip. It was a habit he got from me, a habit I was unable to break, even after seeing myself do it over and over on the videotape of my moot court oral arguments in law school.

"Why do you guys care what *she* wants?" Tara asked. She slammed her glass of water on the table. "This is her fault, right?"

Everyone stopped eating, except for me, and I continued in order to pretend that everything was normal, and to numb myself to the unpleasant realization that everything was different. "It's nobody's fault," Ross said without hesitation, before launching into a speech about love, marriage, and separation. I shot him a grateful look, but he was focused on Tara.

Although I'd known since she was a little girl they were naturally closer than she and I were—closer in temperament, in talents, in senses of humor—it hurt to see the strength of their bond compared to the weakness of ours. I was her mother from the moment she was born, and I was certain that finally I would have somebody on my side in my family. All the dark, tumultuous sorrows of my childhood faded into a distant memory. The immediate aftermath of childbirth had been awash in anxiety, but the misery faded as time went by, and Tara's childhood, by and large, had been a happy one, full of empathic moments when I remembered myself as I once was—my first taste of ice cream and the milky splotches of the galaxies while camping and the new feeling of stepping in deep snow during our first winter in America—but to see Tara now, no stranger would have assumed we had any sort of connection—she was pale, I was dark, her gestures were miniature, mine were expansive. She was born in one of the wealthiest spots in the world, Silicon Valley. I'd been born in the Third World. As a teenager, she ignored or disdained me as if I had a vile stink. I would have done anything to get back to who I was supposed to be—the person I could have been if my mother hadn't died—but she would have done anything to get away from me.

Ross concluded his speech. "Misunderstandings can happen between two people over the course of years, and it's hard to sort out without some space, some distance. Without the clarity of time."

Sometimes Ross's style of speech made me a little crazy. Why did he have to use one hundred words, where one would have done? Why did he have to make such a big deal out of minor mundane missteps? Why did everything turn into a metaphysical or spiritual question? But other times, like that moment, when my daughter shot me an icy death glare, his style of speech reminded me that I loved him and that he protected me from the worst, most meretricious and greedy parts of myself. So I simply said, "Yes, I want this, too, Mike. We'll all gain some perspective this way."

"Why hasn't anyone asked me my perspective?" Tara said. "If you ask me, there's no need to prolong the torture. Doug told me what this separation means." Doug was a skater punk she was seeing with Ross's permission, and my silence. With a heavy chain hanging from his pocket and woolly brown sideburns, Doug reminded me of the boys I'd dated before Ross, slugabeds who made me feel like nothing but meat, lucky to receive their attention, who spoke to me in short, clipped sentences like they were conserving all their words—words that, back then, I was sure they had—to spend on someone better.

Years later, I realized they truly did lack words—they grew up to be mechanics, overly aggressive coaches of kids' sport teams, mousy engineers, stoic carpenters, and deadbeat dads—and my abundance of words had been intimidating, appealing, and annoying all at once, but that wasn't what I knew as a girl, and I was pretty sure the experience of dating those silent boys deformed me. It was all I could do not to outright forbid Tara from dating him.

Ross continued to speak. "How's that saying go? Every family is depressing in its own way? Doug doesn't really know your mother or me."

"But he's already gone through this —"

"None of us know what's going to happen in the future. Our hope is that we're going to work this out. I only have a six-month lease on this place."

"I'm not working right now, so you can stay with me at various points during the week," I said, eating another spoonful of curd rice, the mustard seeds in the yogurt reassuring in their familiarity against the backdrop of this ugly, cheap apartment. "Well, except I've got a new witness and a way to get my job back—"

"Your job? Big surprise. Why don't you run off with your boyfriend and leave us alone?" Tara raised an eyebrow.

"Tara!" Mike said.

"What are you talking about?" I didn't know what else to say. I could feel my cheeks getting hot.

"I know about you, Mom," Tara said, still not looking at me. I tried to remain composed. How did she know? I was so careful. Ross's expression didn't change; he didn't believe her. Slowly I exhaled.

"I don't know what you're talking about."

"Ugh. Anyway, I'm not staying with you," Tara said, as she shoveled her rice pilaf from one end of the plate to the other. "I don't want to hear your shrill voice morning, noon, and night."

"Tara, don't talk to your mother that way," Ross said. His fork hung suspended over the plate.

Tara continued to rant. She made a sound somewhere between a whine and a screech. "It's like fingernails on a chalkboard. . ." I blocked her out. She'd only inadvertently stumbled on the truth, she didn't know for sure about Evers. She was just testing me. But shrill?

"I don't see why not. She's barely with us when she's with us, anyway," Tara said.

"That's not true. I'm here right now."

She turned to Ross. "All she cares about is work. Isn't that why you left? Isn't that why we're living with you, not Mom?"

"No," I said. "We can talk about whatever's bothering you. I want to talk about your lives. Yours and Mike's."

"Stop it, stop it!" Mike screamed. "You're going to make her go away!" He put down his fork and began bawling, his nose running and eyes turning red.

"It doesn't matter what I say. She'll leave on her own. She always does exactly what she wants." Tara's chair fell over. She stood and sprinted down the hall.

Ross glared at me like he expected me to go after her, but I knew that pursuing her would only occasion more biting criticism, and after the conversation with Spencer, I couldn't stomach it.

The new apartment looked like an alternative life, a humble life we were supposed to have had, but didn't, because I pushed myself to work and I pushed us to buy the bigger house, the better television, the luxury car. But I didn't want a small *nothing* life, I reminded myself. I didn't want only an itty-bitty piece of the emotional and material bonanza that everyone else we knew in the Bay Area seemed to have. I wanted everything. Didn't everyone?

After Tara's outburst, the dinner quickly ended, and I was soon alone with my thoughts, speeding home on Highway 13 through the evergreens and eucalyptuses. I refused to think about the pain Mike felt, and focused instead on what needed to be done to prepare the lemur for the meeting with Spencer. I exited the freeway, crossed the overpass, cut back over the freeway, zoomed up Keller Avenue with my foot on the accelerator and sped around the curves at the top of the hill.

When I unlocked the front door, the lights were out and the house was dark. I crept downstairs. The door to Mike's room was closed. I opened the door a crack and peered inside, assuming I'd find the lemur sleeping. But he was nocturnal. He lounged in the middle of the beige carpet with my laptop straddling his lower limbs, typing—hunting and pecking—with a frantic, manic energy.

"What are you doing?" I asked.

"Just checking out the interwebs," he said, without looking up. "I searched your name to see what your reputation as a lawyer is."

"You thought an internet search would tell you whether I could be trusted?" I came into the room and peered over his shoulder.

"If it can't, what good is it?" He pointed at the screen.

The lemur had typed in "Mya Ramesh," but the search engine autocorrected to my name. Surprisingly, the first entry in the lemur's search results wasn't my law firm biography or anything about the mural case, but a blog post on a popular cooking blog, crediting a cupcake recipe to somebody named "Maya Ramesh," a resident of Palo Alto who was married with two children. I hunkered down next to the lemur. He sighed as I took the laptop from him, and scrolled through the results.

The next few pages of entries pointed back to me, an attorney in Oakland, and I breathed a sigh of relief. But when I clicked on the image search, the first was a photograph of me that I had never seen before. Me with blowsy, curly hair, standing by the green-hearted ocean with massive waves cresting behind. For a second, I thought the photo was a snapshot from when I was younger, so closely did my face match the woman's, but I would never turn my back to the ocean. I'd been in Chennai with Tara and Ross just before Mike was born when the tsunami in the Indian Ocean hit Marina Beach near my uncle's house, and I never forgot the unpredictable ferocity of the ocean. You never know when a wave, even a wave smaller than a tsunami, will claim you for its own, drag you flailing into its depths; the name *Pacific* is a deception.

My doppelganger, however, had no such qualms. She looked jubilant, cocky, standing there on the sand, one ankle tucked behind the other, and her gauzy, pale-pink dress blowing up around her knees, and when I clicked, the photo that was ostensibly a picture of me, linked back to the Facebook wedding album of somebody I didn't know.

"What's so interesting about that shot?" asked the lemur, pointing at my double. "Pleasant memory?"

"It's not me," I said.

The lemur pressed his nose up against the screen and then drew back slowly, studying the tiny details of the figure. "Sure, it is."

"No, it isn't, but it could be this woman I saw earlier today when I went to see the kids. Very strange . . . She lives in my hometown, has my name, looks like me, and has the same number of kids, but she's not me. What do you make of that?"

"Maybe you just don't remember taking the photograph," the lemur said.

"I haven't worn my hair naturally in public—all curly and messy like that—since I was nineteen years old and thirty pounds lighter." A pungent, musky odor was floating off the carpet, tussling the curtains, stinking up Mike's room. "Get some sleep," I told the lemur as I stood, but he shrugged, crossing his arms over his chest.

"Nighttime is my jam."

"I'm taking this." I picked up the laptop. "If you really can't sleep, you can watch television upstairs, if you want."

He grumbled and trudged to the nest of blankets in the corner. "There's something about her," he said, as he pulled the covers over his body. "She's more vivid than you are. I guess I should have known it wasn't you, but I just assumed it was you, before you split with your husband."

"Gee, thanks." I left the room and walked into the hall.

Before I pulled the door shut behind me, I heard him call after me, "More vivid the way an original would be."

CHAPTER 4

Upstairs in my bedroom, I undressed and swilled two more glasses of wine, hoping to drink myself to sleep, but no such luck. I tossed back and forth, frustrated, trying to forget about dinner. Usually through the window I could see a scattering of far-flung stars like Lite Brites pegged into a dark paper sky, but tonight, inexplicably, the stars weren't there for me to count. I've never been a good sleeper.

I put on my glasses and started surfing the internet: *lemur, indri, giant lemur, Madagascar lemur, lemur too big to be believed.* Most of the websites spewed the same facts: endangered, strange song, black and white. But a blog post on the Society of Crypto-zoology site caught my eye.

Do Giant Lemurs Exist?

Giant lemurs are supposedly extinct. Why "supposedly"? Because we actually don't know whether they became extinct, or what caused their extinction—if in fact they are extinct.

Many experts believe lemurs arrived in Madagascar forty-five-million years ago on rafts made of vegetation. They had few if any predators and evolved in isolation, becoming extremely unique and diverse. Some of them were giant lemurs. We don't know why the larger lemurs wouldn't have survived into the present alongside their smaller kin, although it's possible the coming of humans to Madagascar is at least partially to blame.

Back in 1658, the French explorer Admiral Étienne de Flacourt reported sightings of a huge animal he called the "tratratratra," a kind of Bigfoot or Sasquatch as big as a calf—in the dense wilds of Madagascar's interior forests. He described it as having a humanoid face, frizzy hair and ears like a man's. What he'd seen terrified native Malagasy people, but there was no further investigation.

Several centuries after the tratratratra sighting, paleontologists began unearthing Malagasy fossils that seem to be the giant lemurs'. Although scientists had believed that giant lemurs went extinct during the Pleistocene Era, the bones showed they had died much more recently, within the past few hundred years.

When the bones were reconstructed, the animals looked like the tratratratra seen by de Flacourt. Cryptozoologist Dr. Bernard Heuvelmans proposed in 1958 that the mystery creature was actually a sloth lemur. However, the mystery creature's face had a snout and was quite different than the tratratratra's flattened face. As an alternative, Dr. Heuvelmans suggested it could be the large extinct lemur *Hadropithecus*, which is known to have existed up to one thousand years ago. To this day, there's no definitive answer.

If scientists were wrong about the timing of extinction before, who's to say they're not wrong about all of it—including whether the giant lemur is extinct at all?

At the Society of Cryptozoology, we believe that

deep in the heart of the forest, giant lemurs exist. Were they hunted into near extinction? Are they hiding from mankind? How many are there? We aren't sure, but it seems likely that they have become adept over centuries at keeping out of the way of humans, and we can only see them by taking extreme measures.

Recently, there have been a few sightings of a cryptid that appears to be a giant lemur, specifically a close relative of the sacred indri, but larger. The sightings warrant further investigation. Nick Evers, an attorney from California with a long-standing passionate interest in giant lemurs, told us that he has organized a collective based outside Perinet to study this particular creature and that his partner, a photographer from his hometown, has tallied more than thirty sightings of these cryptids over the past decade.

He acknowledges that some of the sightings were no more than glimpses, but produced four photographs for us of a giant lemur that looks like both an indri and a man. They do not appear to be doctored photographs. We will report more as we learn more.

Nick Evers, an attorney from California. The blog post was referring to Evers, my Evers, who drank Scotch and ate popcorn each evening in the office, and whose kisses were butterscotch and smoke, a soft, definite pinprick of light at the end of something I hadn't even realized was a tunnel, a burning and a quenching, all at once. Evers, the Francophile art collector I had known for eight years, but had never known to have a passionate interest in giant lemurs, long-standing or otherwise.

I set the laptop on the bedspread next to me and lay there looking at my cell phone, willing it to ring, even though it was the middle of the night. Why hadn't Evers gotten back to me? What other secret life had he been living? Had I known him at all? A collective—of lemur hunters? Could it be the collective who had sent me the postcard?

I opened the drawer in the nightstand and studied the postcard I'd received the day the lemur arrived. The lemurs in the picture looked like they had shifted positions. One was still high in the tree, while the other had moved down. I thought about the last time I'd seen Evers. Over the last week, he'd been out of the office, supposedly at depositions for one of his other cases, so the last day I actually saw him was more than a week before.

It was another sultry summer day and we'd gone to his house to fuck, like we often did on Friday afternoons, sticky and grappling with each under the mind-numbing roar of a stainless steel ceiling fan in his bedroom. Afterward, a mood came over me. I put on his shoes and placing my hands on my hips, I staggered around pretending to be him at trial, gesturing dramatically at a jury the way he did. It was a kind of mockery, but I was merely joking around. Nevertheless, he looked peeved. To turn the mood around again, I suggested getting sorbet in Temescal, a neighborhood far enough away that we were unlikely to run into anyone from work. It was a scorching hot day. He ordered a sorbet sandwich—pistachio with cardamom cookies—and I ordered a scoop of lime mint, which tasted like a mojito. When I kissed him out on the street afterward, his short tongue tasted nutty and creamy.

We were walking back to his Jaguar when he said, abruptly, "Can you take the train home?" He slipped his Kangol over his blonde hair. The cap made him look older, like a daguerreotype of his usual self.

"What? Why?"

"I can't really explain. You have to trust me that it's better this way."

"What are you talking about?" I licked my sorbet, taking pleasure in its coldness.

He gazed at his car like he was dying to jump in and drive away without saying another word to me. "Remember what we talked about. Escape? It's all about the escape."

We'd previously had conversations about starting over. These were more about our mutual longing for a blank slate than romantic feelings for each other. We both wanted freedom from the choices we'd already made. He prompted me, "Madagascar, remember?"

A glossy green smear of pistachio remained at the corner of his lip. I wiped it off, feeling ridiculous, as if he were my son and not my lover. In those earlier conversations, he could have named any place. He could have said Seychelles or Timbuktu, and it would have been equally quixotic. Instead we talked about starting over in Madagascar. Maybe the mural had gone to his head.

We all have a Madagascar, right? A primeval place that seems so far away, so remote, so vibrant, it simply must be better than our own banal, disenchanted, cookie-cutter lives. A place where our imaginations take root, a place that takes root in our imaginations like an earworm, playing over and over in lush detail, until it becomes bizarrely more real than the things around us, and more beloved. Loved into existence like the Velveteen Rabbit. A place that is real to its own population, but not to us, and we like it that way. Or am I the only one?

But lying was my default mode, and so in that moment, I told Evers, "Of course, I remember. Someday, we'll run off, we'll start a vanilla farm."

I didn't mean it. But everyone needs a fantasy place. Based on what my father had told me about my mother (very little), I imagined America was that place for her. She listened to the Beatles, the Mamas and the Papas, the Carpenters, all of this foreign music possessing her imagination, propelling her toward America, even though the real America was nothing like her fantasy, and actually living there without any of her family, with my workaholic father, lonely and starting completely from scratch because her family had disapproved of the marriage—it could only bring disappointment.

I didn't articulate any of my thoughts to Evers for fear of breaking the connection. Our mutual fantasy of a life after the law firm would have been revealed to be nothing more than a cheap carnival attraction if I said our escape would never happen, that I wasn't even sure that I wanted to get away from the firm the way he did, or that escapes were always better imagined than realized.

"Why someday?" he said, smiling. Before getting into his Jaguar, he kissed me, his eyes tender. His expression surprised me, because I'd always told myself that this was merely an affair, a short-term escape for me. In that moment, however, I decided that it must be something more for him. He saluted me and sped off.

Returning the indri postcard back to the drawer of my nightstand, I registered the time on the clock: two a.m. There was something fishy about time and sleep, especially after I'd been drinking. In the moments before sleep came, time adopted a kind of doubleness, the fictional quality of simply being a memory of falling asleep the night before, though actually the memory was still being made. If I were really falling asleep while looking at the clock, I wouldn't remember the moment consciously, the way I later did, since you can't remember the few moments before sleeping. Instead I'd be in a limbo between sleep and reality.

I must have passed out because the next thing I knew, I heard the lemur singing, the cats yowling, the pattering of an unusual summer rain, and the hissing of the automatic sprinklers as a timer brought them to life. Sunshine, cold and bluish through a faint drizzle, lit up the room. Managing to wobble onto my feet despite a headache that bisected my brain and the sensation I was dry-mouthed, underwater, and lost, I slipped outside to turn off the sprinklers.

Taking care of the house, making sure the hilly wilderness didn't creep too far inside, had been Ross's job. I hunted around on my hands and knees, searching the side of the house for the box, getting sopping wet and cold in the mud, crawling among the marigolds, juniper bushes, and the Brandywine tomato plants with their plump, split tomatoes rotting off the vines. Lichen crept up the taupe siding where bits of white root grew above ground, and fat worms gasped and writhed through the clotted dirt. Snails inched forward onto the concrete, their slime crisscrossing in iridescent strings.

Eventually I located the box and turned everything off. A bedraggled mess, I sprinted through the fat raindrops. Inside, the lemur was still singing, but now he was sitting at the kitchen table, looking at my laptop again. I wiped myself off with a tea towel and plunked down next to him. "We need to work on what we're going to tell Spencer," I said.

"Not sure what good that will do." The lemur took his bowl to the sink and shook his head at the stack of dirty dishes that had accumulated over the past day. He started rinsing them. "If you're not on the case anymore, what difference does it make whether your old firm wins or loses?"

"Well, they'll take me back if I fix this for them. I mean, when they see how dedicated I am to their reputation. It breeds goodwill, don't you think, to save the firm from public humiliation?"

"Mmm, I don't see that. You'd embarrass them by bringing me around. You'd be saying *nyah-nyah, you don't have a case.*"

"Not at all. They would want to know that their case has a major hole. You don't know Spencer the way I do—he's very ethical. He'll see I really do know how to be moral." As I said the words, I believed them, in spite of the lemur's skeptical face.

"Were you fired for being immoral?"

"I wasn't *fired*. I was let go."

It seemed important that the lemur should acknowledge the distinction, for real this time, but he rolled his eyes. "If you were fired, I think what they probably want is for you to disappear, poof. Not show up trying to rub their noses in it."

"You're not a lawyer. You don't understand," I said, waving him away from the kitchen sink. "Spencer will be pleased I caught this mistake. It's expensive to try a case. Showing them it's a dud will save them tons of money and maybe they'll reconsider."

That afternoon we ordered Thai food from a restaurant down the hill. I wanted to soften him up, and make him more comfortable about going to see Spencer, but noodles made the lemur throw up, so I drove back down the hill to buy watercress, kale, and lettuce from the little neighborhood market. After he finished his salad, I unsuccessfully tried to teach him Dictionary—a game like Balderdash except without cards, which my parents used to play as immigrants in New York. We also played several rounds of an old computer game called *Myst*, which the lemur pronounced boring. I hadn't had so much fun since before I became a lawyer, when my children were small.

The next day was Labor Day, and the office would be closed, except for a few sad-sack junior associates. I intended to take the lemur to see Spencer the following day. I plied him with diversions to make it more fun to prepare for our conversation with Spencer: kale chips and video game time to reward solid blocks of time spent preparing answers for questions that might be asked about his motivation for leaving the wall, and his delivery of the facts. He browsed the internet, ignoring me as I tried to coach him about his story. Finally, I grabbed the laptop and hid it on a high shelf in the kitchen. "No more distractions. You really don't know how you got off the wall?" I repeated.

He hopped up on a barstool at the breakfast nook and crossed his arms in defiance.

"You must have some explanation."

"Nary a one."

"Americans like reasons."

"I like sunflower seeds," he said, swiveling on his seat.

"You can't be nihilistic. This should be an empowerment narrative." I paced the kitchen, annoyed that he wouldn't cooperate.

"Can you talk normal?"

"You can intimate that you were taking control of your independence from the wall."

"You want me to lie?"

"It's not lying. Just tell your story in the most favorable way possible. As a story of freedom." I found a rag and wiped down the counter. The lemur's baby-fine fur was shedding—long black threads squiggled over the glossy tile surface.

"Err. I'm loath to let you bust up their fantasy that they've got a case, Maya. You don't see it because you're so immersed in this world, but one day—"

"That's what Ross would say. Trust me, I'm sure I'm right on this point of law."

"The legal arguments are irrelevant," said the lemur, spinning around and around on the barstool.

"How could legal arguments be irrelevant to a lawsuit?" I didn't give him time to answer. "Spencer will realize what a tough spot I was in and forgive whatever he thinks I did and he'll give me my job back so that I can get back on track to a partnership. Then Ross and the kids and I can get back to our normal life."

The doorbell rang, and I went to answer it. I peered through the peephole and was shocked to see Evers waiting on the front step, his Kangol askew, looking around furtively, as if he expected Ross to appear behind him at any moment. How could he come to my house? I didn't even know he had my address. I was surprised at how invasive his sudden appearance was, how keenly I felt he didn't belong here, at my family's home. I opened the door a crack.

"Hey," he said in a mock whisper, taking off the Kangol. "Is it safe?"

"Why didn't you call me back?" I asked.

"Nice place you have here," he said.

"I must have texted you a million times. Where were you?"

"I had a few things to figure out after the partners voted me out," he said. "I'm sorry about that." He leaned in to kiss me, but I pulled away.

"Now's not a good time," I said uneasily. What did I really know about Evers? I hadn't even known of his interest in lemurs, much less his interest in cryptozoology.

"You landed a new job already?"

"No, but I have a plan, and I'm busy. Let's meet up for dinner and drinks later tonight. Seven at Luka's."

He looked mildly disappointed, but nodded. After he left, I returned to the kitchen, where the lemur was still perched on the barstool. He wore an expectant look. "What was all that about?"

I feigned nonchalance. "Somebody I used to know from work. Don't worry about it." I didn't want to reveal the complicated story of how I betrayed my husband and trigger the lemur's distrust.

CHAPTER 5

Because reputable scientists had proposed Lemuria,
and Lemuria coincided with the Kumari Kandam of
ancient literature, the idea of Lemuria as a Tamil
homeland took hold in the Tamil imagination. In the
Tamil imaginary, at least, Tamil Nadu might be small in
the postcolonial era, and Tamils might be dispersed
all over the world, but once upon a time, Dravidians
had maintained power over an entire continent. That
continent was also the cradle of humankind.

This origins story of Tamil power was enough to
sustain Tamil devotees through colonial oppression,
as well as postcolonial marginalization within the
nation of India, and the world at large. The notion that Tamil culture and language had once been
dominant in the cradle of humankind was taught in
schools and colleges across Tamil Nadu.

According to the Tamil devotion movement, the
texts and records that would have proven Kumari
Kandam's existence were drowned in *katalkōl*, the
Tamil word for the catastrophic floods that led to
the submersion of the continent.

After reading online articles for a few hours, I drove to Luka's
Taproom to meet Evers. I arrived a little early to dinner. Perhaps

I was too eager. Or perhaps I needed space from the lemur—he had taken over the living room, turning it into his, with the pop-pop of video games, his long dissonant songs, his stench, and his clueless bromides about my life. As I walked through the lilac-gray twilight of downtown Oakland, the restaurant welcomed me with its cheerful yellow translucent glow. Nobody else was waiting for a table, but the place hummed with jovial, drunk patrons in fine suits and dresses. Their raucous laughter and their carelessness rubbed me the wrong way. I needed to come up with a way to hack away the brush, the distracting tangle of weeds that obscured two things I knew to be true—that it was a mistake for Spencer to let me go and that I needed explanations about several things from Evers, a man who had disappeared after helping me destroy my marriage.

I needed quiet. I needed to be able to focus on how to get answers and listen closely to what Evers told me so I could figure out what was true, but the atmosphere at Luka's wasn't at all conducive to my ruminations.

Before I could change my mind and text Evers with a more appropriate meeting spot, however, a server whisked me into the dining room, seated me at a table, and rattled off the specials. I'd eaten there so many times with Spencer, I didn't need to look at the menu to order.

"Remember you're an apprentice," Spencer had told me over lunch the first week I started at his firm. "You understand that, right? I'm the journeyman and you're the apprentice. The problem with law school is they don't teach you anything. Or at least not anything you can use at trial. Juries respond to emotions, not the law. The law is boring." In spite of the crazy lavish fare he served in order to impress at his dinner parties, he'd simply ordered a root beer and a Cobb salad at lunch, citing his cholesterol.

I'd been right there with him through the forkfuls of lettuce. He'd said what I wanted to hear, what I believed about people and the world anyway, but hadn't felt secure enough to articulate clearly in the face of what Ross, my sister Julie, and my undergrad friends thought was important—abstract big picture stuff about politics, physics, literature, art. The more time I spent at the office, the more the office transformed into home, a place where I could be myself, and the more home turned into work, a place where I had to struggle to be the person other people wanted me to be— maternal, nurturing, without needs, always secondary to myself. I knew for a lot of people it was the opposite—those people always complained about office politics or pay cuts or staff, while I complained about family obligations—but knowing how different my priorities were only served to make me feel more lonely.

I looked around the restaurant hoping to order a martini from the waiter while I waited for Evers. Next to me two young men in suits were making ribald jokes and doing shots. One caught my eye and winked. I looked away quickly, feeling simultaneously attractive and disgusted with how vulgar the first signs of aging were—how embarrassing and fraudulent it felt to want to be desirable, to still possess the same mind, imagining everything was the same as it had been at my peak, even though everyone else could observe my body was utterly different.

Evers appeared twenty minutes later, when I was about to give up on him. Even though he was unemployed, he wore pressed slacks and a button-down shirt, and his hair was brushed rakishly to the side. I had so many questions, but smiled and gave him a peck on the cheek. He removed his jacket and sat across from me. "I really am sorry I didn't return your texts," he said. "But you know how it is. I've missed you."

I didn't know how it was, because, unlike him, I almost always responded to texts and emails within twenty-four hours, but I nodded. We made polite chitchat about what we were going to order. I craved an apricot-braised pulled pork sandwich, and from force of habit, I also ordered the root beer I would have ordered if I were with Spencer. Evers ordered a grilled bavette steak and a dirty martini. As soon as the waiter left the table, I realized that what I wanted was stronger, did not fizz. What I wanted was something that would transport me to a place in the clouds, and keep me from feeling the anxiety that had been chasing me ever since I'd seen the post about whether giant lemurs exist.

"So kid, how you been? Keeping yourself busy?" he asked, as if my entire life hadn't been turned upside down. I resolved not to disclose anything about the lemur, at least not until I figured out what his interest in meeting was.

"You know, this and that. Job searching. I'm waiting for Spencer to realize he made a mistake."

Evers laughed, a short bitter laugh. "Keep telling yourself that." I tried not to reveal that I was hurt, but he immediately apologized. "I shouldn't have said that. I mean, I helped found that firm and I wish I could say they recognize talent. But Spence . . . he's always looked out for number one. It's all about appearances to him and to the others, too."

He and Spencer had known each other around thirty years, enjoyed each other's zingers over squash games, showed enough cordiality at meetings, but Evers routinely expressed a certain level of disdain for Spencer, the kind of shrugging disdain you have for someone you know too well through the pressures of circumstance, rather than inclination. One Friday evening the year before when we'd been working late, Evers had said of Spencer, "He's a fame whore that cares more about the limelight than the law. You think he actually likes those politicians he hangs out with?" Evers had never explained why they were partners, although it might have had something to do with Spencer's wife, who was Evers's friend—she even got away with calling him by his first name, Nick, an intimacy he wouldn't share with me.

"Do you know why you were voted out?" I tried to keep my voice neutral, but I wanted to find his weak spot, the most sweet and tender part of his psyche, and press on it as hard as I could. How dare he ignore me for days and then dismiss me right to my face?

He took a long sip of the martini a waiter placed in front of him. "They thought I was neglecting my rainmaking duties. Too many outside interests."

"How many clients were you bringing in?" I said, though what I really wanted to ask was whether Spencer had given him the same lecture about ethics and extramarital affairs that was given to me.

"Why all this interest?" His martini glass was empty and he was fiddling with the stem. "Be honest. What are you really asking me?"

It was my turn to look mysterious. "I'm just asking. I'm confused about why they let me go, and I'm just as baffled about why they let you go."

"Oh, well they let you go because there's a double standard for men and women." He motioned the waiter for another martini. "It's very simple. No need to overthink it."

"But did I do something wrong?" I asked. He barked, another bitter laugh. "Do you know that a double standard is the reason they let me go, or are you just guessing? They were reading my emails, I think. Was it something in my emails?"

Evers sighed. "This is exactly why I didn't want to answer your texts right away. I knew that you'd be obsessed about the why of it. As if *why* matters so much, or at all. It's something that the partners talked about during our last meeting. Some of the partners just didn't think you were cut out for the job. You didn't have it."

"It?"

"No killer instinct."

My heart sank. The waiter arrived with Evers's second martini and, after his disclosure, I ordered a double-malt Scotch.

I watched his face to try and figure out whether he agreed with the other partners about my instincts. "What about Spencer? Did he stand up for me? Did you stand up for me?"

"Well, I mean, for what it's worth, I told them you were a hard worker, the hardest worker we had," he said. "And so did Spencer. We expected you would be, and you were. And we talked about how you were due for the promotion and couldn't be an associate forever."

"But you didn't think I have a killer instinct?" I said, trying to control my facial muscles and the volume of my voice so he would stay relaxed and tell me what I needed to know. I tried to ignore the implication they'd only hired me because they assumed I would be a hard worker—I didn't want to think about whether that was because I was Indian, or because of my father, but perhaps those were really the same reasons.

"Sure, you do," Evers drawled. "But I would think you'd realize preparation and being a hard worker can't take you as far as a killer instinct."

"No, it can't." I tried to keep my voice light. "You've always said that the best trial lawyers are in possession of a killer instinct. They go for the jugular. That's what makes them the best. Evidently you don't think I have *it*."

He reached across the table and took my hand. His was cold. "Of course you have it, Maya. I told you this whole thing is just because you're a woman."

I'd seen him lie before and it involved the same smooth, friendly, impenetrable expression in his sunset-blue eyes. He almost certainly knew I would rather hear I was fired because I was a woman, rather than because I lacked an essential and immutable personality trait necessary for the job. Nonetheless, I decided it was more important to ferret out the information I came for than to get him to agree with me—sincerely—that I had a killer instinct. And didn't my ability to hide my true intentions prove I had *it* anyway?

Soon, I approached the more important reason I'd wanted to meet, the article about his collective in Madagascar. Evers looked taken aback when I brought it up. He said nothing, and then he smiled a sleazy smile, a toothy smile I'd seen him deliver to juries at trial. There's nothing more disturbing than the smile of a practiced liar. He was going to try to snow me, but he didn't think enough of me to consider I might spot his deception. "Oh that. It's just a little nonprofit project I act as a spokesperson for. One of my investments."

"You're interested in giant lemurs?" I prompted.

"Giant lemurs? No, I don't know anything about them. I fund a nonprofit in Madagascar that studies indri—that's what the article was about, right? It's simply a tax write-off. Someone else manages it. Now that I won't be with the firm anymore, I'll probably pull the funds and shut it down." His face was still smooth. I scanned it for tells and didn't find any.

"But you're interested in indri? Just like Brian Turner used to be? How did you guys meet again?"

He laughed. "Oh, it's such a long story. Didn't we already talk about this? Who wants to talk about Brian anyway? He thinks he's God's gift to the art world." His voice was warm, but the warmer his voice grew, the more I sensed he was icy inside, a burning, steaming ice man that would say anything to convince me.

"We never did talk about it. Tell me." My dinner appeared on a warm plate. The pulled pork was tough and stringy; it tasted like dishwater. Evers was sawing his rare steak into tiny bloody pieces.

"We met while I was backpacking through Asia. That was way back when he was blowing through his inheritance, and I was squeezing in one last hurrah before law school."

"When did you find out he was interested in lemurs?" I mashed the pulled pork as best I could, swallowing it down in spite of my anger, while at the table next to us people that looked vaguely familiar chatted and flirted and ate moules *marinières* and drank something dark pink and full of stars, perhaps Kir Royales, in champagne flutes.

"Brian?" he asked. His eyebrows were knit together, but I knew he was faking confusion. I must have looked as exasperated as I felt, because he leaned back and put his hands up. "What is this? An inquisition? How would I know when Brian became interested in lemurs?"

"Is he the one who got you to fund the collective?"

"Nope. I met some environmentalists at a dinner party and they told me about the plight of the indri—they're endangered, you know—and it was my idea." He began dragging the steak bites through bright green chimichurri sauce and burying them in a sculpted mound of summer squash.

"That seems like a huge undertaking—creating a collective. And kind of lunatic, too. A collective to find a giant lemur that only cryptozoologists believe exists. How did you plan to manage an enterprise like that from all the way over here?"

"My only interest was the tax implications. I swear. I knew someone who wanted to live in Madagascar desperately, and I put her in charge and paid her a tiny sum on a monthly basis to run it. You know how I am about money. It was a decent tax strategy." I was certain he wasn't telling me something, but he seemed to be one step ahead of me. "When did *you* become interested in lemurs?"

"I'm not," I said, taking a last bite of my sandwich.

"You're lying," he said. Dread came over me. "I saw that lemur in your kitchen. What's going on?"

My mouth was too full to respond at first. I choked down the slightly sour piece of bread. "You were spying on me?"

"You were acting strange, so this afternoon I peeked inside to make sure you were okay. And what do I see but you hanging out with an oversized lemur. Is that why you got rid of me so quickly? Why didn't you want me to know?" He was smiling flirtatiously, a smile that revealed his crooked incisor, but I thought of him lurking at the window, watching, and waiting all through dinner to pounce on me with his revelation—that he knew I was lying. I was profoundly disturbed.

"No. But can you not say anything to anyone?"

"Why?"

"Just, please keep it to yourself." I assumed he and Spencer wouldn't keep in touch because Evers would feel the other partners had thrown him under the bus. But he didn't appear affected by the loss of his life's work—he certainly wasn't as enraged as I was. His near-complacency made me think he had some other project brewing.

I threw a few twenty-dollar bills on the table and gathered up my handbag. I knew he was expecting a kiss, but I saluted him.

He grabbed my wrist with his large freckled hand. "Hey! Are you freaking out?"

"I'm not. But I have things to do."

"But the lemur." A sly tone entered his voice. "What exactly are you doing with that lemur?"

"Nothing. Just helping him out. I need to find a job where the partners aren't just pretending to believe in me. I need to find a job where I'm valued," I said. "Or else find a way to convince Spencer he made a mistake."

Evers groaned. "I did believe in you. How much reassurance does somebody need to give for you to believe them?" I didn't answer because what I needed was everything. "Look, I know it's a little weird for us now that Ross isn't in the picture, because it seems very real in a way that it didn't before. But even if we can't be together-together, we can still hang out, right?"

He sounded like a teenage boy, like somebody I wouldn't want Tara dating, rather than a man in his fifties. I didn't know I'd been imagining Evers was waiting in the wings, imagining he would simply replace Ross. But I realized in that moment I'd been as-suming there would be a new life with Evers, one in which I would skate over the gaping hole where my marriage had been. Looking at his face, I understood it was more than my cynicism that kept us from transforming into an official couple. He was supposed to believe we were the real thing, otherwise what was the point? Until he said "together-together," I hadn't felt in my gut that all the time we'd spent together was a dirty and knowing lie, rather than a kind of fantasy. Knowing for sure our conversations weren't real made me feel like an absurd figure. We'd frittered away our time, creating a together that was not a together, time I could have spent with my family, exactly as Ross had wanted.

In spite of my thoughts, I nodded and smiled to avoid arousing his suspicion. I swept out of Luka's into the cold dark, and the wind nipped at my ears. The smell of burnt paper and sausages drifted by. I took a deep breath, and hurried to my car, parked several blocks away.

CHAPTER 6

Every trial is made up of five billion moments, both dark and shining, scripted for years in advance during discovery, and what's left, the fixed corpses of these moments, are trotted out at the right time for judgment. This applies not only to legal trials, but to personal ones as well. I often felt that all I'd ever done was to prepare for those moments. If the partners were right—that I just didn't have a killer instinct—preparation for those moments was the only thing I had going for me. I was good at creating persuasive witnesses, because I was good at creating myself. As someone who wasn't naturally powerful, I had learned to channel the charisma and intelligence I'd seen others display, and I was determined I could train the lemur into what I needed him to be when we went in to see Spencer.

The lemur's dirty physical appearance and stench were the first problems I needed to fix. The night before we went to Spencer's office, the whole house smelled like he'd rubbed his armpits against the curtains, the armchairs, the sofa, my son's bed—animalic odors everywhere. After a rousing game of Stratego, I thrust an old bottle of Tara's rosemary mint shampoo into his hands. "Here, doesn't this smell good?"

"Eh." He tried to stick his nose in the bottle, but it wouldn't fit.

"And look, matching conditioner!"

He grumbled, but I gave him a spiel about how a hot shower would make him feel good, and in the kids' bathroom, while he inspected the space, I turned on the shower. He yelped at the blast of warm water as I shut the bathroom door. I sat on the bed in Tara's room, a few feet down the hall from the bathroom, and looked around. I'd seen this room from the outside dozens of times when scolding Tara about her homework or pranks or cutting school or the boys she brought to the house. But I hadn't been inside this room in years.

On Tara's desk sat a framed photograph of my sister Julie and her husband Sean from when they first met in college. Julie looked young, and not yet fat from antipsychotics. Sean's short dreadlocks and deep tan made him look like a Rastafarian. There was a wedding photograph of my mother and father, unsmiling because almost nobody came to their wedding. Next to that photo was another framed snapshot, one I'd taken of my father and my sister when we'd first moved to California thirty years ago. We were standing in the blond meadow under a gnarled oak tree, near the stables where I took riding lessons, and bay ponies were grazing on the grass in the distant background. I hadn't realized Tara cared that much about my sister or my father, and I wondered if she'd framed the photographs and placed them there because they would appear retro and vintage to her friends. The walls were papered in advertisements for older musical performances that I wouldn't have expected her to be interested in— The Mighty Mighty Bosstones, The English Beat, The Uptones. Soccer trophies lined the top of the bookshelf. One was for Most Valuable Player. I'd never seen her trophies.

It was like visiting the room of somebody else's daughter.

Forty-five minutes passed while the lemur sang in the shower. I banged on the door a few times to hurry him up. Finally, he came to the door still dripping, the water running in the background. "Jesusfuckingchrist, what? First you demand I shower. Next you rush me," he said, and stomped back into the shower.

When he emerged, I took a blow dryer to him for over an hour. Under the hot air, his black and white fur lay shiny and silky across his body. He no longer bore the same musky, woodsy odor. He smelled herbal, minty. I convinced him to sleep in Tara's bed, rather than on the floor, so we could change the sheets. "Just for now," I said, tucking the comforter around him. "Soon we'll whisk you back to Madagascar. Promise."

The lemur and I arrived in downtown Oakland early the next morning, hoping to catch Spencer before he went to court or to a deposition. We parked in my usual spot in a lot a few blocks from the firm. On the way, we passed a pair of black men carrying brass instruments and wearing cream-colored tuxedos and bowler hats, and a few joggers ran past us, the armpits of their pastel running suits dark from sweat, ponytails flying in the warm wind. A paper bag blew across the road, followed by a plastic cup.

Once again, I quizzed the lemur on the story we'd be telling, even though we had practiced for hours the night before. After grilling him, I'd discovered no concrete reasons for his abandonment of the mural, but I had trained him to use a few vague statements that intimated he wanted freedom. By the time we walked through the office doors, I was certain Spencer would see not only that he was wrong about Brian's case, but also that he was wrong about my value as a trial lawyer and my killer instinct.

I opened the door and waved at the receptionist. She looked at me with her thin lips pressed tightly together and blinked a few times as I told her I was there to see Spencer. "Do you have an appointment, Maya?"

I didn't. We sat in the lobby, snacking on organic pink jelly beans from the dish on the coffee table and reading back issues of *The Nation*, waiting for Spencer to finish whatever he was doing. I read a piece in the magazine on patent law and social justice that made me think of my father, how much he loved his job, how much he loved the simple act of getting ready for work. Around the house, he'd been a bit of a slob in his *veshti*, drinking his one-tumbler-of-Scotch a day, eating snacks from the Indian store on El Camino Avenue, and working into the wee hours. Back then, what my father called discipline I thought was something that spirited him away from us, forcing me to supervise my goofy little sister, so that I couldn't hang out downtown with my friends. But when he put on his suit and stepped out in front of his colleagues, it seemed clear all those hours reading the latest news in patent law, refining his writing, and keeping up with technology trends were worth it. Julie and I always complained about what we thought we lost—okay, I complained, and like younger sisters around the world, she mimicked me—but other lawyers respected him beyond measure.

I put the magazine down. The phone rang, and after the receptionist answered it, she said, "You can go in now." She eyed the lemur with an inscrutable expression. "Can I get you guys some coffee? Or some red velvet cupcakes?"

"I'll take a cup of coffee," said the lemur. I shook my head no.

Spencer was speaking into his Dictaphone when we walked in. Nonplussed, he clicked it off and stared at the lemur. "And who are you?"

"This is who I wanted to talk to you about," I said.

"I have to say, I'm surprised to see you, Maya. We said everything last week." Spencer was still holding his Dictaphone near his mouth as if he were about to start speaking into it again.

"It's about how you don't have a case," I said.

Spencer sighed. "Look, *Turner* isn't your case anymore. I can take it from here. Brian and I have developed a reasonably good lawyer-client relationship."

"I know it's not my case," I said. "But, we've known each other for years and I feel I owe it to you to let you know about some important evidence that guts your argument. This is the lemur from the painting."

The night before, I'd advised the lemur not to volunteer explanations or give long speeches, explaining they could undermine his credibility, but before Spencer could say anything, the lemur said, "Got off that wall for my own reasons. You don't need to know what they are, but hey, I made the decision to leave on my own. Nobody coerced me, nobody threatened me, least of all those store owners you're suing. Which if you ask me, not that you did, was a bit idiotic from the outset. They've not an artistic bone in their bodies, those two. How can you imagine they replicated the style of the leaves?"

I nudged his leg with my foot to remind him to shut up.

"I see. Interesting. You're claiming to be *that* lemur," said Spencer. He didn't sound fazed, but as he put down the Dictaphone I noticed a barely perceptible, uneasy tremor in his hand, similar to what I'd experienced when I'd first met the lemur.

"How many of us do you think there are in Oakland?" the lemur asked. I could see he was upset, and touched his shoulder to steady him.

"I'm not sure why you've come to me with this. Your decisions are irrelevant," Spencer said to the lemur.

"Don't you see? If he decided to leave on his own, there is no case. VARA doesn't even apply to this situation anymore because it was his choice." As I spoke, I saw the lemur had been right. Spencer was staring at me as if I were trying to taunt him. Rather than interpret my gesture as an effort to get back in his good graces, he viewed us as a threat, and he wasn't going to take the bait. Even though I realized from the glint in his eyes that the lemur was right, I kept going, thinking of all the lunches we'd shared, how much he knew about my family situation, and how much encouragement he'd given me. Why would he tell me I was up for partner, if he didn't think I had the stuff? I was certain that if only I could make him see it my way, make him see how serious I was about getting my job back, make him see me as the daughter he never had, he would convince the other partners to hire me back. "You don't want to prosecute a case like this, Spencer. It would be embarrassing to the firm. It would be embarrassing to you. Not to mention—"

"What about 'it's not your case' is unclear to you, Maya? Listen, you're a bright woman. You're talented and capable. I hope you find your place, but it's not in my firm, and this little parlor trick doesn't change that."

"But the law doesn't support this case. You always told me that the only way to win on the plaintiff's side is to select good cases to begin with. This case is about the biggest loser I can imagine." I sounded desperate to myself, but once I started talking I couldn't stop. He had believed in my lawyering abilities when my own family hadn't. Why would he change his mind so suddenly?

"I don't know why you would bring him here." Spencer gestured at the lemur. "You're threatening the case, aren't you? I refrained from reporting your infractions to the state bar in the hopes you would learn your lesson. That was a gray area, but this is not. You still have ethical obligations to the client, and trying to threaten his case shows me you haven't learned your lesson."

I racked my memory—none of my ethics violations had been that bad. Were he and Evers lying to me for some reason? I felt as if I were being manipulated, a pawn in a much larger scheme. And I had a sinking feeling, a slow spiraling down, an eddy made all the worse because I couldn't find the reason that gave cause to this effect. Before I could say anything, however, the lemur spoke up.

"Listen, big shot," he said, leaning forward with a raised paw. "She's here to help you, but if you're so dense you don't want our help, we'll scram."

I would have continued, but the lemur stalked out of the office, and so I followed his lead. Outside the building, we were blasted with black, dusty exhaust. I pulled out a cigarette and lit up. The meeting wasn't supposed to go down that way. "So anyway. That was a bust," said the lemur. "Told you so."

"You know what's really great about Ross? He doesn't rub it in. He's right a lot more often than I am, but he doesn't come out and say so. Spencer will change his mind. We'll be hearing from him soon." That probably wasn't true, but I couldn't see a way to start over from scratch. Spencer's case was sunk, and if he wasn't going to hire me back, I was sunk, too. What firm would want me now, without even a good reference to recommend me?

"Well, you win some, you lose some," the lemur said, waving a hand in front of his face to push the smoke away. "Can you take me home now?"

"Let me think through whether there's another way to make this work out. But soon, soon."

"You certainly pick and choose when it comes to ethics, don't you?" the lemur said.

The following few days, I hovered by the telephone, thinking about ethics, drinking glass after glass of an aged Cabernet Sauvignon that left an oak taste in my mouth. When I grew bored, I read an online message board where folks were talking about the mural. I hoped Spencer would call and ask me to bring the lemur back. Meanwhile, the lemur ate massive amounts of watercress salad and played games on Mike's Nintendo. My father called to see how I was doing. "Do you want to come stay down here with me?" he asked. "You always have a room here. Your bedroom is exactly as you left it, Maya. We can figure out where you should apply for a job. Maybe I can call some former colleagues on your behalf?"

"No, I'm all right, Dad." I hated the thought of my father picking me up again. In a way, this was all his fault. Would I have been in such a rush to leave his house if he hadn't lied about my mother? If he hadn't routinely shouted me down and forced me to take care of Julie? Would my whole life have been completely different, maybe even normal? Would I have been the person I was supposed to be? Would I have more confidence, maybe even the killer instinct that Evers claimed I was lacking?

"Your sister and I are worried about you. Are you and Ross working this out?"

"Why are you talking to Julie about me?" I asked. The thought of them pitying me together, commiserating about what a failure I was, made my skin crawl almost as much as the thought of him and Ross doing the same. Ross would have told me I was over-reacting, but without him there to curb me, I could react to my heart's content. "There's nothing to be worried about. Seriously. I'm fine."

"Well, you should be worried," my father said. "I'm not sure I've ever seen you lower in your life."

"Why? I'll get my job back; I'll get Ross and the kids back. I just need to regroup and strategize." I paced back and forth in front of the glass sliding door, eventually opening it and stepping out on the balcony. Down below, the hill was parched, drying into a sad golden-brown, and monarchs were flitting through the yellow wood sorrel blossoms. Tiny jewel-bright cars buzzed around the bend of Keller Avenue, far below our hill.

"There's no need to strategize about something like this, Maya. It's pretty simple. You love Ross. You should be spending your time working it out." I waited for him to say something about Spencer. "As for work, let that go. Whatever happened, happened. I don't think litigation is the right thing for you. You should think about a career change."

He didn't take my side, or even try. He'd never done so before, and there was no reason for him to start now. But I'd never heard him say that litigation wasn't right for me. I saw red for a second, but I pushed it down. "Why would you say that? I've been litigating for years. I was about to be partner. Why would I stop now?"

"Litigation—law firm life—is not a good life," my father said. "You can give up everything for it, especially yourself, and still wind up with nothing. Just look at my life." He let out a small, sad, unfamiliar laugh.

"You love the law," I said, still confused. "You've never once said this was a bad path."

"Would you have listened to me if I told you to stop?" he asked.

Although the answer to this was no, I pressed further, asking him what prompted his statements. The lemur had turned the volume up on his video game. Guns firing onscreen, *pow, pow, pow.*

"Turn that down," I mouthed to the lemur, but he ignored me, just the way my children did. "Spencer told me he doesn't think you have it in you to do this," my father said. "And after seeing how hard you've worked for so little gain, I'm inclined to agree."

"The good old boys club," I said, even though I wasn't sure that really was the source of these comments or that my Tamil father was truly part of that club. "Predictable." I hung up on him.

After, I started thinking about my mother again. I went to look at a photograph of her that I kept in the bedroom. Her death seemed to me a dark wrenching scream in the background of my life, the source of everything: why I couldn't seem to fulfill my potential, why I couldn't deal with my father, why my sister's struggles with sanity made me so angry, why it was so hard for me to connect with Ross, why life, for me, was always elsewhere until elsewhere was here, and above all, why it seemed so much harder to be a mother to Tara and Mike than to focus on work, the work that kept me on top and in control.

I didn't want my kids to feel as abandoned as I had felt the day I'd found her lying on the bed, pills nearby. And so I called Mike from my bedroom to say goodnight. By the end of the conversation, his reedy voice was cracking.

I leaned back on the headboard of the bed and tried Tara on her cell phone, but she wouldn't pick up. In spite of all the wine I drank to anesthetize myself, I was still painfully aware she wasn't going to cut me slack any time soon. She possessed a vague notion I'd been cheating, and she was right. She thought I didn't understand her or Ross, or give them enough of my attention, and this viewpoint wasn't entirely unfamiliar to me. My sister and I spoke only occasionally for the very same reason: she'd never really forgiven me for not understanding about a mental breakdown she'd experienced in college. I never apologized, because I didn't think there was anything in particular to apologize for.

I did understand why she and Tara didn't feel they could confide in me—I could be harsh—but I didn't understand why they thought it was wrong to tell the truth and why they wanted me to pretend. Like in Julie's case: she'd made a series of terrible choices and it seemed to me, at least a little bit, it had been her choices that had broken her and landed her on psychiatric medications with adverse side effects for years. Why did she hate to hear that? Didn't it give her more power to claim she'd made at least a few choices? It gave her no power to say an illness had entirely stripped her of her agency. She'd moved off the continent claiming that parochialism and racism were at the root of her troubles. But by choosing to be an artist, she'd picked one of the hardest things in the world to be successful at, and she simply couldn't tough it out in the competition of the American work force.

I returned to the living room and the sounds of a video game. "You're not a help to anyone starving yourself and getting wasted," the lemur said from his perch on a blue cushion on the floor. He'd abandoned the watercress salads for potato chips, claiming that his interest in junk food was purely anthropological—he was a tourist trying to understand America, and he would be back to leafy greens once I took him home to Madagascar.

"I'm just not a good cook." This was partly true—I had never bothered to learn to cook because Ross liked doing it, but also I hated the idea of doing so-called women's work. I wanted to be the one in control, and it always struck me that cooking and laundry and all the little things you needed to do to maintain a house were what made women more vulnerable in relationships. Whoever earned the most money had all the power.

Later that afternoon, I staggered back to the kitchen to retrieve another bottle of wine. Through the kitchen window, I saw someone hovering at the door with his fist drawn back, about to knock. I opened it.

"Does the lemur live here?" Without waiting for my reply, the man handed me a sealed envelope. My heart sank. This couldn't be anything good.

When the lemur opened the envelope, he found a deposition subpoena issued by Katie Snow and a cover letter addressed to me.

Dear Ms. Ramesh,

We understand that the lemur from the mural has taken up residence with you. Since he is a material witness to *Turner v. Eustachio*, we'd like to take his deposition. I assume you are serving as his counsel and will produce him? Although we have set the deposition with sufficient notice, we'd be happy to reschedule to a mutually convenient date.

Please advise as to the status of his representation at your earliest opportunity. Thank you for your professional courtesy and cooperation.

Yours very truly,
Katie Snow

I stomped around the house, disgruntled at the idea that the lemur and I would have to postpone our trip to Madagascar so he could be deposed. How had Katie Snow known about the lemur? Spencer wouldn't have told the opposition about my trip to his office—the lemur's existence would have been a piece of information he kept close to the vest, especially since trial was so close. As I opened the kitchen window for a breath of fresh air, the realization that Evers must have betrayed us sank in.

Evers and Katie had been opposing counsel on numerous cases together, but over the last couple of years they'd developed a special rapport. Perhaps they were more than friendly; perhaps they were intimate, as well. Katie was six or seven years younger than me, and Evers was certainly not someone who denied himself the pleasures of youth or youth as pleasure.

In the living room, the lemur was curled up on the couch. He watched me, his amber eyes gleaming by lamplight, and no doubt was thinking *I told you so, I told you so*.

"As long as I'm stuck here dealing with this shit," he said, holding out the computer. "Can you open one of these accounts for me?" He was on Twitter. Reluctantly, I opened his account.

"Here, take a selfie," I said, handing him my camera phone. The lemur strolled around the room, trying to find the clearest shot of himself in the mottled light from the skylight. Finally, he touched the screen and the flash went off. He dropped the camera. I picked it up and showed him the picture.

He said, "I don't look good in this."

"Oh, you! You look fine," I said. But once I had the phone in hand, I could see there was something different, mutant-like, about him in the photograph. We uploaded it to my laptop. The lemur's selfie popped open on the screen.

I'd opened a Twitter account for myself about a month earlier, primarily to spy on Tara, who was a prolific tweeter. Through Twitter, I learned my daughter's interests were ska, typewriters, perfume, and Lauren Bacall. She was a bit of a flirt, but tweeted nothing so dismaying that I would have been required to discuss it with Ross. I'd tweeted only once (*"Hello world"*). The lemur followed me first, then scrolled through avatars, clicking "follow" willy-nilly. While he crafted his first tweets, I took my cell phone downstairs to call Evers and tell him off, but he didn't answer. I left a message asking him to call me back.

In the backyard, I weaved between the rosebushes, pausing to press up against the chain-link fence where I'd first seen the lemur. He'd seemed so vulnerable and trusting with his back against the fence, asking for my help. The clouds spiraled. Beyond the chain-link fence, the drop from the top of our hill seemed vertiginous, a giddy, golden whirl of grass and weeds. I gathered myself together: I needed to cooperate with Katie Snow if I wanted to stay involved in the case and prove myself.

A few hours later, the lemur asked, "Do you have another account?" He was tapping an arrow key on the keyboard. I shook my head and stood behind him. His face bore a quizzical expression as he passed me the computer. The web browser was open to a Twitter timeline. My doppelganger was there under the handle @RameshM. Most disturbingly of all, she seemed to be tweeting about aspects of my life, but in a way I found foreign.

> No, actually I *don't* care that you took the kids.
> Have fun!
> lover, lover burning bright, in the forests of the
> night
> Bossman fired me today. boo hoo
> something wicked this way comes

She was following over one thousand accounts, but she had only thirty followers, most of which seemed to be logorrheic spambots. Her avatar was a blurry profile pic, in which I recognized my own features.

"Is she your cousin or something?" the lemur asked.

"I don't know my cousins," I said. As far as I knew, they were all in India, and from the few times I'd met them on trips, they were neither particularly interested in me, nor similar to me. @RameshM identified her location as Palo Alto, where my father lived. Perhaps I should have paid my father a visit after all, if only to try to locate and interrogate my identity thief.

"Want me to tweet her?" The lemur reached out and took the laptop back. I watched as he tweeted: *Whattup?* We waited, eyes fixed to the screen, but no response came.

CHAPTER 7

Long ago, two brothers lived together in the
rainforest. One brother wandered out of the forest
into the bright sunshine. Wet dirt squished between
his toes—his toes were vulnerable like little roots in
the soil. Hot light warmed his head. By accident, he
discovered the wonder of seeds: a week after one
dropped a seed in the soil, a tiny pale green shoot
would poke forth, tunneling through the darkness
below the ground toward the light. He transformed
into a man by falling in love with this fact, by calling
it magic. All right things gravitated toward light. He
cultivated the land outside the forest, digging up
the black soil and planting rice and vegetables. He
kept zebu for milk and later raised them for meat.

The man's brother did not share his wonder. He
took no enjoyment in the light, the rice, the zebu.
He stayed deep in the dark forest. There he grew his
fur long and lived on leaves and bounded across the
canopy created by the tree branches. Every morning
and every twilight, he still cries a song of sorrow for
the brother who abandoned him for magic.

"Nice," the lemur said, peering over my shoulder at the laptop
screen. "All right things gravitated toward light. Light! The thing

that causes skin cancer. Humans are the worst. Are you falling for this?"

"It's only a legend," I said, closing my laptop and setting it next to me on the couch. "I'm just trying to understand where you come from, to figure out why you're here."

"Google doesn't know everything." He walked to the sliding glass door and gazed out at the hillside. "That's the trouble with humans. You place all this wild faith in metal and circuitry."

Needing his cooperation, I decided not to point out he'd trusted online research a week before. We hadn't decided what to do about the deposition notice yet. The lemur shambled around the living room, pausing occasionally to look at the view. He loped from the balcony to the foyer, and back to his video game, paused on the TV, wondering out loud whether he should make a break for it. I offhandedly suggested he place an online ad to see if someone traveling to Madagascar would take him, mostly so he would perceive me as generous and helpful, and cooperate accordingly. But when I observed he was seriously considering my suggestion, I balked. If he took off, I would have to deal with the legal consequences—and the vast echoing emptiness now that Ross and Evers and my job were gone. I was starting to feel like he was my only friend, as if I could keep going so long as I had him.

When he started to type the ad copy, I said slowly, "On the other hand, you are rare, maybe even endangered. Strangers might claim they're trying to help you, only to trap you and send you to a zoo or something." He jumped off the chair and backed away from my laptop.

In a transparently self-serving gesture, Spencer did call later that evening, but not to offer me my job back. His voice was suffused with sunny warmth, the way it had been when he was recounting war stories over lunch. If his tone were to be believed, we were old pals again. "I've been thinking about this deposition that Katie

Snow requested. Why don't you file a motion for protective order, Maya? It's kind of a hassle for you and the lemur, isn't it?"

"You worried about her taking his deposition?" I asked, sipping a glass of Prosecco.

"Certainly not," Spencer said. "But you still have a duty to Brian, you know. Not to do anything that would jeopardize his case."

"You should file the motion," I said. What he wanted was to foist onto me the work of writing a brief, even though I was no longer his associate. "I'll write a paragraph joining it."

"It's up to you, I guess. I don't have time to file frivolous motions." No longer assuming the mannerisms of a raconteur, the warmth left Spencer's voice like air leaking from a balloon.

After we hung up, I thought about his suggestion. I knew the lemur didn't want to be deposed, but I didn't think the judge would grant the motion. It was just a delay tactic. Spencer had explained to me numerous times that one of the strongest defense tactics was to delay and delay and delay some more. But that strategy worked only when an insurer or a wealthy client was paying the defense attorney's bills, and the plaintiff's attorney was working on a contingency fee basis. The lemur wasn't paying me. And Brian had money to burn. On top of that, Spencer had humiliated me in his office twice in seven days, two times too many. And I was absolutely right about the law on this one. If Spencer didn't think it would hurt the client, if he wouldn't simply admit I was right about this case, I saw no reason to seek a protective order to suppress the deposition. As much as I wanted validation, another part of me wanted to see Spencer fall flat on his face.

In fact, since I needed to return the lemur to the Andasibe Preserve within a matter of weeks, the deposition had to happen relatively quickly, more quickly than usual. The lemur was fond of reminding me in grandiloquent terms that no indri had survived more than one year outside of Madagascar. Although he couldn't offer a concrete symptom, he grumbled his health was suffering. "It's a feeling I have. The same kind of feeling that motivated me to leave the wall. A burst of energy. Only it's a bad burst this time." It was true, he looked fatigued and harried.

"We made up that story about the energy, remember?" I reminded him. "It's not real. And you're a giant lemur, a cryptid. According to what I've read on the internet, you're not any old normal indri. For all we know, you could live hundreds of years."

"Hmph. You know, bigger dogs have shorter lifespans than little dogs," he said. "So it stands to reason I have less than a year to live, not more than the average indri, being a giant lemur." He was getting carried away, but now that he would be deposed, we had to make up even more details to support the original story. My double had never responded to the lemur's tweet, but I followed her on Twitter to see if she tweeted about what the lemur and I were doing, strategizing and preparing for his deposition. She didn't. She tweeted cupcake recipes and short clever comments about movies and made veiled references to her relationship with her lover—I wondered who that was. Evidently my polar opposite, as she commented that she was happier without a job, with all the free time.

I hoped the edifice of lies the lemur and I were building wouldn't all come tumbling down. I had a paranoid thought that kept circling my mind like water around a drain, made worse by wine. What would happen if reality fell away around us? I was starting to wonder if that was what my doppelganger was hoping—that it would all fall apart so she could take over my life. Would I even know I'd been replaced by my double? Was Evers in on it, too?

I didn't let my anxieties show in front of the lemur. "Believing the story that you felt a burst of energy that propelled you off the wall doesn't make it true."

"Well, but it *could* be true and you want me to sell it, don't you?" he said.

I had no answer to this. I poured myself another glass of Prosecco. Outside the window, the hillside was turning bluish with autumn. Hoping to smoke him out, I texted Evers. *Last chance to give me some advice. Come out come out wherever you are.*

Ten minutes later he texted back. *On a trip. Back soon. What do you need?*

Surprised at his quick response, I decided not to accuse him just yet. *The lemur's deposition has been noticed. Do I produce him?*

Who noticed it? Do you have something to hide? Evers texted back.

Nothing to hide, but the lemur really wants to go home.

A small violin is playing somewhere. Just produce him.

Of course, what had I expected Evers to say, since he was probably the one who'd revealed the lemur's existence to Katie? With civil courts backed up the way they were, bringing a motion would have taken over a month, plus an ex parte appearance to get it heard on the date that I wanted, and I would have had to spend my own savings on the filing fees. It was unlikely I would win, a consideration that had weight. There were some lawyers, like Spencer, who filed motions with little substance, even if they knew they would lose, because it would accomplish a longer-range goal, like getting a case in front of a judge first to establish their versions of the facts in his or her mind. I had no such long-range goal, and I had no desire to get sanctioned and pay the sanction out-of-pocket for bringing a frivolous motion.

At Mike's insistence, I went to dinner at Ross's again the next day. Tara didn't show up, and I was monosyllabic, still racking my brain for strategies to get the lemur out of the deposition. Ross was in the mood to lecture. "You put off working on the marriage, you put off everything real until the next day, but tomorrow is here already."

"I don't know what you mean. I'm here today," I said, even though I understood what he was talking about. I'd always believed there would be time for my family later, after I was done making partner; they were a fixture in my life, like appliances or furniture, and until Ross had left, I hadn't even imagined a life where they weren't simply *there*. Should I tell him about the lemur? Should I explain that I had found a way to return things to the status quo? It was on the tip of my tongue, but he turned to Mike, who looked terribly disappointed.

"It's getting late, kiddo. Go get ready for bed," Ross said.

Mike ran at me hard, and wrapped his arms around me. I could barely breathe, and not only because of his vise grip. He was thirteen, but his cheeks still hadn't lost their baby fat, their soft apple roundness. "I don't want you to go," he said. "Don't go, don't go."

"Remember, I'm nearby. I'm really nearby." Other than the lip biting, I no longer had tells. But watching Mike fall apart while being able to keep myself from crying, too, it seemed a monstrous condition to be so in control, and to have control as a life objective.

Ross shook his head and I saw something shiny under his eyes. Most of the time, I was pretty sure that he and the kids were exaggerating the adverse effects of me working so many hours, the way my sister Julie exaggerated her aversion to America—to provoke, to compel a reaction. I always held it together, which meant they had the freedom to fall apart. But in that moment, looking at Ross tearing up, it sank in. My children and husband genuinely believed I was the bad guy, that I'd utterly failed them, even though I'd worked so hard to make our lives spectacular.

"Don't worry, sweetheart," I said with a confidence I didn't feel, that I never felt. "Hopefully, you guys will be moving back in soon. We'll work it all out."

When Mike left to get ready for bed, Ross and I cleaned up the kitchen. "You don't have to do that," he said. I shelved the *garam masala*, the mustard seeds, the dried chili peppers, the turmeric, and the kosher salt, all neatly arranged in small glass bottles on a rack, as if he'd been living here for years. I mopped up the counter, something I'd never done in our ordinary life together, because usually I'd been busy hurrying back to work.

Ross was another one of those people who kept it together.

Even when everything was falling apart, he did the right thing. Sometimes, before I had a chance to check my own thoughts, I found myself musing he was so together because he was adopted and he believed he had to do everything by himself—and well— to make sure love stayed. He did the laundry. He paid the bills. He cleaned. He made dinner. Although I'd never broken the way my sister and mom had, all of me was sunk in work, and had to be, to get anywhere. It was Ross who kept all the clunky little wheels and gears of family life turning.

When we were done cleaning up the kitchen, he said, "That was an intense dinner." He wanted me to care enough to initiate conversation, but I couldn't. Even from a couple of feet away I could smell him—a comfortable smell, a trustworthy smell. It wasn't a smell that made me think about fucking him, but one that reminded me that if we were together, no matter where we were, we were always at home.

Instead of diving into the fight we surely would have had about using the lemur, I told Ross about my doppelganger. "The strangest thing is that when I saw her, she was brighter than me."

"Like brighter-smarter?" he asked. "Did you talk to her?"

"No. Brighter as in more vibrant, like a painting when it's still wet and new."

"I told you. You've been spending too much time with that case."

There was a lull in the conversation. He probably wanted to tell me again that I'd been too obsessed with the upcoming trial, and that my obsession was what had broken us. I excused myself to use the bathroom.

In the hallway, I noticed my sister's painting—the one missing from the hall at home—hanging there. The canvas depicted a huge group of brown people congregating under the broad boughs of a live oak tree near the hills by our childhood home. Ross liked the painting so much she'd gifted it to us. I'd been thrilled when she first unveiled the painting to us—before she put it in her exhibit—thinking she was finally, *finally* making pieces I understood, instead of dicking around with philosophy and conceptual mindfuckery. But later I realized the painting was the result of the brain-dulling medications she took, combined with the structure of school. When I looked really closely, I discovered that each of the people was made up of infinitely tiny humans in different shades of tan, black, and white. Even when she tried to make a normal painting, it came out strange.

When I returned to the kitchen, I grabbed my purse from the kitchen counter. "I've got a lot of work. We can talk about this later."

Ross groaned. "Maya, you don't work there anymore. You need to figure out what you're going to do next, not stew about how to get that job back. It was a terrible job for you, a pointless money-grubbing job."

"You don't understand. Spencer has clout. If I don't mend what's broken, I'll never work in this town again," I said. "Or I'll have to start all over with the worst cases at some crappy nothing little practice. I don't want to be clawing my way up, doing document review and answering interrogatories at my age." It struck me that his take on using the lemur could be useful—his take was always an "objective" take—but I also needed to shut him down and prove I was right.

"Better you start at the bottom with a clean slate. You were always coming home from work complaining about trouble, Maya. Things that would go wrong that you would fix in some way that had you typing emails at three a.m. Or sitting at dinner with glazed eyes, not hearing a word we were saying."

I couldn't really deny either of these assertions.

"So tell me, what did you do?" he asked.

"I don't know," I said. "Spencer wouldn't tell me."

"Why not?"

"I don't know and I probably wouldn't be able to tell you anyway. Attorney—"

"Client privilege," he finished with an air of boredom and sneered, "I know, I know what you do is *top secret*. And I'm equally certain you think you did whatever you did in this situation out of some misguided loyalty to the client."

"At least I am loyal," I said. Then I realized this wasn't strictly true, so I changed my tack. "You are so frustrating! What do you know about the law? I owed my client that loyalty. That's what my license is for. It's not misguided, it was a fucked-up situation." Sanctimony was creeping into my voice, and if I'd been speaking to anyone but Ross (whose own holier-than-thou tone I knew too well), I would have suppressed it, knowing that most people found it unpersuasive.

"Okay, do you hear yourself? 'It was a fucked-up situation.' One, you're still not taking responsibility. Two, you were fired over this. You don't want to be back with those people. Even if what you did was wrong, what they're doing by suing every Tom, Dick-head, and Harry? It's insane. Three, our marriage ended over this. What does it say about us that you would choose a job like that over your own family?" Ross flushed as he spoke. He was pacing around in his socks and slipped on the hardwood, catching himself by grabbing hold of the counter, but I kept going like a fire was burning beneath me, saying all the things I hadn't said before because I'd always poured all the energy it took for me to speak honestly into my work instead.

Finally I said, "You saw how hard I worked. I'm not going to throw eight years away without any sort of fight. It's not like you, with how you knew what you wanted to do."

"What are you talking about?"

"Physics just landed in your lap. Numbers, ideas—everything came easy for you and you didn't even care. You're just talented like that. You're one of a small number of people for whom the American Dream was invented. Men. Men who are so talented, they barely have to try. You don't understand what it's like to never be that person, not even in elementary school when everybody's supposed to be special."

"Of course, I cared," he said. "You think you're the only person who's had a dream? What did you think I was doing, those early years of our marriage, when I worked late?"

I shook my head, knowing he didn't get it. "You didn't care like I cared. I worked my ass off to become a lawyer, to make something of myself when I was nothing and nobody. Invisible."

"You're every bit as talented as me," Ross said. He'd paused before he said it, and I knew he didn't quite believe it, although he was probably as desperate as I was to think what he was saying was true.

Outside, I got into my car and slammed the door, hoping Ross could hear it all the way inside his apartment. I turned the radio volume up, letting blare The Pixies, the music of my youth, which I still secretly listened to. My anger had been coiled up, silent, waiting for the right time to erupt. In my early years of practice, I would have to argue a trivial point in front of a judge. Spencer would send me in to make some hypertechnical point about a motion we filed. He famously used power plays against the other side to rack up their fees or to get our version of the facts in front of the judge repeatedly—if you repeated certain facts often enough, they wormed into people's brains and became a kind of truth. Often, the judge would see through the strategy and punish me in front of the other attorneys, humiliating me with a tongue-lashing or threatening to sanction the client or the firm. I'd want to let go, whether the result was tears or not, but I couldn't. Instead I clammed up, letting the coldness of my anger guide me, and this allowed me to articulate my points more clearly, often changing the judge's mind about the merits of the motion—even though his first instinct was usually correct—and I won more often than not.

But disappointingly, the same techniques never worked on my family. "You're trying to lawyer me again," Tara said, echoing Ross. "That's really annoying?" I tried to dissuade her from talking like a Valley girl, tried to make her understand that other people wouldn't take her seriously if she were always asking and yielding, never taking up space. But she kept on the way she was, occasionally adding she would never work for "the man" the way I did.

I cooperated with Katie Snow and arranged for the deposition to take place even earlier than her notice demanded, hoping I could hustle the lemur onto his flight faster—and because I was dying to prove Spencer wrong. On the afternoon after I finalized the details of his deposition, the lemur lolled on his stomach in front of the television with a can of Coke, resting on his elbows and hitting the buttons on the console with his thumbs. "Bam, bam, bam!" he mumbled as he rounded a corner and shot at an assassin. I put my conversation with Ross out of my mind, replacing the memory with thoughts of impending victory. It would all be over soon.

"Come on," I said, taking pity on the lemur. "Let's go to the passport agency."

The almost-white sky was luminous rather than drab as we drove across the Bay Bridge and into the City. We stood in a long queue with nothing to eat but spearmint Lifesavers and stale protein bars while waiting to file for an emergency passport and visas.

CHAPTER 8

I'm not a superstitious person. I never saw any signs of impending failure or ruin in the gray-bellied clouds as the hottest days of summer morphed into a muggy autumn, as the star jasmine plant growing next to my front door cascaded over the sidewalk and curled over the doormat, as neon-green moss metastasized across the siding of my house for lack of maintenance, as the lemur came to believe his story. In fact, I thought it could only help us that he believed more and more in the tale of empowerment that we'd made up together.

Years later, I would be able to see that there had been another way to hold at bay the insanity that ensued—we could have simply disobeyed the subpoena and left—but in the days before the deposition, I felt as if I were following the right script. Victory seemed to be so close. I didn't see how what I was doing could be wrong. I was sure that in no time I would be the one saying, "I told you so" to Spencer, to Evers, to Ross, to my father, to anyone who'd doubted me.

On the morning of the deposition, a secretary at Katie Snow's office seated us in one of their largest conference rooms with the court reporter, a videographer, Katie, and Spencer. From the window I could see the indigo blue spire of a church, the neon signs on the shops of Koreatown, the pale tops of cars like sticky sugar pastilles, crammed together in the heated traffic. No birds were out. An assistant passed around mugs of coffee, plastic thimblefuls of creamer, and pink paper packets of sweeteners. Katie picked up a cup with her name scrawled on the side in black marker. She'd bought her own coffee from a nearby café, and once I started drinking from the mug of bitter sewage that was passed to me, I understood why.

At the start of the deposition, she ran through the standard admonitions and began to make her way down an outline of questions to examine the lemur. Her version of an outline, however, wasn't simply topics to be covered, but a massive list of questions, twenty pages or so long. Apparently, she assumed this way she covered everything, discounting the likelihood that the lemur would say something unexpected that required follow-up. I looked at Spencer, hoping to see his expression of disapproval toward someone other than me. He didn't like lawyers who used detailed outlines for their depositions, claiming these were either new lawyers or hacks who didn't really know the facts of their cases and that reading from a list was a surefire way to miss crucial follow-up and details. The use of outlines irritated him so much he tended to throw out objections in order to intimidate opposing counsel, irrespective of the legitimacy of the question. Even the background portion of the deposition lasted an hour or two longer than it should have, with Spencer objecting between every question and answer. Despite his past lectures to me, he showed no sign of disapproval toward Katie. Anxiety buzzed inside me, but it was too late to change my course.

Katie took a sip of her latte and read the next question on her list. "And so what prompted you to leave the mural?"

"Vague, ambiguous, assumes facts, irrelevant," objected Spencer. "May call for an expert opinion."

"Can I answer?" The lemur looked at me.

"Yes, remember, you can answer unless I instruct you not to," I said. During our prep sessions, I'd told him objections were voiced simply to create a record, but he still wore a confused expression, rubbing a knot in the surface of the oak conference table with one hand. It looked like he had a tic, moving his hand back and forth. I wondered if he were trying to stifle one of his songs.

"Okay. So what was the question again?"

"Can you read the question back?" I asked the court reporter.

"What?" the court reporter said. She jumped a little in her seat and pushed her glasses up on her nose. "Read what back? I haven't been typing anything. I mean that monkey keeps talking!"

"Can we get another steno in here?" Spencer asked, groaning.

"For the record, I'm not a monkey," said the lemur.

The court reporter apologized for not realizing the lemur was the witness, and the deposition started all over, until we arrived at the question, "What prompted you to leave the mural?"

"That's kind of a stupid question. Would you want to be on a wall?"

"What I want is irrelevant," Katie said.

"Listen, I had enough of watching plastic bags blowing up the street and getting peed on by homeless guys. Just wasn't made for that, you know? And so I thought, hey, I'll swing off this wall, see what else is out there. Turned out there wasn't much *there* there. You know?"

"Just answer the question," I said.

"Sorry," he said.

"Did my clients ask you to leave the mural?" asked Katie, who appeared to be taking notes verbatim on her laptop instead of listening to his answers. Spencer rolled his eyes, and I started to feel more comfortable.

"No. Though truth be told, I don't think they dug the mural. They were standing in front of it one morning, talking with a painter about whitewashing over it and complaining how the paint had faded. Neighbors thought it was an eyesore."

"If I may, Counsel. I have questions about that," Spencer said. "Was that—?"

"Write your questions down and ask when it's your turn,

Counsel," I said, interrupting him. "Keeps things orderly." He rolled his eyes again, and wrote something on the yellow pad in front of him.

"Did you ever learn why they didn't paint the building?" asked Katie.

"Oh, they wanted to, all right. But that isn't why I left. Not that I wanted to be painted into oblivion or anything, but it was more important to me to get back into the wild than to avoid being painted over. In fact, I'd already be there if you hadn't subpoenaed me."

"I'm sorry about that. You know how lawyers are." Katie smiled through too much baby-pink lipstick. Then, surprisingly, she winked. By flirting, she hoped to relax him into volunteering more information, something that would help her case. The videotape was trained on the lemur, so it didn't pick up her wink. "We'll get you back as soon as we can. Now, let me get through a few more questions. What was your goal in leaving?"

"My goal?" the lemur asked.

"Yes, what did you hope to accomplish by leaving?" she asked again.

"Asked and answered," said Spencer. He leaned the office chair so far back I thought, and hoped, he would topple over.

"Goal was to get out of the painting," said the lemur.

"Is that because you thought there was something wrong with the painting?"

"I dunno. I can't remember." The lemur's face contorted. I sat on my hand to keep from reaching out and touching his arm.

"You hesitated a little bit before answering. I'll ask again, and remember, you should answer by using real words—was there something wrong with the painting?"

"Nothing was wrong with it, really. It just looked like other painted murals."

"So then, you believed it was derivative? Lacking in value?"

"Objection, that's outside the scope of his deposition," Spencer said. "He's not an expert, is he?"

"We haven't designated him as such yet, but maybe we will. Who knows the painting better than he does? He's a percipient expert witness. Your objection is noted, Mr. Clark." Katie looked at the lemur expectantly. "You can answer."

"I'm not an expert. I don't know anything about art," the lemur said, following the script we'd rehearsed.

"But you knew about this painting, surely. Did you believe that it was derivative?"

"It was copied from a photograph, so in that sense, yes." I'd asked the lemur during our prep session to avoid volunteering anything that could be construed as an attack on Turner, who after all, had painted him, and to whom I still had an ethical obligation. I assumed the lemur was talking about the photograph of an indri that Turner had taken on his trip to Madagascar and used as a reference point for his mural. Before I could think too much about this, Spencer's eyelids were fluttering down as if he was about to fall asleep.

"Were you uncomfortable being a copy?" asked Katie. Spencer's eyes opened again.

"Objection, Counsel, what does his comfort level have to do with this case?" he asked. He voiced a few more objections, and it seemed plain he was trying to rattle Katie.

"I wasn't uncomfortable . . . But I mean, come on."

Katie repeated herself, but her voice wobbled, revealing Spencer had gotten to her. Inside, I cheered. "So you were uncomfortable with the fact that Turner painted your likeness based on a photograph?"

"More like, I didn't see the point of it."

"And so you didn't think that the painting was a work of recognizable stature? Something you could be proud to be a part of?"

"Objection, compound," said Spencer.

The lemur looked at me. I nodded for him to answer.

He sighed. "Good artists borrow, great artists steal, right? Or as Steve Jobs said, good artists copy, great artists steal? So I guess it was as recognizable as any other work of 'art' in that most work is derivative. Most artists do copy. And you know, what's the value of art anyway?" He was starting to ramble and I put out a hand to signal that he should stop.

"I'm sorry? You don't think there's value in art?"

"The value of art is in the experience of the people who engage with the art. The people who make their own art from it, even. There's nothing to be gained by preventing them from engaging, and there's everything to be lost." He recited the words we'd developed together, but I cringed. Even I could hear how canned, how rehearsed they sounded.

"Counsel, is this going somewhere?" I asked.

"So, you self-identify as a copy?" asked Katie.

"OK, you got me. I'm a copy."

"And you believe that willful copyright infringement is acceptable?"

"Objection, assumes facts, calls for a legal conclusion, may call for an expert opinion," I said.

"Yes."

"And you *intentionally* left the painting?" asked Katie, smiling again and picking up her latte. She was no longer reading from her outline. I had almost the same sinking sensation I'd experienced when Ross told me he was moving out, and I realized that my gambles—not to fix my marriage immediately, to bring the lemur to Spencer, to cooperate with the deposition subpoena—all involved a far greater risk of failure than I'd imagined.

"Well, no, I didn't leave it with the intention to leave. I left because I couldn't stay."

"Would you say you left without thinking about the ramifications?"

"Yes."

"And was that because you didn't believe the painting had value?"

"I don't think it had value, but that's only my nonexpert opinion. It clearly had value for Brian and the art students from California College of Arts and Crafts who came to draw it periodically. A lack of value isn't why I left." The lemur looked from side to side, like he was hoping for an opportunity to escape.

Spencer interposed more objections. He leaned forward in his seat, his tie falling slant on his crisp white dress shirt. I waited for him to see that I was right, but she pressed forward with her questions.

"Counsel, how much more of this is there? I think we should break for lunch," I said, looking at my watch.

"It's only eleven thirty," said Katie. "Can you hang on for a few more minutes? And then Spencer gets his turn." I had no choice but to let the deposition continue, though I now regretted producing the lemur at all.

After many more questions that all sounded like variations on the same one, Katie asked, "Did you discuss the decision to leave with Maya Ramesh?"

"Objection, that's attorney-client privileged information," I said, irritated.

"So, you represent the lemur?" asked Katie. "I thought you represented Brian Turner?"

"I'm the lemur's attorney for this deposition. And there's no conflict of interest, from my perspective." The lemur was my ticket to returning to my old job or to acquiring a new one. It was a fine line I hoped to walk, between implicating him just enough to convince Spencer of my points and not implicating him too much.

"We'll see about that."

She asked a few more questions before we broke for lunch. I excused myself, ostensibly to freshen up in the bathroom, but truly to collect my confidence. Here were the facts: I was fired right before I would have made partner, I'd barely dodged a state bar inquiry for unknown ethics violations, and we were in the middle of a legal recession. But years of litigation had taught me that facts, at least the way the public thinks of them, are usually less important than spin. If I could make this lemur important to resolving the mural lawsuit—how, I wasn't sure—then Spencer's firm or some other powerful firm was bound to give me a chance.

Katie followed me into the bathroom and stood at the sink, smiling toothily at her reflection in the silver-framed mirror, the smile reading as a taunt. She retouched her lip liner and smeared more pink gloss over her thin, dry lips. "I'm loving this deposition," she said, as she dropped her gloss into a small Coach bag.

"Is this the first case the partners let you take the lead on?" I asked. The partner she worked for was a control freak, a micromanager. I'd been invited to interview with her myself way back when, but had decided my career would be better off in the hands of a male partner. Less jealousy, less suspicion. Sounds sexist, but it cuts both ways—unlike many women, Spencer hadn't seen me as a threat, and that perception was what had allowed me to advance.

"No," she said, blushing. I wasn't sure if it was a blush that indicated I was right, or a blush in response to me suggesting she wasn't good enough, but when she narrowed her blue eyes at me and wrinkled her nose, I was reasonably certain I'd pushed the right buttons. "I like your shoes," she said. "I love platform heels."

"Okay, that's one strategy." I smiled. Then I repeated something bleak my former legal assistant, a surgically enhanced fifty-year-old Bettie Page look-alike, had told me my first day of work, something that replayed in my head like a pop song earworm every so often: "See how far being sweet will get you." Years of exposure had softened my assistant toward me. During the last office Christmas party at Spencer's sun-flooded mansion in the Berkeley Hills, she'd pulled me aside and offered me eggnog made of more rum than egg. Hovering by the elaborate Dickens village that Spencer constructed and disassembled holiday after holiday, we watched an electric train circle the rickety tracks around plastic cobblestone streets and miniature Victorian slums in an infinite loop, while in the background the Mormon Tabernacle Choir trilled "it's a marshmallow world." She advised me to watch out for Evers, that he was the partner that most frequently gave a thumbs-down to Spencer's proposals to advance female associates.

"And don't think that being 'nice' will make things any better. It's usually the sweet ones he throws under the bus. See how far being sweet will get you in this business," she'd repeated. At the time of that Christmas party, I'd been secretly happy about this. The last thing anyone would ever have described me as was "sweet" and in the law, I'd finally found a place where that was a good thing. After repeating Patti's words to Katie, I wondered for the first time whether it would have been better to have ignored what she'd said.

The lemur and I chose Luka's for lunch. Though I was ravenous, we split only a roasted beet salad, Belgian-style fries, and a curried vegetable stew. I had enough savings to last for some time, but was starting to tighten my belt, still living well beyond the way my parents had lived when we first moved to America, but less well than I had as Spencer's associate.

"How am I doing?" the lemur asked. He was sipping his iced tea. The mint leaf floating on the surface stuck to his nose and he shook his head trying to remove it. The waitress came by with a refill.

"Keep it shorter. You're giving them too much material to work with. The more you give them, the more they have to spin in their favor. Stop lecturing them on your theory of copyright. You're not an expert in this. I saw them giving each other looks. We need to make them turn on each other, not seize upon your words for more ammo. And Katie Snow is trying to make it seem like she's your . . . friend . . . but she's not."

He looked sheepish. "I know, I know. I'll try to keep it shorter. Why does she keep asking me about the value of the painting?"

"She's trying to get you to say it wasn't valuable, that it was a trivial piece."

"She doesn't need me to say that. Anyone will tell you that it was just an okay mural, nothing to get worked up about."

My skin heated up with embarrassment, since clearly, I'd gotten worked up about it. "We don't know that for sure. History may place things in a different perspective. Like van Gogh's paintings. They were worth nothing in his lifetime because nobody recognized his talent, but after his death, they gained a following and look at his legacy now. He's on coffee cups! And key chains! With a little distance, we may see this mural as the one that galvanized Oakland's art scene."

"You think a little distance will turn a mural depicting Madagascar, a country America doesn't know anything about beyond a Disney movie, make that a few Disney movies, into the galvanizer of an art scene? Shit, man. That's reaching."

"Stranger things have happened," I said. "Who would have predicted there would one day be a Banksy London walking tour? Who would have expected Duchamp's toilet to spawn countless copycats? Success will always breed copies."

Inside the conference room after lunch, I sensed with dismay the alliances in the room had shifted. At one end of the conference table, Katie and Spencer were smiling and chatting over sandwiches from the same deli, their wrappers and a small stack of paper napkins strewn over the blond wood of the conference table. The videographer trained the camera on the lemur again, and the court reporter reminded him he was under oath. We went back on the record. Spencer wiped his hands, gulped one-quarter of a root beer, and took over the questioning. Unlike Katie, he asked questions so rapid-fire there was no time for me to object to anything, there was almost no chance to breathe.

"Earlier you testified you left the painting intentionally, correct?"

"Yes. I—"

"So you no longer consider yourself part of Brian Turner's imagination. Is that correct?"

"I guess."

"Yes or no?"

"Yes. I became part of the world after he painted me. Is that what you're asking?" asked the lemur.

"Strike that please," Spencer said to the court reporter. "I didn't ask you that. Stick to answering my questions. You went rogue, is that correct?"

"Yes, I guess."

"But you had no judgments about whether the painting was good or bad, correct?"

"Correct."

"Did you consider the damage to the integrity of my client's work that would occur as a result of you leaving?" asked Spencer.

"Damage? No," said the lemur.

"Did you think about the damage to his reputation as a result of leaving?"

"Um. No?"

"Is that your answer?"

"Yes. I mean, yes my answer is no."

"Do you believe you belong to the Eustachios?" asked Spencer.

"No, I don't belong to them either."

"Is it your contention you are now a free agent, belonging to no one?"

"Yes."

"Objection, belated objection," I said. "You can't ask contention interrogatories during a deposition in California, Spencer. *Rifkind v. Superior Court.* That's a legal conclusion, something he would need my help with. And he's not even a party."

"Not yet," said Spencer. He continued with a magnanimous

shrug. "That's not a federal case citation, Ms. Ramesh. But I can rephrase. Sir, do you think you belong to someone?"

"No, I don't belong to anyone," said the lemur, looking puzzled.

"Do you feel you were driven off that wall by the fact that the Eustachios considered you an eyesore?"

"An eyesore. Something offensive to the eye, but it could just as well be an actual sore on the eye, something that disrupts vision."

"Answer the question, please."

"I guess."

"Yes or no?"

"No," the lemur said. He was clutching his head between his hands, as if he had a headache, and I wasn't sure he really knew what he was saying. Spencer continued to pummel him with questions.

An hour later, Spencer was still going strong, and I wanted to lay my head on the table from exhaustion. "Do you see yourself as a product of Brian Turner's imagination?"

"You can choose to see me that way, but I don't see myself that way. I got out in the world and now it's anyone's guess what I'm a product of."

"But you understood that it was Mr. Turner's intention that you stay inside the mural."

"I guess . . . Yes."

"And you thwarted that intention purposefully. Did you want to harm Mr. Turner?"

"No."

"But you recklessly disregarded his intent? Fair enough?"

"Objection, argumentative, calls for a legal conclusion. You can't do that, Spencer," I said, noticing that Katie was looking at me with an untoward amount of glee. They were ganging up on the lemur, and that could only mean one thing. We were in danger of ending up implicated in this lawsuit. There was nothing I could do about it. If I suspended the deposition, they would move to compel the rest of it, which could take another month. The ship by which I planned to sail right back into my old job was sinking. The ocean was darkening. We were fucked.

"I'll rephrase. Did you care about Brian Turner's intent for this mural?"

"I don't know," the lemur said.

"You were entirely unconcerned with what it might look like for Mr. Turner, you leaving the mural. Fair?"

"Yes."

"Did you consider whether you were damaging Mr. Turner's reputation?"

"No."

"Did you contact Mr. Turner, to give him notice and the opportunity to make a copy of his mural before you left?"

"No."

"Do you have any intentions to return to the mural?" Spencer asked.

"None."

"Did you learn at any time that your appearance in the mural was intended to break the picture plane?"

"Break the picture plane?"

"Yes, did you realize that you were painted in such a way as to make the painting seem to come to life?" Spencer was leaning forward with his arms on the table, like he was about to seize the lemur and eat him.

"Yes."

"So you understood that it was critical you remain in the painting in that semi-suspended state in order for the meaning of the artist's work to become clear to viewers?"

"Well, no. I mean there were other lemurs who sort of came off the wall, too, I think. I wasn't the only one Turner painted in trompe l'oeil."

"Really? You sure about that? Let's take a look." Spencer pulled out photographs and marked them as exhibits to the deposition. He handed each of us copies. The photograph depicted the right side of the mural as it had originally existed. The lemur was still snug in his place in the painting. I'd never seen that version of the mural in real life.

"Do you see that?" he asked the lemur. "Do you still think that the other lemurs were painted in the same style as you?"

"Yeah, I guess I am the only one painted fully in trompe l'oeil," the lemur conceded.

"Most of the other lemurs are quite a bit less realistic. They're flatter, correct? More two-dimensional?"

"Objection, calls for an expert opinion. Is he here as an expert or a percipient witness?" I flipped through the copies of photographs. I was hoping to buy the lemur some time to think about the answers he was lobbing back. One of the photographs of the original mural, before he left it, chilled me. The picture showed the back of my head and upper body. A woman that had the same curly hair as mine, as my doppelganger's: same shoulders, same curve to the top of her spine. I shivered. I had never seen the mural before I was assigned to handle the *Turner v. Eustachio* lawsuit, had never even been on that street, but the photograph said otherwise.

"Yes," the lemur said. They both ignored me.

"Did viewers spend more time engaging with you than the rest of the painting?"

"I guess they did," the lemur said. Spencer started to admonish him and he answered, "I mean, yes."

"In your opinion, is the painting better because you're in it?"

"Objection! There's no foundation for this line of questioning, Spencer," I said. "He's not an expert."

"You would have us believe that the subject of the painting is not an expert on it?" asked Katie.

"No, simply because he was in the painting, he's not more knowledgeable about it," I said, clenching my fists under the table. It sounded laughable even to me. Of course, he should know more about the painting, but in reality, he didn't. I should have told him to be totally honest. "Don't answer that."

"You can't instruct him not to answer," said Spencer.

"He's my client. I can instruct him as I see fit."

"Your client is Brian Turner. Not the lemur. And to the extent their interests are in conflict, you can't represent them both. You're already on ethical thin ice, Maya." Spencer sat back, root beer in hand, and smiled.

"Actually, their interests can't be adverse, Spencer. You just spent the last hour suggesting he is part of Brian Turner, a part of his imagination. You can't have it both ways," I said. I wondered what would happen if I knocked the smug root beer out of his hands. I looked down at the photograph of my doppelganger standing in front of the mural. What did she have to do with the lemur leaving the wall? I realized then that I might never know.

"Perhaps you two can resolve this issue off the record," Katie said. "I just have a couple more questions to follow up before we finish. Were you aware that this mural was insured?"

"No," the lemur said.

"Did you realize, by taking off the way you did, you were essentially making a false statement about the mural?"

"Objection, argumentative," I said, groaning. "I don't even know what that means."

"I didn't make a false statement."

"Didn't your actions essentially say, hey, I'm not really a part of this mural?"

"Maybe that's reasonable, but I didn't lie with words," said the lemur.

"And wasn't that a false impression?"

"Objection, calls for a legal conclusion," I said.

"No, that wasn't a false impression. I'm not part of the mural, as you can see. I have a life of my own," said the lemur.

"All right. I can't guarantee that the insurance company won't ask for a separate deposition on the policy coverage issues. But that's all I have, Maya," Katie said.

"That's it?" I asked.

"That's all we need." Katie turned to the court reporter to order a transcript.

"Should I note him as a monkey on the transcript?" said the court reporter.

"I'm not a monkey," said the lemur. "Lemurs and monkeys and apes are all primates, but lemurs are prosimians, whereas monkeys are monkeys."

"Note him as 'Lemur,'" I said.

"We'll need that transcript expedited, please. Can you get me a rough?" asked Katie.

Katie and Spencer left the room. The court reporter shook her head and murmured to herself. I asked the lemur, "While I was in the bathroom, you didn't tell Spencer and Katie anything off-record, did you?"

"I didn't. Did you want me to?"

"Definitely not," I said. Dispirited, we left the office.

"It wasn't that bad," said the lemur when we were home.

"Trust me, it's plenty bad. It's definitely not going the way I planned. Katie and Spencer have joined forces."

Lawyers, perpetually focused on climbing ladders toward the ever-elusive sign that they are the best, whether that's having gone to a top-ten law school according to the *U.S. News and World Report*, or appearing on the cover of a magazine, or being dubbed a Super Lawyer, are often attracted to what's hot and popular; it's a sign of status to be associated with whatever has won in the marketplace of ideas. So much of tort law is built on what a reasonable man would do—as if the reasonable thing is the same as what the majority would do—that lawyers are always looking for verification of their worth from others, others that are assumed to be reasonable rather than moblike: rash, brutal, and cruel.

If I could sell the lemur's story, I would be relevant again, not a has-been associate who didn't make partner, but the kind of trial lawyer who wins even the most unwinnable cases. Ross and the kids would come home. I would retrieve my old life. Then again, although I missed Ross and the kids, I didn't miss feeling perpetually discontent.

"You're freaking out about nothing," said the lemur. He grabbed a carton of milk from the refrigerator and dumped in instant pistachio pudding mix. I poured a glass of wine. "Let's do something. We got to get your mind off this shit."

I showed him the closet with the board games. He pulled one out, and we sat cross-legged on the living room floor, unwrapping red and blue Stratego pieces from two plastic bags. I showed him how to play. The game was Mike's favorite, and our family had spent many holidays playing tournaments. I could tell pretty quickly where he had hidden his flag, but it was surrounded by bombs.

CHAPTER 9

Early in the mornings as the sun crept over the
mountains, villagers would send a honey hunter
to venture among the rosewoods in the eastern
forests. The villagers needed to determine where
the swarm had settled, where the honey flowed.
The honey hunter would examine the bee droppings
on the leaves. He would watch wild bees as they
swarmed by, dark against the glowing red sun. When
he found the dark hole in the tree where the swarm
made its home, he would light dried sisal and smoke
the bees and their queen from the hole. When they
were out, he would gather honeycomb.

In one village, a man named Koto was the honey
hunter. Early in the morning, Koto took his son with
him into the woods to gather honeycomb. The villagers waited for his return. As night fell, he still
hadn't returned with honey. The next morning, an
elder organized a rescue party. They followed the
large, toe-heavy footprints of the man and the
light, nearly invisible footprints of his child in the
muddy woods. Deep in the forest, the footprints
disappeared. Up above them two indri leaped from
branch to branch.

The villagers believed these indri were the man

The lemur had no interest in the legends about his kind that kept
turning up on the internet. He had reached the next level on his
video games. Next to him on the carpet were three empty, crum-
pled red Coke cans with claw marks where he'd grabbed them
mindlessly and chugged.

Our flight to Madagascar via Paris was scheduled for two days
later. I wanted to admonish him about the Coke cans, and explain
how unhealthy soda was, a lecture I'd given my children numerous times, but I thought I might as well let him indulge since he
would soon be on his way. I went to the bathroom adjoining my
bedroom to wash my hands for dinner and to check my phone for
messages from Evers or Ross, without the lemur asking me why
I was checking again. I heard a knock on the front door. "What
now?" the lemur asked in a grouchy voice.

"Can you get that?" I shouted.

I heard him unlock the door. Someone said, "You been served."

I dried my hands on a towel and went out. The lemur was
clutching a sheaf of pleading paper. I took it from him. The caption on the face page read "Cross-complaint of Peter Eustachio et
al." The causes of action listed were (1) Violation of Visual Artists
Rights Act, (2) Violation of California Art Preservation Act, (3)
Intentional Property Damage, (4) Negligent Property Damage,
(5) Nuisance, (6) Indemnity, and (7) Declaratory Relief.

I sank into the couch and flipped through the cross-complaint.
Since they weren't the artist that created the work, the Eustachios
couldn't recover for a violation of the Visual Artists Rights Act
or the California Art Preservation Act, but Katie, ever the diligent and niggling insurance defense attorney, had asserted these
claims in order to protect the possibility that they were somehow
viable.

The lemur paced back and forth, muttering, "What the fuck. I do you one little favor and what do I get? A lawsuit. That's right. A lawsuit. What the fuck?"

"Shut up," I said, examining the papers for technical errors. "I need quiet, so I can think about what to do." Katie had brought us into this lawsuit, but was Spencer next? If so, what duties did I have to my former client? Could I even represent the lemur? He trudged into the kitchen, his head hanging. I heard his loud rummaging through the cupboards. He returned with a stiff bag of salt-and-vinegar kettle chips and a bottle of ghost pepper sauce.

"I'm not going to shut up!" He sat down beside me and pulled out a fistful of chips, drizzled the ghost pepper sauce over them, and stuffed his mouth. I expected him to wince with pain from the spicy heat, but he kept munching. "I'm never going to shut up again. This happened because I listened to you. Because, like a moron, I thought we'd now be on our way to Madagascar, but you're so selfish and self-absorbed, you dragged me into your mess instead. Fuck fuck *fuck*." As fistful after fistful of chips doused in pepper sauce entered his mouth, I remained amazed he didn't burn his tongue off.

"This, or something just as bad, might have happened regardless of what I did. If I hadn't taken you in and put a roof over your head, you might have been taken to the zoo. I'm not sure how that would be any better. All the alternatives were bad." This wasn't strictly true, but I wanted to defuse his rage.

The lemur continued muttering. He gulped down some hot sauce and bounded around the room, slamming into the sage-colored walls. Worried that he'd punch a hole through the drywall, I rose and placed my hands on his furry shoulders. He shrugged me off. "Look, I came to you because I saw you as a chance to go home," he said. "I thought if I helped you, you'd help me. Instead, I get this."

"Let's just step back a minute, okay? How did you find me in the first place?"

"What is this, another deposition? Are you even allowed to be my lawyer?"

"I think so. You're not being sued by Spencer's client. Yet."

"Bananas. This is bananas. Why don't you make sure before you go questioning me?" He stomped off to the kitchen again.

"Okay, yeah, that's probably a good idea." I pulled out my cell phone and called Spencer half-cocked. I had no idea what I would do if he said, oh, actually, we're preparing a complaint against the lemur, too, and I was expecting voicemail, but the receptionist put me through directly to him.

"Maya," he said with the commanding voice I'd once found comforting. "What can I do for you?"

"Katie Snow just served the lemur with a cross-complaint. Is this what you two were plotting about during lunch?" Through the glass door, I saw a hawk circling the sky above our house, around and around as if he couldn't veer off his preset path.

"Don't be paranoid. I had nothing to do with it. She believes the lemur is responsible, and her clients are footing the bill for what's proving to be an expensive lawsuit. I can see her point of view."

"Do you plan to follow suit?"

He laughed. "No pun intended, right? Not at this time. I think the Eustachios will be successful in obtaining insurance coverage, and all this business with a lemur just distracts."

"You're not going to take issue with me filing an answer on behalf of the lemur and probably representing him, too? Because, like we talked about, he's really a part of Brian Turner and so—"

"Not at this time. Brian already signed off. I'll send you his agreement to your little arrangement in writing. But we'll be seeking a continuance of the trial, so that we can handle this new aspect of the case."

I hung up feeling only mild relief. It was perplexing that he and Brian Turner were letting me represent the lemur without any sort of fuss—perhaps they found me harmless, no kind of threat.

That would certainly fit with what Evers had told me. Or was their nonchalance part of a greater malevolent scheme? I shoved those concerns to the back of my mind. "Everything's fine," I told the lemur. "He's still pursuing insurance. It shouldn't be a problem for me to file an answer for you and continue to represent you."

I searched through the sheaf of papers, which included a rough copy of the deposition transcript. In among the attached exhibits, I found the copy of the photograph from the deposition that showed the other Maya and examined it.

"Fine? You're not getting it. I'm dying! I'm slowly *dying*. None of my kind has ever lived more than a year outside Madagascar. I want to be where I belong, not in this industrial wasteland you call home."

"Okay, okay. I understand you're upset. But it's really not so bad. I can totally handle Katie Snow. I'll answer the cross-complaint on your behalf. I'll figure out a way for you to get out of this." I put the papers down and turned to face him. He'd eaten through half of the bag of chips and his mouth and nose were greasy.

"I'm not just upset," he said, dropping the second bag of kettle chips. "What kind of sadist are you? You pull me into this mess and think it's all better because I'm stuck with *you* as my attorney?"

"A bit of a low blow, isn't it?" I grabbed the bag, rolled it up, and took it to the kitchen and stored it in a cupboard.

"Not low enough, if you're still yapping." He flicked on the television, but I could tell it was from force of habit. He wasn't watching.

We spent the rest of the evening not speaking. He tried to play video games, but kept losing, while I surfed the internet and sent out my resume to every contact I could remember from prior cases. I needed the financial resources of a big firm if I was going to fight Katie Snow on an issue like this. Though I wanted to have nothing to do with Evers, I didn't know for certain he'd betrayed us and, since he was the person most likely to give me a job reference, making a big firm's backing possible, I texted him. I poured a glass of wine and stared at the phone, willing it to beep. Eventually, I fell asleep on the couch to the sound of explosions on TV, trying to figure out how I was going to fund the lemur's defense.

The next morning, my phone rang with the underwater submarine tone that alerted me I didn't know the caller. I jerked awake on the third ring, my mouth slow to open as if it were plugged with cotton, and sat up on the couch. Hoping it was a law firm calling to offer me a job, I answered with as much ebullience as I could muster.

"Is this Maya Ramesh?" asked a low, treacly voice.

"Yes, who's this?"

"My name is Jill Sutherland. I'm an editor at the *New York Times*. You have a lemur living with you, correct? And he's just been named a defendant in a copyright infringement lawsuit?"

"This is a joke, right?" I thought it best not to admit anything to the person on the other end.

"No, this is real. Do you have some time to answer some questions? You're the attorney representing the lemur, aren't you?"

"Is this really the *Times*?"

"Yes," she said.

"Yes, I'm representing him." I wasn't convinced that a newspaper as prestigious as the *New York Times* found this a matter of interest and wondered who might want to play such a baroque prank on me. "How did you find us?"

I heard her breathing, a gauzy pulse over the wire, an inhale and exhale that were barely perceptible. "I can't reveal my sources."

"This doesn't seem newsworthy," I said in confusion.

The woman laughed. Her laughter wasn't sinister, but it definitely wasn't friendly, either. "I understand he may be a cryptid and that scientists have never previously admitted his existence. I'd say that's newsworthy, wouldn't you?"

"Listen, I'll have him call you back if he's interested in going public. Thank you." I hung up.

"Who was that?" asked the lemur. He'd gone to sleep in Mike's bedroom the night before, but was now standing, arms crossed, in the living room, eyeing me with suspicion.

"A reporter. From no less than the *New York Times*."

The lemur grunted. "*Times* isn't relevant anymore. I read it on Twitter. What did they want?"

"She wanted to interview you."

The lemur looked like he was ready to jump through the window, ready to jump into the eucalyptus trees and bound off screaming, and he might have, if I hadn't reached out to steady him. "About what?"

"About—don't panic—but somebody told them you're a cryptid whose existence has never been verified by scientists."

"Holy fuck," he said. "I need to get out of here."

"Calm down. Let's take a minute and think through this." I patted his shoulder. His fur was becoming matted again and he would need another shower. After the last one, the drain had been clogged with black-and-white fur, so I'd been procrastinating the arduous task of convincing him to take one again.

"Take a minute? I gotta start packing!"

I didn't think Katie would have told the *New York Times* about a cryptid. The last thing she wanted was publicity. Similarly, Spencer was out. That left Evers, who had never given me a true account of his collective. He was the one who'd advised me to let the lemur go to the deposition. He may have been the one to tell Katie Snow about the lemur. I thought about how he'd spied on us through the windows, and broke out in goose bumps. I looked around. The cold dawn light frosted the tops of the coffee table, the sofa cushions, and the wall-mounted TV with a white clarity. I felt we were being watched. I tiptoed through the house looking for a face behind the window glass, certain I would see someone else's two eyes, a nose, lips looking back at me.

When I couldn't spot anyone, I returned to the lemur. "I'll get you out of this," I said. "And I really think doing this interview could be a good idea. Good press could be exactly what you need."

"I'm going to die if I don't get home. There's nothing good to be gained from this."

"The system can work. Seriously, I'll do my best to make it work for you." I placed my hand on his shoulder.

He wrenched away. He jumped on and off the chairs and couches in a kind of frustrated dance. I wasn't at all sure that I could make the system work for him or for me.

Although I was sitting on my own couch all day every day, with my computer on my lap, wedged between a pillow and a stack of books on art checked out from the library, I had a sudden inexplicable longing for home. That night, I decided to drive over to Ross's place to say hello to him and the kids. It was a clear, cold night with no stars, and I climbed into my car to pay them a surprise visit. I wanted to apologize for what I'd done. Taking up with Evers, letting our marriage slide away like it was nothing.

When I arrived at the apartment, I parked across the street and stayed inside my car outside the dingy building. The place was the color of a swamp after the fireflies leave, and the closest streetlight was half a block away, but there was one window with the lights still on, and it was my husband's.

I got out and walked to the middle of the quiet street. The first floor was slightly higher than the ground floor, but I could see into the apartment through the living room window. Someone had trimmed the ivy that had been covering the facade. The kids stood in the kitchen, which was golden, illuminated by tiny white Christmas lights even though Thanksgiving hadn't happened yet. Mike was washing dishes by hand, rubbing them methodically with a red-and-white-checked rag. He looked older somehow, his silky brown hair falling over his glasses, his pale gold skin glowing, as he rinsed dishes before putting them into the dishwasher. Tara was off to the side, chopping a lump that looked like a potato or misshapen vegan meat. She had a long thin purple stripe in her hair that reminded me vaguely of a period in my adolescence when anything new involving my appearance gave me a thrill. My black hair was chemically fried by the time I'd met Ross because I'd bleached it so frequently.

The air smelled incredibly sweet and fresh, something twisted and green, star jasmine perhaps—a row of it grew in front of the apartment. I heard the sounds of some kind of futuristic ska that had to be Tara's. Ross walked across the kitchen, looking completely relaxed, rather than vigilant and ready for an attack, the way he so often looked when I was around. He wore a Bon Iver T-shirt that Tara had given him for Father's Day, and was smiling and joking with her. I walked up to the edge of the lawn, hoping one of them would sense me there and look outside. When I was little, just after my mother died, I felt certain that people who were deeply connected, true family, had a psychic connection. The feeling never quite went away that there were people out there who would sense my presence, know what I was thinking, and understand me. Over the years, the lack of psychic connection to my father or sister made me want to grow up fast and leave to find my tribe, to make my own family. I had made my own family, but even after all these years, they were more bonded to each other than to me. As I stood there on the sidewalk, watching them in their kitchen, I didn't know why I'd thought Ross and Tara and Mike would sense my presence.

They spoke animatedly about something they thought was funny, something I probably wouldn't have thought was. Tara was dancing a little bit, bobbing her head in time to the music and laughing. She and Mike had Ross's sense of humor, his sense of right and wrong. What had they gotten from me? I'd breastfed them and been their chew toy when they were toddlers. Carrying them had changed my body almost beyond recognition—my feet had remained swollen, my nose had grown, my stomach muscles had permanently slackened. I'd listened to their stories of school-yard rivalries and kissed their boo-boos and dispensed time-outs like Pez candy. Ross had done more, but I had done a lot—at least I had before the last few years when I was desperately trying to make partner. And yet they couldn't sense my presence. I didn't matter at all.

Fifteen minutes passed this way. When they left the kitchen and turned out the light, I climbed back in my car and drove home. I prepared for bed, saddened at how different the routine seemed, now that there was nobody to witness it.

I wanted to text Evers before I went to sleep. *How could you betray me? We're done.* But it wouldn't have mattered to him, either. I lay in the dark, empty bedroom, staring into its blackness as if I could divine answers from the absence of stars, clutching the cell phone to my chest, waiting for a sign, waiting for someone to tell me what I should do.

PART II

MUTATION

"What a chimera then is man! What a novelty! What
a monster, what a chaos, what a contradiction, what
a prodigy! Judge of all things, feeble earthworm,
depository of truth, a sink of uncertainty and error, the
glory and the shame of the universe."

Blaise Pascal

CHAPTER 10

A large-hipped songstress with black-and-white hair
lived deep in the eastern forests of Madagascar. She
gave birth to so many children, she couldn't keep
track of them all and couldn't feed or care for all
of them. Some of them left her and went to live as
farmers, cultivating the land and raising zebu. Others
lived by their wits in the woods, gorging on berries and
leaves. Over time the two groups of children fought
miserably, as all siblings do. The ones who lived as
farmers drove the others deeper into the woods and
higher into the trees.

As the years passed, many of the siblings and
their descendants, who lived high in the trees,
shrank, becoming ever more lithe and agile. They
lost the power of their larger form, became small
shadows of their original selves, developed their
own music. Meanwhile, the siblings and their descendants who lived as farmers grew larger and fatter.
But they, too, were mere shadows of their original
selves.

A Frenchman named Sonnerat visited Perinet in
1782 and asked to see the source of the green howls
that came from the forest. The farmers led him into
the woods and told him, "indri" or "there it is" in

Malagasy. The Frenchman thus believed that the name of those that lived in the forest was "indri."

There were no signs in the sky, nor any in my house, that I could decipher, and yet I persisted in trying to convince the lemur that we should give the *New York Times* the interview. It was the only solution I could conjure—he needed public sympathy, he needed people to want to help him, he needed politicians fighting for him—he certainly needed more than I could give him as a former associate. But no amount of rhetoric would convince him that he should go public.

"If we do it right, we can leverage the public interest to get you out of the lawsuit," I tried. "We'll just expand on what we did for the deposition. We'll create a spectacle, a narrative about freedom and your right to leave the painting, your right to interact with whomever you please. People go wild for that sort of thing these days. They'll want to support you."

"You been drinking the Kool-Aid," he said, shaking his head. He had found a bag of stale marshmallows in the cupboard and was squishing them with his fingers, evidently delighted by the way each marshmallow bounced back into a cube. "You think everything can be solved with publicity stunts and the Constitution. System's jacked, man. The sooner you realize that, the better for both of us."

"You have to trust me," I said. I was sipping a glass of Pinot Noir. At nine a.m. it was too early to be drinking, even for me, but otherwise my anxiety would have shot through the roof. "I get paid—or I used to get paid—to work the system, to find its weak points and exploit them. There's no set of facts a good lawyer can't get around. Trust me."

Actually, I wasn't sure of this. There are too many variables in any given lawsuit to say with any certainty that you can manipulate the outcome. No lawyer can honestly offer that guarantee. Still, I'd taken a number of cases to trial and I'd been on a winning streak. Notwithstanding my confusion surrounding Evers's true intentions, I'd always possessed a sixth sense, or maybe it was more apt to call it a radar, for phoniness—lies, frauds, charlatans—anything where the surface of someone didn't align with the truth of what they were. Lies—inconsistencies, really—caught my attention; they were like the edges of a sticker that had been removed and sloppily replaced, slightly off the original placement.

"How do you get along like this?" He was channel surfing now, clicking through channels as fast as he could, having shifted from a fascination with video games to one with television programs. "Alone here in this big house, drinking wine, and plotting and believing in this corrupt 'system' as if it were the second coming."

It sounded crazy when he put it that way. "I don't know what you're talking about. It's not corrupt."

"If it weren't corrupt, you wouldn't have to work so hard to persuade the public we're right," argued the lemur. He turned on a cooking show and hopped off the sofa to sit closer to the set.

"All cases involve work. Work is the human condition." Although my cases were mostly lower-profile matters, I remembered Spencer advising me that eighty percent of lawyers are lazy, losing their cases due to lack of preparation and care, so I worked as hard as any human could. I'd observed that many attorneys like Katie Snow were rarely prepared in any real sense. Perhaps she was skillful at case evaluation—I could only imagine her reports to the insurance company were as pedantic and niggling, as laser-sharp about trivial, legally irrelevant details, as her conversations with me were—and spotting dull procedural loopholes, but that wasn't what generated trial wins. Good plaintiffs won trials. Diligent preparation won trials. Showmanship won trials. Spencer had taught me that. I clung to his advice, though I was starting to feel doubt. Left with nothing but your wits, wouldn't you?

On the screen, a chef was preparing a kale salad. "This is what I'm talking about," the lemur said.

I snorted. "You've been living on chips and Coke and a bag of old marshmallows. If you wanted something healthy like a kale salad, I could make you one, but the truth is you'd rather have junk."

"You don't have the patience to massage the kale leaves with lemon juice for thirty minutes," he said. "I'm assuming your husband did the cooking around here."

"He did," I said, feeling attacked. "But not because I couldn't or didn't have the patience. I was just busier."

"I'm getting the impression lawyers always think they're busier than other people. Didn't you say you grew up taking care of your sister? Did you feed her this garbage?"

"Julie and I ate healthy. Not that it saved her from anything." I couldn't keep the bitterness out of my voice.

He started channel surfing again. "What happened to her?"

"She lost her mind."

"How so?"

"What is this, twenty questions? She lost her fucking mind, okay? She's fine now, though. Artists can get away with having a screw loose. She lives in Europe with her husband, a playwright."

"Do you see her?" He paused again on the cooking show.

"At Christmas."

"What kind of art?"

"She paints. She's always painted these kind of weird canvases and had performances around them, calling it conceptual art. She's a big deal genius in Europe, but in America, which is a more competitive place, nobody knows who she is."

"You sound jealous of her."

"Jealous of someone with a history of psychiatric breakdowns?"

"Jealous of how other people perceive her."

"Look, give me that remote. I've had it with you looking for the perfect show and coming back to this over and over again." But after he handed me the remote, I figured out my strategy and started typing. I was going to draft a Rule 12(b)(6) motion to dismiss Katie's cross-complaint against the lemur.

I would confront Evers. I had to get to the bottom of his involvement in this lawsuit. I had to know whether he was helping Katie Snow, and I also wanted to see if he was sleeping with her. I swung by his apartment building. The morning smelled like rain ready to coat the concrete streets, and the sky was dark gray. The sidewalk was dull, the sun barely visible behind an ice-white cloud. Evers lived on the penthouse floor, and from my vantage at street level, I saw that the curtains weren't drawn on his windows. Inside, the doorman recognized me from the year's worth of afternoon visits. I leaned against his desk and gave him my most charming smile.

"Hola, Maya. Comó estás?"

"Bien." I took a deep breath. "Juan, listen, I left something in Evers's apartment. Is he home?"

He shook his head, but his eyes were still twinkling, inviting me to lie. "He hasn't been home in a few weeks."

"Do you think I could run up? For a minute?"

"You know I can't let you into that apartment."

"Are you sure he still lives here?"

Juan's pitying expression indicated he thought I was in love with Evers and hoping for signs, any small signs Evers would be returning, as opposed to what I was really looking for—signs of treachery. Perfect. I put on a forlorn expression to enhance his sympathy. He pulled a large black binder from behind the desk where he sat. "I'm not supposed to do this, but you've come by so often . . . ," he said.

"Thank you! You know how much I appreciate this, Juan." It was all I could do not to hug the man. Then I realized that he had phrased his words as if he'd seen me recently, which he hadn't. My doppelganger?

Juan said, "He does pay rent still. Name still on the lease, no sign of a sublease, no notes that he plans to let the place or break his lease."

"Can I please run up? Just for five minutes."

"Three minutes." He handed me a key.

I rode the elevator to the top floor. The inside of the elevator smelled like pumpkin spice and bleach. I stepped out into the hallway and a frisson ran up my back, the way it did when I was listening to a really good song, or while I was working out. From the grimy crimson carpet in the hallway, with its dark spots like blackened chewing gum flattened into the weave, a person might not guess what a luxurious apartment it was. Two potted ferns still flanked his door. I rapped the brass knocker from force of habit. I stuck the key in the lock and opened the door. I didn't know what I was looking for. Partly, I was still thinking about Katie Snow, about whether he was now sleeping with bumbling Katie, who relied on that young, unlined face of hers to get her out of a jam. She never followed up at depositions; her discovery questions were so much an exercise in the popular legal saying "don't reinvent the wheel," that nine times out of ten she would serve wholly irrelevant discovery for an automobile accident in a real estate or intellectual property case. I searched her name online once as research and saw overexposed photographs of her life before law school as a tambourine jingler in a folk-indie band, and every time I saw her after that, I pitied her, thinking the disinterested, lazy way she ran her cases was probably the result of thwarted musical ambitions. I supposed none of this meant she was also bad in bed.

Possibly Evers was hiding out in the apartment, without Juan knowing it, hiding out from all of us, but as the door creaked open, I saw that the spacious apartment was stripped bare of most of its furnishings. It had a slightly different smell, too, a wonderful smell like cedars in winter, though it should have smelled musty without Evers living there. The gigantic orange rug and coffee table were still in their places, but the couch was gone, as was the TV. Perhaps he'd spirited them out on a different doorman's shift.

Several open cardboard boxes sat along the back wall by the window. Was Evers packing to leave? Juan had given me minutes, but the boxes were perplexing.

Inside the boxes were documents. I rifled through the papers, and found a pile with clippings about Brian Turner's career, some dating back more than ten years. There were press releases about the mural that I'd never seen and various tax documents. Cryptozoology papers, a binder of them about giant lemurs. I flipped through it. There were the legends I'd already found on the internet and legends I hadn't read. Watercolor and ink illustrations of both indri and giant lemurs, one species known to be real, and the other only glimpsed and speculated about. Underneath the binder was a stack of yellowing correspondence. I carefully unpeeled one of the envelope flaps, but old age had evidently made the adhesive sticky. Just as I managed to pry it open, the buzzer rang. Juan told me my time was up.

I grabbed several of the envelopes and stuffed them into my leather hobo bag. I needed to make some sense of what was happening, and, hopefully, the papers would help. I glanced at my watch. I had scheduled an expedited Rule 12(b)(6) motion with the court and Katie had agreed to shorten the time it was to be heard, given the looming trial date. The hearing was less than an hour away.

I glanced into the bedroom, where oddly, the silk sheets were still in an elegant heap on Evers's bed. The room smelled not like his cologne, but like something else: the cedar trees, but stronger. Mixed with the smell of a strange man, I thought, someone with whom I hadn't had sex. I caught a glimpse of myself in the mirror, my dark hair brushed and straightened, and a memory crept into my mind, a memory of a twilight many months ago, walking around in Evers's shirt, naked underneath, while Jobim's "The Girl from Ipanema" played on the record player by the window. Evers's arm wrapping around me, his hand slowly caressing the soft inside of my thigh as the room darkened.

I found no pictures of Katie in the apartment, and for a moment that seemed like a sort of vindication, until I realized he might have taken such evidence of their relationship with him, if he'd left town. I picked up a hairbrush from the dresser, one I'd used. In it were twisted long dark hairs, no long hairs of the sort I would expect to find if he were sleeping with Katie, nor any of Evers's own short blond hairs.

I hummed as I rode the elevator down. When I stepped into the lobby, someone was standing there. A black man wearing a lamba. I saw recognition in his eyes, but he said nothing, brushing by me and jumping into the elevator. As he passed, I smelled it. The smell that had been in the bedroom. His sweat. The cedar trees. I swiveled. The doors were sliding shut, but before I could think to push them back open, they closed. Juan watched me, looking considerably less friendly. He said, "Everything okay? Get what you came for?"

"Yes, thank you," I said. "I'd left some important correspondence from work the last time I was here." I was too shaken to smile or to make him feel like he had done a good deed by letting me into Evers's—or that man's?—apartment.

Outside the building, rain was pouring down, and the acrid odor of exhaust whipped into my face with the wind. I pulled out my red umbrella and walked in the direction of the courthouse, holding it in front of me like a shield. I hurried through the long streets, dashed up the dove-gray marble steps of the courthouse and through the heavy dark wood door.

Inside, I opened my bag and pulled out the three envelopes from Evers's apartment. I'd always been of the opinion that eavesdroppers never heard anything good about themselves, and it seemed the same would be true of people who read other people's letters. Nonetheless, I started with the large envelope I'd pried open earlier. I hadn't noticed when I grabbed it that a Malagasy stamp was affixed to the corner. Not the same stamp as the one I'd seen on the corner of the postcard sent to me on the day I met the lemur, but still, it seemed like a clue. The post office's date stamp indicated the letter had been sent twelve years earlier. Inside, there was a single page, stained a disturbing shade of brown. Coffee? Tobacco? Blood? Someone had written in blue ink:

NE,
Yesterday, the last of our supplies arrived by truck. F and I have been working nonstop to unload the furniture and set up the pieces. So. . . . (drumroll) the warehouse is finally set up. It looks beautiful and clean. We're in business!

You'll also be glad to know, the staff has already had several sightings of one or more giant lemurs. They seem to be just as curious about us as we are about them! Enclosed are a few snapshots. One of them is by yours truly! As you mentioned he would, Brian Turner contacted me to send some of these to him for his work.

Hope the legal world isn't treating you rough.

X

NE. That was Nick Evers. *X.* Who was *X*? I rifled through the photos. Indri swinging out of the electric rainforest in just the same positions as in Brian Turner's mural. Same colors. Same expression. Compared to the leaves on the trees they were flying through, the lemurs in the photograph were even larger than the ones on the mural by the lake, giants about the size of people, with mesmerizing amber eyes almost the size of my head, staring straight at me. The mural I had thought moving and magnificent and notably original was . . . a copy.

My heart slowed. What the fuck?

Before I could decipher this, or open another letter, a small, male court clerk wearing a white button-down shirt and a disgruntled expression pushed the doors of the courtroom open, kicking down the doorstops. The judge hadn't yet arrived. The sign-in sheet included a short list of motions, and my 12(b)(6) motion was first up. I signed in for my appearance and sat down at the front of the courtroom. A minute or two later, I heard a familiar voice—Spencer chatting on his cell phone. He sauntered up the aisle in a navy suit and hunkered down in a seat on the other end of my row. Katie still hadn't arrived.

He looked over and said good morning politely, while pulling a newspaper from his brown leather briefcase.

"Are you opposing my motion to dismiss?" I asked.

"No," he said. "I'm just here to get the lay of the land."

"You didn't want to send an associate?" I expected to see my replacement, his new senior associate. I wanted to know who had moved into my place and hear the office gossip. My life was quiet without the little colorful stories of office life—an office that had always seemed to me like a second family, one whose dynamics I understood better than the interactions inside my home. Stories of the romantically dysfunctional associate dating and breaking up with our copy guy, another senior associate's wedding to her girlfriend, the paralegal's online dating experience, the misadventures of one of my fellow senior associates trying to buy his girlfriend a diamond ring, and how chemotherapy was coming with the partner battling cancer. All the mundane junk I missed.

"We're so close to trial," Spencer said, opening the newspaper. "There's no associate assigned to this case."

Katie arrived. "Good morning, good morning!" she chirped.

"All rise. The Honorable Darren Stewart presiding." The judge entered the room. His cheeks were marked with gin blossoms and his immense jowls sagged like a bulldog's.

"The matter of *Turner versus Eustachio*. I see it's a Rule 12(b)(6) motion." Katie, Spencer, and I walked up to the counsel's table.

The judge continued, "I've read both the briefs very carefully. This is an unusual case. Evidently there's a lemur. And even more rare in America, a rich artist. Two angry small business owners. I'll tell you all now that based on this brief by . . . Ms. Ramesh, I'm inclined to dismiss this cross-complaint. There's no basis at all for the Eustachios, the building owners, to bring VARA or CAPA claims. Moral rights belong to the artist, not the physical property owner. An animal doesn't have intent. An animal can't be negligent by law, because "negligence" involves what a reasonable man would do. Animals don't have reason, so they're exempt from that. And it doesn't look like there's any precedent for holding an animal responsible for indemnity. Even if we assume that he could be held responsible, just for the sake of argument, what kind of indemnity could you hope to get from the lemur? He has no assets, no money. He's judgment-proof. But let's hear what you all have to say. Ms. Snow, let's start with you."

Katie stood up at the counsel table. "Your Honor, with all due respect, this is a special case. This is not an ordinary lemur. He doesn't fit the taxonomy of a lemur. He's not any old animal without volition of his own. With the court's permission, I'd like to play portions of the videotaped deposition, so you can see how cognizant he is of his motivations."

I jumped up. "Your Honor, I object to the use of the videotaped deposition. That should have been presented as part of her opposition papers, so that I would have a chance to respond. This is just counsel's attempt to . . . unfairly surprise me."

"Ms. Ramesh, I assume you had a chance to object to the deposition in the first place. If you had objections to the use of the testimony, those should have been raised in a motion for a protective order before the deposition," the judge said. His eyes looked watery, rheumy. I had been before him only one other time, on a motion I'd brought as a young associate. I couldn't remember the outcome.

"Yes, but I'd ask that you consider the lemur's condition. I didn't bring the motion for protective order because my goal is to return him to his natural habitat. He is in a significantly weakened condition living here."

"Isn't his natural habitat the painting?" the judge asked.

"No," I said firmly, although I'd been wondering the same thing. "His natural habitat is Madagascar. No indri has ever lived more than a year outside of Madagascar."

"I've seen lemurs at the zoo," Judge Stewart said.

"Yes, but indri are special. They are fragile and endangered."

"What about Ms. Snow's argument that he isn't really an indri?"

Katie said, "Yes, he's not exactly an indri. He's not quite the right size, though he otherwise meets the criteria. I think it would be fair to say he's some other unknown type of lemur. We don't know how long he'll survive, but that's not my clients' problem, in light of the damage they're being held responsible for."

"And what about you, Mr. Clark? You're uncharacteristically silent," the judge said.

Spencer laughed like they were drinking or hockey buddies from way back, and they probably were. "Your Honor, this is a special case, but the issues of taxonomy that Ms. Ramesh and Ms. Snow have raised are irrelevant. He's a creation of my client, but he's also got a will of his own. When you take a look at the videotape, you'll see that the lemur is a material witness who is involved in this lawsuit due to his own choices. There's no reason to exclude him as a witness for purposes of this motion, though I reserve the right to exclude him in other contexts." Even when Spencer was saying things I hated, I had to admire his confidence. I would have given anything to have that much self-assurance, to always feel right instead of simply blustery. To walk away from a confrontation feeling resolved, instead of vaguely ashamed of my own boldness without knowing why.

"All right, I'll take a look," the judge said. Katie gave the videotape to the bailiff. One of the clerks wheeled in a television and inserted the deposition tape. The lemur appeared on the screen.

Katie Snow: What was your goal in leaving?

The lemur: My goal?

Katie Snow: Yes, what did you hope to accomplish by leaving?

Spencer Clark: Asked and answered.

The lemur: Goal was just to get out of the painting.

Katie Snow: Is that because you thought there was something wrong with the painting?

The lemur: I dunno. Not really.

Katie played a few other clips from the deposition. The judge was riveted to the screen. He laughed a couple of times. When Katie was finished playing the tape, the clerk wheeled the television out of the courtroom.

"Your Honor, you'll see that both Mr. Clark and I objected several times during the deposition," I said. "Will you be ruling on those objections?"

The judge overruled all of our objections. "The videotape is fairly powerful evidence, Ms. Ramesh. I can see you're concerned about your client, but he seems to be integral to this lawsuit. As such, I am denying your motion with regard to the intentional destruction of property claim, the negligent destruction of property claim, the nuisance claim, and the indemnity claim. I agree with you, however, that there's no basis for the copyright claims by the Eustachios, and as to the cross-complaint only, those are dismissed."

"Your Honor, can you make it part of the order that the lemur not leave the country?" Spencer asked. "We need to reevaluate our approach to this lawsuit, and I'm afraid that he may simply leave."

"There's no need to put that in this order," I said loudly, turning to Spencer. "We've done nothing but cooperate with you!"

"Nobody's questioning Ms. Ramesh has made the lemur available," Spencer said. He was still facing the judge, as if the judge had spoken, not me. It reminded me I was in a courtroom, and needed to speak with the right modulation and decorum to get respect. The legal system was one created and run by WASPs—straight hair, modulated voices, suppressing all emotion, never talking about anything big, focusing on the small and manageable and "reasonable." Even though my father was an attorney, how lawyers acted was so different from the tiny Tamil household in which I had grown up, a household full of noisy gesticulating, dramatic statements, and eccentricities. The only thing these two worlds seemed to have in common: rarely did anybody admit those feelings that could make them too vulnerable.

In addition to ruling the lawsuit could proceed, the judge added a notation to the order stating the lemur could not leave the country until the lawsuit was resolved. Katie and Spencer were huddled together like old friends as I left. Energized by rage, I burst through the courthouse doors into the tense sunshine and damp autumn, the smell of salt and seagulls staining the air after the short, heavy downfall.

When I returned home, I suggested the lemur accompany me on a walk to pick up some apples and lettuce from the grocery store on Keller Avenue. It was a long way down the hill, now an autumnal gold that contrasted with the evergreens in the distance. The juniper bushes were starting to brown. There were sparrows and crows in the few oaks and sycamores next to the sidewalk, even though the trees had lost their leaves. I explained what happened at the motion, and what a long shot the motion had been to begin with. After we bought food and emerged from the store to the parking lot, the lemur jumped with a fierce movement onto a nearby overhang and bounded across it. For a moment, I thought he was going to run off, leaving me in deep trouble with the judge—I wouldn't have blamed him—but he turned and waited for me to catch up. He began singing. A woman pushing her walker up the hill on the opposite side of the street stopped and stared at the sound.

I interrupted the song. "Slow down! Look, I know you don't

want to do an interview, but trust me. The only way to get you out of this is to create public pressure for a specific outcome. We must get public opinion in your favor. If this remains a tiny, private lawsuit about a neighborhood mural, it won't mean enough."

"Mean enough for what? For you to make a name for yourself? No, thanks, I've seen what happens when I try to do you a favor." He was frighteningly calm as he hopped off the store overhang and stood next to me, staring me down with his yellow gaze, his unblinking round eyes. They fixed on me like two dim flashlights before he started jogging slowly up the hill. I gave him a minute to cool off, and then I ran to catch up with him. He stopped at the top of the hill and waited. As I approached, panting, he shook his head, "I know your intentions were . . . if not 'good,' not 'bad' either. But I'm already sorry that I came to you."

When we went back inside the house, he loped down the stairs. I took off my shoes and sat down on my bed. I opened my laptop. I played a video clip of an indri in the wild on YouTube to see if it sounded the same as him. When I first met the lemur, the sound was unlike anything else—at times a scream with neither fear nor anger in it, at other moments a chilling rhapsody of green leaves and light. There weren't any words for the kind of transportation the sound offered. But lately his song sounded threadbare, like the video clip, all the primal power drained out of it, the way any number of haunting songs become pedestrian after they're played to advertise smart phones or luxury cars.

CHAPTER 11

Later that evening, the lemur was watching another cooking show and I was drowning my intense disappointment about the 12(b)(6) motion with too many glasses of a Cabernet Franc that tasted like spearmint and moss, when I remembered my shock about the original photographs of the giant lemur by somebody—"X"—in Evers's Malagasy collective. I showed the lemur the photographs attached to the letter. "No shit, Sherlock," he said. He was staring at a pastry chef demonstrating how to make and pipe a Swiss meringue buttercream.

"What this means is the work's not original," I said, thinking he'd misunderstood. "That means we have a good argument that it shouldn't be protected under the relevant statutes."

"I already knew that the work wasn't original," the lemur said calmly.

"You knew? Why didn't you tell me?"

"I tried to tell you that first day when I saw the newspaper article where you said something dumb, but you were too full of yourself. I knew you wouldn't listen."

I pulled out the other letters, both single-page missives. The second one wasn't as old as the first letter, but it had clearly been read many times. Fingerprints obscured the words in blue ink. The letter was written on translucent stationery, presumably to reduce the international postage rates.

Dear N,

You asked why I haven't been updating you as frequently as we initially agreed. I'll be straight with you. I'm disturbed that my photograph of the GL is being used for some crappy mural. I know Turner's been your friend for years, yadda yadda yadda, but I agreed to send it to him for use as inspiration—to advance the cause, our cause. To bring more public awareness, more American awareness anyway, to lemurs, to the mysteries of the forest.

Inspiration! That was all it was meant to be and all you told me it would be.

Instead, I visit you and discover that you actually authorize your friend's plagiarism as "appropriation art"!!! "It's all been done," you say. "Remix is the hot new thing." Well, the thing is, everything hasn't been done. Maybe for you in your first-world consumer culture, it's all been done and there's nothing real and new and exciting, but excuse me if I thought we were doing something different with this collective.

Let me remind you. Our mission has always been to do the new: to capture one of these guys, dissect him, see how his song works, prove that this giant creature, this Bigfoot of Madagascar, exists, for fuck's sake. We talked about the thrill of discovery, about making a huge discovery that the world would recognize. We talked about fame.

We did not talk about helping some shitty wannabe artist rip me off. You may be a big shot attorney in the States, but you're not God. You don't make up the rules. You're just another person and you're subject to the same laws—international laws—as everyone else. This is not a threat, but a warning.

X

I felt sick. I didn't give the letter to the lemur, but sat there in a queasy confusion. "What's it say?" he asked.

"Oh, nothing," I lied. "It's just routine stuff." I'd suspected Evers had lied to me, but I hadn't imagined it was for such nefarious purposes. He was far, far more interested in a giant lemur than he'd let on—he'd wanted to dissect him, study his song, use him to get famous. I suppose when you believe it's all been done, you have to push the frontier out a little further, and as a wealthy trial attorney, Evers had the means, the money, to do that. Tax shelter, my ass.

I opened the third envelope, an ivory-colored business envelope. The address was typed—it appeared, from the Courier font and uneven quality of ink—on a typewriter. It contained only a note on a quarter page and had been sent only a few months previously. It was from Brian Turner.

Dear Mr. Evers,
Your legal services are no longer required. I received a cease and desist letter from your associate in Madagascar making a number of wild accusations. I will not be taking my mural down. I will not "admit" anything. I'm not sure where this is coming from, but if you had a conflict of interest in my representation, you should have alerted me to that fact. You're lucky I don't bring a legal malpractice suit against you.

Best,
Brian Turner

Was that why Evers was fired? For conflicts of interest? For not telling the other partners about his side business? For losing a client? How many other conflicts did he have, and how many other associations? I thought about how many times we fucked over the past year. I couldn't count all the occasions, but sex had occurred more than once a week most of the time—between fifty-two and two hundred times in total. It seemed like all those instances of physical intimacy should add up to something, not much, perhaps, but *something*. I'd assumed the time Evers spent away from the office and me, he spent rainmaking. That's what the other partners did. Instead, all sorts of things were happening without my knowledge. Of course, I had a secret life, too. I reminded myself that Ross thought I was working during times when I wasn't. But still!

"Anything interesting in that one?"

"Nope." I didn't want to alarm the lemur, and I decided to keep what I'd learned to myself. "Nothing juicy there."

"I think the more immediate issue is me, anyway."

"You're right," I said in a soothing tone as I folded the letters up and put them back in my purse. I sipped the glass of wine. "I've been wondering whether any of the art blogs wrote up what's going on with this case. Let me take a look." Within minutes, I discovered that either Spencer or Brian had leaked misinformation to bloggers.

Dangerous Lemur Escapes Mural

Something strange is happening in Oakland. One of celebrity Brian Turner's earliest works is a mural featuring the lemurs of Madagascar. Last year, Turner noticed one of the lemurs was missing. He immediately filed a federal civil suit against the building owners, Peter and Paula Eustachio. But according to legal paperwork that was recently filed, the lemur left the mural of his own volition.

According to Turner, the lemur is out and about— and extremely dangerous. He may be violent, and he is almost certainly vicious. If you are in the Bay Area and spot this creature, it is advised you avoid contact and call Animal Control, as well as the police.

"Vicious?" the lemur said before I could finish reading the blog post aloud. "But I'm a vegetarian." He shook his head.

"I told you if we don't spin this, we're asking Turner and the Eustachios to do it for us," I said. The lemur went outside for a moment, claiming he needed the air. Meanwhile I skipped the rest of the post and read the comments, wanting to know if the public believed the lemur was a threat. The online names of two commenters discussing the post in an artificial way caught my eye.

Konakoffee: What's interesting is that they haven't arrested him yet. Wonder if the OPD is scared.

Cornflake Girl: I know I'm scared! Po-poz incompetent.

Konakoffee: yo. I guess when he kills someone they'll have to pay attention.

Cornflake Girl: !

Konakoffee: I know, I know, innocent until proven guilty.

Cornflake Girl: Yah. It's pretty clear that he over-stepped. Literally. But just imagine.

PrincessLeia: That lemur defaced the mural! He was essential to it. Who defaces a Turner like that? I love Turner. : (

Cornflake Girl: Me, 2. It wasn't all that original a move.

Konakoffee: Leaving the wall or defacing it?

Cornflake Girl: Either. Or.

Konakoffee: Yah. Someone not paying attention to art
over the last half century, clearly.

The exchange caught my attention because Kona coffee and cornflakes were a running joke between Evers and me. Early in our affair we lamented the fact that we would never wake up together at dawn—that magical, pink-gray time that still feels off-kilter and wonderful like a dream. Looking back, I don't think either of us was truly sad about this, but like all lovers, we believed early mornings were romantic in a different way from night. We had talked about what we would have as our first breakfast together, if the opportunity ever presented itself, and he had revealed that his perfect breakfast included Kona coffee, shipped directly from the slopes of Hawaiian volcanoes, where it was grown.

When I was very little, my mother always made dosas for breakfast, but even though that was my ideal breakfast, the breakfast I wanted to repeat, I didn't want to get into all the implications with Evers of preferring South Indian food because it reminded me of my mother. After she died, my father fed us cereal for breakfast, usually Lucky Charms, and I hated cereal. Rather than saying what we would have at our perfect breakfast together, I went with what we wouldn't have. "Never was a cornflake girl," I'd said to Evers, brushing a lock of his hair out of his eyes. He leaned back on a satin-encased pillow and began singing the Tori Amos song.

As I scrolled through the comments, most of them asinine, searching for further commentary by Konakoffee and Cornflake Girl, theories swirled through my mind. The one that came to the forefront was that Evers and my doppelganger were somehow in this together.

Not finding anything further, I relocated the Konakoffee comment and clicked on the tiny picture icon next to his screen name to see not only what he wrote about himself, but also whether he commented on any other articles. The picture gave me pause. It was an image of an indri, one of those old-fashioned eighteenth-century affairs, lithographed and filled in with watercolor. The profile contained no biography and, suspiciously, the only comments associated with the account were the ones on the post about the lemur.

I clicked on the icon for Cornflake Girl. It was the blurred profile of a woman hovering in the darkness, a photograph in which I could see the blackened obscured edges of my own profile—the straight nose, the two curls of the lip, the long lashes against gray twilight—although it was possible that I saw my likeness because I wanted to see my likeness. I had only ever seen my profile in photographs, and perhaps that was the reason for the identification. Still, once you see a likeness, it's hard to un-see it. After a few moments, I realized it looked quite similar to the shot for the Twitter page associated with my doppelganger.

I decided to confront Konakoffee and Cornflake Girl. I created an account for myself and a user name: TheRealOne. I took a blurry profile pic and applied a filter to it so that I wouldn't be immediately recognizable. I responded to Cornflake Girl's claim *It wasn't all that original a move*, typing in a question of my own: *How is entering reality/the world ever anything but an 'original' move in the strictest sense of starting from the origin or existing from the beginning?*

A minute or more passed. I listened to the ticking of the clock. Was I wrong about Konakoffee and Cornflake Girl? If I were, I would look like an idiot, but my ridiculous user name and the Instagram filter would protect me. I could be anyone. That was the thing. Cornflake Girl could also be anyone. Why had I thought she was my doppelganger? And what did it matter, really, if I had a doppelganger? Supposedly everyone has one.

And then the comments rolled up and a new one appeared.

Cornflake Girl: You believe that defacing a work of art is original in the history of art? LOL

TheReal0ne: Actually, I'm taking the position that the lemur being alive isn't the travesty this post makes it out to be. It's not defacement.

Konakoffee: According to the dictionary there are at least three definitions of "defacement." There is the obvious: to mar or spoil or disfigure the appearance of. There is the less obvious: to impair the utility or value or influence of. And there is the third, an obsolete definition but applicable to this context: to obliterate or destroy.

Cornflake Girl: Exactly. By your logic, @TheReal0ne, the lemur didn't spoil the appearance of the mural?

TheReal0ne: Thanks, Evers, for clearing up the definition of defacement for me. No, the lemur didn't spoil or obliterate anything. He is simply more than the artist's intent. He lives! That's the critical part of all this. He's living.

Cornflake Girl: Who is Evers?

TheReal0ne: Evers is Konakoffee. Just as you are pretending to be Maya Ramesh.

While I waited for her to respond, I looked up to see what the lemur was doing. He was still outside, pacing. When he saw me looking, he came back in. I looked down at the screen. Neither Konakoffee nor Cornflake Girl was responding, but that didn't prove anything.

"All right, I'm ready to read the rest of that god-awful post," he said. The way he settled himself on the couch with a sense of resignation, contrasted with his petulant tone, reminded me of my son for a moment.

I handed the laptop to the lemur, and he scrolled through the post. I jumped up and rifled through the papers on my desk in the corner of the room, and tracked down the slip of paper on which I'd written the reporter's number. I said, "Do you trust me now? Can I go ahead and set up the *Times* interview?"

The lemur sighed. "All right. Maybe you're onto something. I'm going to go wash up, and then I'm dying to eat a salad with something other than your iceberg lettuce and mealy tomatoes. The least you can do is buy some decent grub."

I called and arranged the interview. Jill Sutherland was going to send a journalist to my house. I hesitated, thinking that my home—the home with Ross and the kids—was a sanctum. Once I let reporters into that space, once they passed the threshold and became part of my mundane life, I would have pretty much relinquished any private space I had left. But I had gotten the lemur into this mess, and I had to do what was necessary to pull him out.

Or that's what I told Ross a few minutes later, when I phoned him to explain that perhaps it would be best for me not to spend time with the kids this week. As usual, he didn't understand how humiliating it was to be a failure when I'd grown up with so many economic advantages, and how important it was for me, for our family, for everything, that I prove Spencer wrong.

I told the kids I would see them after I had a few things sorted out with a work situation. Tara admitted no reaction, other than to mumble, "Whatever, Maya." Before I could complain, she handed the phone to her brother.

Mike's voice sounded small. "I thought you said you weren't working and we would see each other more."

"Absolutely," I said. "And that's still true. We will be together more. The first thing I'm going to do after I figure out the next step in this case is to see you." I felt a sharp pang in my chest, a flicker of doubt about what I was saying, realizing that my words could seem like a lie to my son later, when he looked back on this, perhaps the way I looked back at my father's late nights working. Since I wasn't working, I had time to think those thoughts. He handed the phone back to his father.

Ross said, "So this lemur just showed up at the house? What's in this for you?"

"What do you mean? The lemur needs me to represent him and take him home. That's it."

"Come on, Maya. You don't do anything unless there's some sort of benefit to be had. What do you hope to gain?"

"Nothing." The silence made me uncomfortable, so I added, "I mean, I suppose I do feel like maybe I can convince Spencer that I'm right he has no case."

Ross whooped. "I knew you weren't doing this out of the goodness of your heart." He laughed.

"Okay, well, if that's all, I'll be going," I said, trying to retain my dignity.

"Are you sure it's safe?" Ross said. There was still a little bit of glee in his voice, but also the faintest edge of concern.

"What?"

"The lemur. Is he violent? Do you feel safe being alone in the house with him?"

"He's harmless," I said. "I'll hire someone to clean the carpets after he leaves."

After I hung up, I lay down on the couch. Rain spattered the skylight overhead, and white sunlight cast shadows of droplets on the lemur's silky black-and-white fur, as he sat cross-legged on the floor and browsed Twitter on my laptop. Eerie theremin music played in a video game he had left idling in the background. "Truly, as a cross-defendant, you can't get away with hedging and abstractions, like you did at the deposition when you were just a witness. You need not only the story of who you are, which we've already developed, but also a concrete reason for leaving that mural," I said, tapping my pen against a yellow legal pad. "You need motivation, you need purpose."

"Can I just say that these are awesome spiced pecans?" he asked, not looking up. He popped one into his too-small mouth and pressed one muddy nail against the keyboard to scroll down. The sound of guns fired in the video game.

"Stay on task," I said, grabbing the tin of pecans and dusting the flecks of cumin and brown sugar off the long dark fur that padded the tops of his wide paws. He made a small whiny sound, the way my children did, when they were shrugging off my tendency to pluck stray hairs from their sweaters or wipe food off their faces. "Give me a reason."

"That's like asking a monarch why he migrates to Mexico," the lemur said. He laughed at something he saw on the screen.

"What's so funny?" I stood and looked over his shoulder, but he had switched screens and was looking at his Twitter timeline. The tagline beneath the selfie that he used as his avatar was ripped off from a famous celebrity's: *There are so many fakes of me. But you can be sure I am real.*

"So how do *you* get followers?" he asked. I didn't answer.

We didn't know it in that moment, but in a month's time, the lemur would be mentioned hundreds of times a day, and he would have many more followers than the celebrity whose tagline he had plagiarized.

"But we know why monarchs migrate. To stay warm," I said.

"OK. So it was pretty cold on that wall that night," he said and went back to crafting a tweet. *I think, therefore I am,* he typed for his hundredth tweet.

CHAPTER 12

I didn't hear back from Konakoffee or Cornflake Girl at first. Acrimonious comments continued to accumulate on the post, but none of them seemed to be written by either Evers or my doppelganger. With the *New York Times* interview a couple of days away, I hunted online for other posts to gauge the public temperature. None of the blog posts referencing the case were positive. Some had gotten a quote from Spencer. Others had quotes from Katie. Essentially, Turner was a god and anyone who dared to question his supremacy as a white American male artist was shouted down. According to the comments, the Eustachios were good, hardworking immigrants and wouldn't be in this mess but for the viciousness of the lemur.

I felt protective of the lemur, but I was also resentful of the way he'd forced me to fight with one hand tied behind my back this whole time, refusing to let me set up the *New York Times* story right away, refusing to believe that the right thing to do was to be the first to put the story in front of the public. Now he looked like a criminal, and I looked like a chump. I thought briefly about what a relief it might be to abandon him—not representing him, letting him fend for himself—and then I felt enormous guilt, because he was reliant on me, more reliant in some ways than my children were.

And I needed to win. I had needed a case like this for years, ever since law school. All I'd had by the time I graduated was potential. And that was still what I had to this day, years later. Potential. If you're anything like me, potential is a ticking bomb deep in your stomach that will eventually detonate, pronouncing you *loser*, if you don't act fast.

I went down to his room and tried to convince him to wear some of Mike's old clothes so that he would look more innocuous at the interview. I pulled items out of a wardrobe in the closet—band T-shirts, shorts, a couple of button-down shirts, a tie I'd made Mike wear to piano recitals back when I had some sort of say over the kids' lives.

The lemur tried on a bright blue T-shirt, but instead of making him seem more innocent, paradoxically there was something vaguely threatening about the familiar softness of the folds of cloth over his bushy dry black-and-white fur. "I'm not fucking wearing this shit," he said, and pulled the shirt off. He left it on the floor, and instead of telling him to pick up after himself the way I did with Mike or Tara, I took it into the hamper in my bedroom.

The phone rang. "Spencer called me," Ross said. I could hear the sound of his shoes clicking against the linoleum. "He was under the impression that my words have some sort of effect with you."

"He called you?"

"He wanted me to talk you out of harboring that freaking lemur."

"Shh. Calm down. Don't scare the kids. This is just the sort of nonsense Brian thrives on, all right?" I had never known Ross to use the word "freaking"; perhaps all the time spent with our teenage daughter was affecting him. I put the empty bags of kale chips into the trash.

"Not all right. Not even a little bit, Maya. How could you bring that lemur into the house? It's downright reckless and dangerous."

"Ross, you know I wouldn't endanger the kids."

"What I know is that you're obsessed with getting the job back that destroyed our relationship. You have to let this go, Maya. It's unhealthy." In the background, I could hear Mike asking to talk to me. He was upset that he was going to miss our time together this week. I felt a twinge of conscience, thinking of all the soccer games I was missing, the classical music piano recitals, and the embellished playground tales of conflict and power that Mike usually recounted at dinner while letting his rice grow cold.

"It's not unhealthy. I need to help this lemur. After that's done, I swear I'll be different. Better. I'll be better."

"I don't think you know how to be better. You barely see the kids as is, but you're now creating a situation in which you can't see them at all? Send the lemur to an animal shelter. Or ask him to find someone else to board with. You don't have to do this."

"He's freaked out. And scared. And alone. I want to do this for him. I'm the only person who can and will navigate the legal system for him and win."

"Don't be a narcissist. Millions of lawyers could take this case. Ask one of them."

"None of them will care as much as I do," I said, and I knew this was undeniably true. I couldn't bear the thought of entrusting another lawyer with the lemur; it would be like sending away Tara or Mike.

"And that's your basic problem with being a lawyer right there. Listen to yourself. You're not objective. Your obsession with winning obscures your better judgment," Ross said. He puffed and cleared his throat like he was short of breath or angry.

The first year we had been together, we hadn't fought once; our courtship had been a whirlwind of dance performances, art openings, stargazing, films, and passionate, breathless crawling-out-of-your-skin-onto-the-walls sex, more of it than I'd had with Evers, I remembered now in a way I hadn't in years. Listening to the sound of him rage at me for being myself, I wondered if I changed myself that first year to make sure that we stood a chance, if I suppressed all the ways in which my personality didn't fit his so that he would see me as perfect. I couldn't hear Mike in the background anymore.

"All lawyers are obsessed with winning," I said. I thought he might be right, but I wasn't about to admit it. He'd pointed out the most obvious flaw I had as a lawyer, one both Spencer and Evers had tried to train out of me.

"Not like you. If you do this, if you throw away your family over a case again, I'll . . ."

"You'll what?" I made my voice smooth. I waited for him to threaten to turn our separation into divorce, something I was both dreading and expecting.

"Nothing." He exhaled, a faint hiss built up over years of pressure. "Maybe this separation will lead to divorce, maybe it won't, but I can't force you to value us over your cases."

"I don't value the case over you or the kids," I said. "He needs me. And he's in trouble." I was caving, wanting to apologize again, to tell Ross I had made a gigantic error in judgment and ask for his forgiveness. But then I reminded myself it was an enormous privilege to practice law, to be the person that other people relied on to fix their problems. I'd underbilled my time, used methods that were extralegal, worked on my acting skills in order to give my clients an edge, all the while letting my life at home crumble into nothingness. I never really understood how the utmost loyalty to a client that all lawyers swore to maintain was compatible with "objectivity." Ross's argument made no sense to me in that moment, and I didn't want it to.

The day before the *Times* was set to interview the lemur, I went back online to check if Konakoffee or Cornflake Girl had posted. No response to my attempts to unmask them, but at the very bottom of the comments, I saw that Konakoffee had started commenting again an hour earlier.

Konakoffee: Representational art is dead. All we have left are ideas, the traces and not the things themselves.

I hesitated before joining the fray as my alter ego, "TheRealOne."

TheRealOne: Representational art is only dead to pretentious snobs who care more about critical theory than real people and their real art. There's real beauty in things. In the warm glow of lights, in baskets of fruit, in cake dripping with frosting.

Konakoffee: Ah. I see we have a Thomas Kinkade fan in our midst. You probably think Wayne Thiebaud was really painting cakes in order to paint cakes, yes?

TheRealOne: What's wrong with painting cakes? That's what I want to know. You just hurl your shit every which way, as if there are no repercussions to ideas in the real world.

Konakoffee: Interesting.

TheRealOne: And stop with the smug! Who are you to be watching, judging my opinions from a distance?

Konakoffee: I'm not at such a distance, Maya. Physically, bodily, maybe. But not mentally.

Strange to see my name set out there in type, in a black silhouette against the paper white of the chatroom. He had revealed himself.

"Evers?" I typed. I had a flash to the way it had felt when we first started having sex, the immense weight of him, compared to the leanness, the light ephemeral touch of Ross. My heart quickened. I knew: he was the source of the leak to the *Times*; he spied on us; he wanted to capture the lemur and study him, use him to achieve the kind of fame and fortune that proved so elusive in the law. And yet I wanted to see the best in Evers, wanted to believe that the bad could be fixed, that he could find redemption. I wanted to be wrong about him; otherwise I would have lost my marriage for nothing. It was hard not to react differently to Konakoffee knowing he must be Evers.

Konakoffee: And who is Evers?

TheRealOne: You know who you are.

Konakoffee: Even assuming I am this person, Evers, what would that have to do with anything?

TheRealOne: It means you're out there. I know you're why the lemur is now in the lawsuit.

Konakoffee: I have nothing to do with anything.

TheRealOne: See, that's what I mean. That's a very Evers thing to say. Or think, anyway.

Konakoffee: So you're going to trial?

TheRealOne: How do you know that?

Konakoffee: That's the word on the street.

TheRealOne: Yes. Any advice?

Konakoffee: Go to trial. Don't be scared of Spencer. Don't be scared of Katie. Don't back down. You want to be a known trial lawyer? A real trial lawyer lives for the fight. A litigator pushes paper. Whatever you do, don't back down.

TheReal0ne: You are dating my doppelganger. Why?

Konakoffee: What?

TheReal0ne: You know who I'm talking about.

Konakoffee: Nah.

TheReal0ne: Are you serious? Go to trial? Don't stall?

Konakoffee: Don't stall. If you stall, they'll think you're scared. That you have something to hide. Do you have anything to hide?

TheReal0ne: No.

Konakoffee: Then face them. If you want to win a war, you have to go to battle.

TheReal0ne: I have no resources. I've got no money. Spencer and Katie have offices.

Konakoffee: LOL OFFICES! It doesn't matter. Really. Resources are only necessary if you don't have the popular vote. So get the popular vote.

TheReal0ne: How?

Suddenly Konakoffee logged off. I was alone in the chatroom. "Dammit! Fuck. Fuck. Fuck. Evers, what the fuck?" I said out loud.

There was no point in typing it. So many other questions needed answering. I wanted to ask him about the postcard, whether he was the one who sent it. I wanted to ask him whether he had run away with my doppelganger—if she was the Cornflake Girl, and I wanted to ask what she had that I didn't, but I also didn't want to ask such a humiliating question. It didn't matter what I wanted. He was gone. And I was left to make sense of his cryptic message: Get the popular vote. Okay, it wasn't all that cryptic.

Evers and Spencer had been at odds since the firm's founding. With Konakoffee/Evers's directives, I was just another pawn in Evers's war with Spencer, but I couldn't see anything inherently wrong with his advice. It seemed so much like the kind of advice Spencer used to give when I was in his good graces. In the beginning Brian Turner was Evers's friend, but he was also his client, which meant Evers had a responsibility to advise me in a way that was ethically compatible with Brian's interests. At least from a legal ethics perspective, he couldn't and wouldn't advise me to do something that would hurt Brian's interests. Or would he?

If the lemur stood for something, if he wasn't merely another defendant in the legal system, maybe his fame could serve a larger purpose. Maybe I could get my job back, make something of myself. No, there was probably no chance that Ross, Tara, or Mike would come back, but at least I could redeem myself in their eyes by being successful; I didn't have to be the bad wife and mother who got fired and wrecked her career.

For the past year, I'd believed that Evers and I were two of a kind, though he had grown up in the rural Northeast and I had grown up in the suburbs. Like most trial lawyers, we were obsessed with beating out the competition and hungry for accolades. Unlike Spencer, neither of us was especially concerned with the right or wrong of an approach, only whether it was workable. We would fuck during late lunches in the afternoon on top of the blue silk quilt that covered his king-sized bed and after, start working again, reading bits of deposition transcripts to the other and talking strategy over Burmese takeout from a place around the corner from his apartment. I was enamored with what Evers knew of trials—I wanted to *be* him, to be some kind of cross between him and Spencer. I never wanted to be myself, some powerless brown woman. Though Evers routinely said he had grown cynical about trial work, about trials meaning anything more than gladiatorial matches with words and appearances, he liked sharing what he knew. Had our relationship been about sex? Love? Identification? How did anyone know the true value of anything?

I spent that night sleeping fitfully, certain that in the morning I would see Evers's directive more clearly. I dreamed that he was rigging the entire thing—he had sent me the lemur, advised Katie to sue the lemur, and tipped off the *Times*, just to see me fail. But when I awoke, his advice seemed genuine, only, in the light of day, I saw he might be trying to help me get the lemur out of this monstrosity of a lawsuit, not because he was interested in the lemur's safety, but so he could take possession of the lemur and destroy him.

The *Times* sent a reporter named Flora Lucchi, who looked more like Audrey Hepburn than any journalist should look—especially a journalist for the story of oppression we wanted to tell. Accompanied by a pale, lanky photographer whose name I didn't catch, she carried a red designer bag that matched her lipstick and wore big retro sunglasses tinted brown. When she removed her sunglasses to look around, eyeing my house with an initial flash of skepticism, I was embarrassed. Maybe her article would note the darker patches on the wall where the removed paintings and photographs once rested. Maybe it would draw embarrassing conclusions. I found myself wanting to explain about the separation, but fortunately she was so shiny and cool, I recognized the impropriety of oversharing and simply watched her.

Other than that immediate surprise, her gaze drifted over everything without any judgment, or at least, she didn't pull out a notepad to comment on the inadequacy of what she saw. She sank back into the couch, crossed her legs, and smiled brightly at the lemur, as if she were at a job interview waiting for a prospective employer to ask her questions.

The lemur perched at the edge of the couch with a surly expression on his face. I nudged him. Before the interview, I'd told him that his public face was supposed be that of someone who was wronged, but not resentful. People like to root for a scrappy underdog who still has hope. Bitterness is a turnoff. He tried to smile, but the effort yielded more of a grimace. I nudged him again. "All right, all right," he said. I turned to beam at Flora, to make sure she had the sense that we were optimistic about our chances at trial, rather than desperate to turn this whole thing around. When I looked back at the lemur, he'd smoothed out his naturally surly expression and was attempting the smile of a plastic doll.

"It's nice to meet you both," Flora Lucchi said, pulling from her purse a slim, shiny tape recorder and a black spiral-bound notebook. She pressed her thumb against the tape recorder to start recording and held it there as the tiny red light flicked on. "You came to Ms. Ramesh a few weeks ago? You went missing almost a year ago. What have you been doing in the meantime?"

"Yes, I came to see Maya not long ago." the lemur said. "Before that I was trying to figure out how to get to Madagascar in other ways."

"Forgive me, but what makes you think you should be in Madagascar instead of back in the painting? I mean you're not actually *from* that country, are you? You're from Oakland, aren't you?"

"I'm from Oakland only because I happened to be trapped in this painting there," the lemur said. "But I existed before that. My kind has existed since ancient times, longer than America's been a country, if you want to know."

"But you as an individual, you don't predate the mural do you? I was reading about lemurs. The working theory seems to be they floated away from Africa to Madagascar and evolved in isolation. Originally, though, they were related to humans."

The lemur nodded. Flora continued to ask questions and they ping-ponged back and forth as the lemur's eyes glazed over, a hazy yellow like melted butter. It was her responsibility as a journalist to be objective, but I couldn't help but think she was unduly skeptical, too willing to assume that the lemur didn't know what he was talking about because he didn't fit her preconceptions. Perhaps I was wrong about this strategy. Perhaps I couldn't control the media message as much as I thought I could. Evers would approve of this strategy because he agreed with me that fame was worth almost anything. But what would Spencer do? He would probably play by the rules, knowing that the addition of an outsider—a journalist—into the mix could easily poison the narrative and ruin the jury pool. Then again, Spencer didn't believe in me, and I didn't want to run this case his way, because winning his way would only prove that I'd lost everything in losing that job.

The photographer was in the corner, fiddling with his equipment, occasionally taking a picture. Outside the window a hawk was hovering over the gentle pink and green eucalyptuses, probably scanning the rumpled earth below for a mouse to eviscerate.

Flora was asking, "And now they've brought you into a lawsuit?"

"Right. But only on a cross-complaint. I think they're targeting me for being a lemur outside the place they've prescribed for me."

"You believe the lawsuit is bogus?"

"Yes. The Eustachios, and maybe Brian Turner too, see me as this out-of-control figure in a story they've already told themselves, that hundreds of people tell about curiosity. Humans who are curious are explorers, you'll remember. But animals who are curious, who get out of their place, are killed," said the lemur. His composure was remarkable and I kept expecting him to lose that phony facade so I could save him, but it never fell off.

"Oh, I'm so sorry! I forgot to ask—can I get you something to drink?" I asked Flora. Talking about drinks was the cue we had worked out ahead of time as a sign to the other that things might be veering off-message.

I went to get her a cold Aranciata from the refrigerator, keeping one ear trained toward the living room. In a measured tone she said, "That's an interesting angle you have, sir, but what I wonder is where Brian Turner got the idea that you were dangerous. You've read his warnings, I'm sure? Sounds like you're saying he made them up. Are you really saying that he has it in for you because you're a lemur, something seen as other than human?"

I poured the bright orange liquid into a tumbler.

"Well, yeah. Shit, there's nothing dangerous about me. But I think there are three common views that Americans might have about me: one, I must be dangerous, two, I must be exotic, or three, I must be nothing at all. The first warrants control. The second says I am controlled. The third is what would apply to me if only Brian Turner's ego weren't involved."

"You think this lawsuit is a matter of ego?"

I returned to the living room and handed her the drink, glaring at the lemur over her head to make him stop expounding on his theory. It seemed a poor strategy for getting the public on his side—to reduce what they might think to three choices. Would it read as condescending? And she was feigning interest, I thought, hoping to find a more sensational story, and to my dismay, he was actively supplying that story by spouting all that anti-America stuff. Our oppression narrative didn't appear to be sparking her imagination the way I had hoped it would. The liquid in Flora's tumbler glittered under the thin beam of sunlight pushing through clouds outside the picture window.

"Yes, this is very much about his ego." The lemur ignored me, as I shook my head at him vigorously.

"I apologize, but I have to get back to my original question, then," said Flora. The leather creaked as I leaned forward in my seat, listening carefully to make sure the lemur wasn't about to say anything that could be used to impeach him under oath when we got to trial. The photographer, lurking in the corner of the room by the television set, took a photo of me as I stood, anxiously, before slumping down again, realizing that I could do nothing. "Does Brian Turner have any basis for calling you dangerous?"

"Can I be honest with you? I came to Maya to see if she would take me back to Madagascar," said the lemur. This wasn't part of our script, but he sounded genuine. Flora's expression relaxed, so I decided to let him run with this story. "There was nobody else I asked. She visited me—the mural—thirty-nine times before I left it so I thought she'd be sympathetic." I hadn't gone anywhere near thirty-nine times even after I began handling Brian Turner's lawsuit, and was about to say so, when I remembered my doppelganger had visited the mural without my knowledge before I began handling Turner's lawsuit. Perhaps she'd been even more obsessed with my case than I was.

"You counted?"

"Yes. It can get boring as hell sitting there on a wall. I thought anyone who loved the mural that much, who stared at me so much, was the natural person to turn to for help once I made it off."

"Did you ever consider asking someone else for help? Say, the embassy or one of the other visitors to the mural?"

"No. I immediately trusted her and so it didn't seem to me to be necessary to seek out other authorities."

"Is it that you didn't think it was necessary, or that you thought they might exploit you in some way?" The lemur paused. He looked at me for a moment before answering. "I thought they might exploit me. I mean, anything that's different loses its agency, gets exploited and funneled into the consumer economy. The megaplex that is America."

"And you see Brian Turner as part of the consumer economy?"

"I mean, he's a byproduct of it. He doesn't take any real risks, he just makes the things he thinks that people want. Nothing wrong with that, though. It's the American way, isn't it? "

Flora laughed, but I was starting to see my limits as the lemur's attorney. Why would anyone trust me over Spencer, when it came to this animal? He hadn't stuck to our story about agency, but had gone off on a rant criticizing America. I wondered if I should present her with the photographs and letters showing that Brian had ripped off Evers's partner "X" in Madagascar, but decided against it. I remembered a sexual discrimination case early in my career where a private investigator we retained found out about the opposing party's nasty sexual exploits. That was the first but not the only time Spencer had told me I needed to keep something in my pocket for trial.

"I should say that there are great Americans who might support me if they realized that I want the same things that they do. I want freedom. I want to be able to move around and live where I want to live and associate with those I want to associate with."

Flora nodded and I glimpsed a cool blue light in her eyes. Finally. She was buying our story. I could breathe again. The lemur went on; now that he had gotten some of his rage out about being seen as dangerous, he could speak at length about the loss of autonomy, the wall as a kind of prison, all the things we'd rehearsed. And I was right about the story we'd crafted—it was one that Flora wanted to tell.

CHAPTER 13

The article was posted to the *New York Times* that Sunday. Almost immediately, the telephone started ringing. It rang nonstop, a hungry bleating, a call for more. The people bought us. More reporters wanted comments for the stories and op-eds they planned to publish about *Turner v. Eustachio*, the legal battle of the year. Somebody wanted to buy the movie rights to the lemur's "life" story, not quite comprehending that his life story was all of one year old, at best ten years old, depending on how you calculated it. Perhaps the confusion arose because Flora used the quote about how lemurs were ancient and older than America. A musician wanted to compose a guitar ballad about the lemur, and his agent wanted to make sure the lemur wouldn't sue for rights of personality or a cause of action along those lines. A flood of emails from art bloggers around the world asked for a comment for the posts they were writing as a result of the article. By and large, I ignored these requests, having neither time nor inclination, but the lemur grew increasingly excited at all the attention and tried to learn how email worked so he could respond on his own to his public.

After a while, I stopped answering the phone. The situation had blown up. While I was accustomed to manipulating any given situation for maximum popularity, I'd never dealt with anything on this large of a scale. All the ringing started to sound like one long demand: *look at me, look at me, look at me.* And wasn't that essentially what we had asked for? At the risk of losing it entirely over the awful sound, I yanked the telephone cord out of the wall and the phone hit the wall. Everyone would go to voicemail. The house fell silent. The lemur stared at me. I drew the curtains; even the brightness of the autumn sunlight grated on my nerves.

The art, ecology, and cryptozoology chat rooms were buzzing with activity. People were arguing over copyright terms and whether the right works of authorship received enough attention. They were complaining about how little people cared about the environment, how little people cared that we would soon need to create a settlement on the moon. They were debating whether there was another frontier waiting to be discovered, and whether there were other undiscovered animals out there. I couldn't have orchestrated a better public response if I'd tried. Flora Lucchi had left out most of the lemur's theories about how animals are treated, how America treated things that were different, but she had warmed to the idea of freeing the lemur and written about it as eloquently as if it were her idea. I was relieved she'd left out the lemur's theories; the more I thought about his off-the-cuff comments, the more I realized what a risk I'd taken in trusting him to do the interview. The theories could have made people uncomfortable, and there might be nothing worse for our reception with an American jury than discomfort.

"It's working," I said to him. Instead of celebrating, he was staring at the television and sipping a diet Coke with a faintly melancholy air. Every once in a while, he would tweet something about the program he was watching, or laugh a little at something someone else tweeted to him. He looked bigger, heftier even, but he didn't look happy. I wondered if the Coke was making him obese and depressed, all that corn syrup and sugar drugging him, transforming him into a bit of a beast.

As I lay on my bed that night, staring at the ceiling, overtaken again by insomnia, I realized that for all that I had fought his efforts to sell his viewpoint to the reporter, if I really sat with the events of the last few weeks, I agreed with the lemur more than I would have thought just a year before. You could work hard, force yourself into colorblindness, buy into all the myths of free speech and justice and liberty for all, and mind your own business when, with a few cruel words, someone on the inside would remind you that you were other, that you were outside, that you would never be inside. It had happened all the time when I was growing up, tiny social grenades blowing up that I wasn't allowed to even remark upon. You weren't supposed to notice anything that other people—white people—didn't notice, or feel any more than they would in the same situation—that was what people seemed to think assimilation really meant. It was an unspoken rule, of course—best for plausible deniability.

At the end of high school, a friend and I had been Christmas shopping in downtown Santa Cruz. I was queued up, waiting inside a bathroom of a bookstore. There was one painted metal stall and a line of shoppers behind me. Ahead of me, a blonde woman pushed open the stall door, shooing me even though I wasn't blocking her path and snarling, "What the fuck. Stand back. This isn't India! Here in America we wait outside."

Hot humiliation flooded every part of me—I'd thought I was just enjoying an afternoon of shopping, but the whole time that I'd been walking around oblivious, other people were watching and thinking I was different, an alien from another culture. When I finished using the bathroom, I told my friend what had happened, and I never forgot her nonchalance, the way she shrugged. A chill came over our outing. I knew enough not to say anything more, but when she asked what was wrong, I said she didn't understand how humiliating it was to have someone make assumptions about you based on your skin color. She said, "What are you talking about? I get it's kind of annoying, but it's just some stupid woman. Relax."

I nodded to be polite, but over the years it had been an onslaught of daily stupid remarks that reminded me I didn't fit in, and that I never would. It was the drive-by "Hey, Gandhi!" shouted by a young white suburban male; the random "Namastes" on city streets from older men that might have been intended as marks of respect about honoring my soul, but seemed more like an unearned familiarity or a way to show off; it was being asked mockingly about reincarnation by bored students in a science class; it was the "shit" jokes made about my skin color; it was the white girl friends who said I wasn't pretty enough for the white boys; and it was the white boys who sexually harassed me privately, but ignored me publicly; and when I was older, it was being mistaken for an administrative assistant at the office, no matter how designer my suits were; it was being mistaken for a store clerk in stores where clerks wore uniforms; it was being mistaken for my daughter's nanny over and over again.

Then, too, after years of being told these differences didn't really matter in America and that I was too sensitive if I let it bother me, I started to wonder if I was simply making it all up— all the snubs, the slights, the friends and relatives that weren't interested in learning what I really thought about anything, and who wanted me to lie routinely. Eventually, I felt my sister was making up her reasons for wanting to leave America, too. I told myself that once we had enough money, I would outrun all of the shame and confusion of displacement, but you can never really outrun yourself.

On the Tuesday after the article appeared, a geneticist emailed us.

Dear Ms. Ramesh,
I read with great interest the feature article in the *New York Times* about a lemur who is fighting off a claim of vandalism by asserting his independence from a mural in downtown Oakland. Of particular interest to me was the claim that the lemur is an indri, a type that is rare and endangered, or at any rate, that he is related to the indri. I'm sure

we can agree that a rare and endangered animal requires special protections.

Let me get to the point. I'm a geneticist at Stranger Labs. I would like to sample the lemur's DNA for possible cloning. I see cloning as being potentially a great advance in the fields of conservation and preservation, as well as genetics. If we can use your lemur's DNA for study, what might that suggest for cloning a wild indri's DNA? What might be possible in terms of preserving all sorts of rare animals?

I hope you will do the right thing and assist in my research efforts. Please contact me at your earliest convenience,

> Yours truly,
> Marcus Spiegelman
> Stranger Laboratories, LLC

"What do you think?" I asked the lemur. I didn't know what to make of this letter. I'd been expecting some interest of this sort from the *New York Times* story, but the letter had arrived quickly after the article, and by snail mail, rather than an electronic message.

"Eh. 'I hope you will do the right thing?'"

"What's wrong with that?"

"Doesn't that seem over-the-top? Heavy-handed? You know, it's not likely I even have the right DNA to help preserve the indri out in Madagascar." He continued to eat salt and vinegar potato chips from the bag, a dusting of crumbs spilling in his fur like dandruff.

"What do you mean?"

"You know I'm already a copy. I have no problem with helping out some geneticist, but I don't fit into his predetermined plan. I probably have no genetic material."

"But what if you do? You brought up the issue of endangerment while we were doing the interview. Don't you have a responsibility to help with this cause?" I wasn't sure myself, but there was something a little cavalier about the lemur's attitude that made me feel like playing devil's advocate.

On the third day, we still hadn't made up our minds about the cloning, but Ross called, throwing me for another tailspin. "Hi," I said. Part of me wanted to admit that perhaps he was right, that I had become somebody unsavory as a lawyer at Spencer's firm, but I waited for him to announce the purpose for his call.

"Hi. Listen, I still don't approve of what you're doing, defending that lemur. You're going to run into ethical problems even worse than what you've created so far, but Tara wants to talk to you, after reading that *New York Times* article."

"She does?" I was so surprised I spilled my wine.

"I'll put her on." Ross said.

The phone crackled. "We read about your case in the papers, Mom." Tara sounded shy. "I think it's really cool what you're doing. Representing the lemur. Working against The Man. Finally!"

"Really?" I asked, momentarily impressed with myself for impressing my daughter. It's funny how I could feel so proud of a kid and congratulate myself on how well she turned out, though I had little to do with the aspects of her that pleased me so much. For one thing, she was really smart, like genius-level smart. Maybe her intelligence had something to do with Ross or with my dad, something to do with genes, but it certainly wasn't my fault, the way we think of fault as being something you actively do.

"Yeah. Think about slash—the fanfic I write. What good would *Twilight* or *Harry Potter* or *whatever* be to their readers if the readers couldn't put some of themselves in the books, you know?"

"They'd still be good," I started to say before I realized that it mattered more that she tell me what she thought, that she *like* me again than that I be right. I had no idea that she wrote fanfic. I always thought Mike was the writer in the family. "But yeah, I know."

"What's special about books is the room the reader has to help create the work. It's not like movies, which are more physical, more spelled-out for the viewer. If the readers couldn't use the books somehow, what would be the point? And I think it's the same thing with art, like the lemur was saying. It's not an issue of what the artist wants, that's all ego. It's what's good for society. Aunt Julie says the reason painting has become less popular is because it's a field where there are too many hierarchies and the avenues for entry into that world are too rigid. There's not much space to maneuver and that's why it's not as successful at finding its audience. All the famous artists are thieves, but they totally guard their work. Who cares what an individual is *entitled* to, you know? That's not why the Constitution was written how it was."

"Oh, totally," I said, as if I knew what she was talking about. I found cleaning solution under the kitchen sink, and began working on my wine spill. Obviously, a popular expression of an idea wouldn't even exist without the artist's labor, but I knew that wasn't what I was supposed to say. The bit about entitlement, however, did sound like something I would say, only smarter coming from my daughter. I was confused that she wanted to talk to me, but also grateful. It wouldn't be a good idea to alienate her and this random burst of goodwill in order to seek clarification as to why she thought her aunt was more reliable in her interpretation of the law than I, as a lawyer, was. "*Harry Potter*, right on."

"I always thought you represented the assholes—you know, the corporations and the institutions and the one percent. The egomaniacs, like that artist Brian Turner. But I was just telling Dad—you actually are one of us. You're representing the people."

"I'm definitely one hundred percent behind the lemur, behind the little guy. Definitely."

We hung up the phone with the understanding that we would get together soon. The lemur was looking at me askance.

"Did I hear you compare me to Harry Potter?" He looked both puzzled and irritated.

"Not exactly. Tara compared you to a Harry Potter fanfic. I just kind of agreed. You're popular now, thanks to me." I put the cleaning solution away and threw out the red-stained towels.

"I'm a fanfic? What the—? Isn't that kind of trivializing? And I have to say this, I know it sounds narcissistic, but I don't want to be *trivial*. People shouldn't think of me in conjunction with fandom," he grumbled. "This is all the fault of that stupid article. I told you."

He sank into the couch and resumed racing an aqua blue Corvette in his video game. The console was oily from the potato chips he'd been eating for the past week. He was gaining weight, and his spryness had disappeared, leaving behind a lumpy, hugely misshapen creature. "I want to be one of a kind."

"You are one of a kind," I said smoothly. I placed some freshly baked kale chips in front of him.

"That's why it probably doesn't make sense to go in for genetic testing," the lemur continued, his ears twitching. He left the kale chips untouched, clicking wildly on a button. "Right? Because I'm not representative of something that's already in the world, the indri as it exists in the rainforest. I'm not exactly part of that species."

"But that's just it. You are and you aren't. You have what makes the indri distinct, the song."

"Oh, that," said the lemur. The Corvette crashed into a concrete wall and ricocheted to the other side of the screen.

"What, you don't think that's unique? There are other things, but that's chief among them, in my opinion. It's like a whale song or a dissonant jazz saxophone."

He said, "It's not that. The whole uniqueness angle is a bit idiotic, if I'm honest." I tried not to make a face, or at least to make my face look receptive after his insult toward my strategy.

"I mean, it's a question of biodiversity right? Isn't the point that there are enough different life forms to improve pollination and water and air quality, not that one particular type matters more than any other? It's not important that it's unique, it's important that there are enough different forms to—"

"Okay, okay," I said. "I get it. Get on with the rest of what you were going to say."

"When I woke up this morning to take a shower, I opened my mouth. This came out." When he opened his mouth, a strange, strangled scream floated between his lips. A cloud of black sound. It was so different from his usual ravishing song, so stripped of what made him special, that when he closed his mouth, he seemed completely altered to me.

"Yeah, so I'm right, right? It's bad?"

"It's really bad. Try again."

He did, but with his repeated attempt, the cloud of black sound only expanded. Instead of diffusing, the warbling seemed to acquire power through repetition.

"Are you sure you're trying hard enough? Or maybe you're trying too hard?"

"Effort's nothing to do with it. You trying to make your voice sound a particular way? Me neither. That was my sound. It happened for me without my intervention. So to speak."

"Maybe if we cooperate with Spiegelman, he can tell us what's wrong with you?" I asked. What I was really thinking was that contacting Spiegelman, involving the scientific community, would offer additional publicity that could help us get out of the case, but the way the lemur was handling everything, letting fame go to his head and openly insulting me, told me he still didn't understand that ramping up public support any further was necessary. My last chance to save him was keeping him partially in the dark with regard to strategy.

"Nobody can tell me what's wrong with me," the lemur said.

He lay down on the couch and stared at the ceiling. I sat down and began eating the kale chips as fast as I could. In that moment, I realized I was starving.

"I should tell Marcus Spiegelman you're not interested. Tell him to shove it?" I asked, my mouth full of crispy baked leaves.

My cell phone rang and I swallowed the chips. "Maya, I'm calling as a courtesy," Spencer said when I picked up. I assumed he was calling to talk about the article, maybe not to congratulate me, but to concede that, on some level, I had done a good job. I was thinking *finally*.

"I'm letting you know that we're adding the lemur to our complaint as a defendant and going in ex parte to amend the complaint and make sure the trial goes forward," he said.

"I thought we agreed that if you sued him directly you'd be attacking a part of Brian Turner."

"What? What's going on?" asked the lemur. I waved him aside and opened the sliding glass door. Out on the deck, the air was putrid. A skunk had sprayed in the backyard.

"There's nothing for you to worry about. Brian agreed to waive the rights he has to prevent you from representing the lemur at trial. He wants to expedite matters so as to stop the injury that's occurring every minute that lemur is out in the world. It's clear after the *Times* article, we need to be fighting the lemur much more aggressively than the Eustachios. More publicly anyway. Brian needs to protect his brand."

"He didn't even have a brand when he painted the lemur. The lemur is definitely not part of Brian's brand. And Spencer, come on, that's not really what copyright protections are for." I clunked down the steps that led from the balcony to the patio. I'd thought a newspaper article would calm things down, make it clear that we had the public favor, but Spencer seemed to see the article as damaging, as a reason to step up his game.

"Oh, don't worry. We'll be adding some trademark claims, too."

"Is this for insurance reasons? Are you settling with the Eustachios' insurance company?" I started digging into the jasmine bush, breaking stems with my nails and letting drops of white pus dribble down my fingers.

Spencer paused. "We're talking about it."

"You're kidding. You can't do this. The judge isn't going to let you tack on claims at the eleventh hour!"

"You're welcome to oppose, of course. I'm sending a messenger with the papers over to you as we speak. But Maya, you might remember that if the lemur really wants to get out of the United States and believes he did nothing wrong, he should welcome the earlier trial date, not oppose it."

"You know that the lemur has no money, right? You won't get a dime from him. You're throwing a whole lot of money after nothing." The melancholy spray of faded green from a neighbor's willow tree hung over the fence, encroaching onto our property. I made a mental note to ask them to trim the tree; it did not look healthy. It was the color of a faded mimeograph. Then again everything— from the moon to the streets—looked dull as simulacra.

"We know."

"Then what are you doing this for?"

"We want that lemur destroyed. Killed. We have no idea how to get him back in that painting, so the only thing to be done is to simply destroy him. We made him and we can destroy him."

I picked up a pair of rusty garden shears and snipped at the air. "Do you have any idea of how bloodthirsty that sounds? Not going to happen." First Evers, now Spencer. I had to admit that the lemur seemed to be right—all humans wanted to harm anything that got out of line.

"Listen, between you and me, I told Brian not to develop a vendetta about this. But he's angry. He believes this is an injustice. He wants that lemur destroyed. It's the principle of the thing." Spencer sounded genuinely sympathetic, but I knew he was always on, always acting. He was telling me what I wanted to hear so I would let my guard down.

"You always told me clients shouldn't make decisions based on the principle of the thing. You told me to change their minds."

Spencer laughed. "That's when you were my associate and I needed you to put my cases in order. This is what it is."

I cut the offending willow branches myself, bringing a step-stool from the garage to snip the high branches. When I glanced up, I spotted the lemur standing on the balcony outside the sliding glass door upstairs. He'd overheard. He shook his head, his white-and-black fur unkempt and ringed by sunlight.

CHAPTER 14

A few days later, a judge granted the ex parte application, allowing Spencer to add the lemur to the lawsuit and to amend the papers to ask for the injunctive relief that the lemur be destroyed. The lemur didn't want me to oppose. I told Spencer over the phone to have the judge continue trial for one to two months, so I could bring a couple of experts together. After I hung up, I sat paralyzed, wondering how I could possibly prepare a new strategy in such a short period of time.

The lemur moped around the house, barely looking up from a shoot 'em up video game, one of Mike's favorites, even to eat meals. The sound of the games was starting to drive me nuts, but what bothered me most was his defeatist attitude. He didn't appreciate that my efforts to make him a star had—well, kind of—worked. He didn't believe I could get him out of the case, so he was simply going to cooperate with Spencer until some sort of miracle happened.

All the muscles tightened around my heart, and my stomach was empty and sour. I'd spent so much energy wanting my old job back that I'd forgotten that this feeling of malaise was familiar. It was how I'd felt every day practicing law for Spencer's firm. Even when I won, the partners didn't see how good I was, and then I'd lose sleep and stop going out to lunches with the other associates, so focused on topping myself, so certain I needed to be the best because otherwise nobody would acknowledge my contribution. I'd missed this all before, but now I wasn't sure why.

A few days after the complaint was amended to add the lemur as a defendant, the other shoe dropped: the insurance company paid $20,000 to Brian Turner to settle the Eustachios out of the case the week after the *New York Times* article ran. This settlement, the lemur let me oppose, but only for the sake of form, only because I insisted we would look weak if we let them simply parade out of the case, grinning and triumphant.

I appeared in court the following Monday, ready to argue the merits. Judge Halloran was hearing motions in Judge Stewart's place. I'd barely gotten out two words about how important it was that the judge find the settlement in bad faith, when Judge Halloran turned to Katie Snow and said, "Well?"

Katie whipped out a familiar report. She glanced at me before addressing the judge. "Your Honor, this is the report created by the art appraiser Ms. Ramesh retained on behalf of Brian Turner. $20,000 is the value of the painting, according to Turner's expert. She can't claim this settlement isn't in good faith because—"

"Where did you get that?" I interrupted.

"Spencer," Katie said. She didn't blush or turn away, but looked directly at me and lifted the corner of her mouth. I wanted to slap her.

"Your Honor, she can't use that report. It's from a potential expert who Brian Turner is no longer using, an expert that stated the mural was worth less than what Turner claims it's worth. Mr. Turner's attorney retained another appraiser that is going to testify at trial and claim the value of the mural was much higher. This report was never even disclosed, as far as I know." I bit my lip hard, as the judge scanned the report.

Katie said, "Your Honor, whether or not the report is going to be used at trial, Spencer Clark said it would be fine for me to look at this now that we've settled. In fact, he specifically gave me permission to use the report to show you the good faith of our settlement. I have an affidavit signed by the expert who authored the report, too."

"He what?" It's not like I expected Spencer to help me since he was now suing the lemur, but I hadn't anticipated that he would actively, affirmatively help Katie, regardless of their settlement. We'd worked on cases with her before and he'd always encouraged me to go for the jugular when dealing with her. Hadn't he been the one who told me that she had no future as a trial lawyer because she never went off script, even when the moment called for it? Hadn't he scoffed at her stiffness and lack of verbal dexterity, and encouraged me to do the same? He didn't respect Katie, but now he was helping her crush me. The enemy of his enemy was his friend.

And I couldn't help but think it was because of her image, rather than her lawyering—to the extent those things could be considered different—because she wore expensive tailored suits and her earlobes were pricked with hard little blood diamonds. My knees felt weak. I wanted to crumple to the floor and give up then and there.

I said, "Your Honor, this settlement wasn't conducted at arm's length. In fact, I'd go so far as to say the two opposing attorneys may have colluded for the purposes of destroying my client."

"Do you have any evidence of that?" the judge asked. He was bald with a soft, friendly face. I'd been in front of him before, with good results. He was still flipping through the appraiser's report, stopping to look at one of the close-up shots of the mural.

I shook my head. "It's self-evident, Your Honor. It isn't fair to admit that the mural is worth only $20,000, while continuing to sue someone else for significantly more—a life. If the plaintiff is receiving the correct amount from one defendant, why isn't he dismissing us?"

"I can't rule on the basis of your hunch, Ms. Ramesh. And I'm sorry, but I don't think that permitting one appraiser's evaluation necessarily means the plaintiff is foreclosing his right to seek other damages from your client. It seems to me that the settlement is fair, even by the standards of your former expert. I'm going to approve it."

And just like that, the trial strategy I'd been planning disappeared. I told the court reporter I would need a transcript, hoping that the judge would see that I might appeal. Katie followed me out into the Indian summer. "Busy day?" she asked brightly, as she kept pace with me, moving toward the side street where my car was parked.

"Not exactly," I said, turning to face her. A ziggurat squatted on top of the building behind her, and I focused on its steps, so that I would avoid grabbing her by the shoulders and shaking her. Downtown Oakland was the same as it had been when I worked for Spencer, but today I didn't feel like it was my town. It felt like some sort of simulacrum of Oakland that I'd been caught in by mistake. "What do you want?"

"There's nothing to be upset about. My eleven-year-old niece plays soccer with a bunch of other girls and I'm always so impressed with the sportsmanship, the way they shake hands and say 'good game' afterward. It's how it should be."

"I'm going to take a wild guess there is no scheming and collusion at an eleven-year-old girls' soccer game."

"I resent you saying that. This was a simple deal. A straightforward one." Katie looked at me, and I could see the corners of her lips twitching like she thought our conversation was amusing.

"It isn't at all straightforward."

"Don't be a sore loser." Katie smiled smugly, a smile I'd seen too many times before, the smile of the empty-headed, the smile of someone who, like a dog, understands enough about power to know she has it, but doesn't understand enough to analyze what that power means or doesn't mean.

"You're an incompetent attorney who flips her hair to get ahead. You're not going to be young forever. Grow up." I thought of the lemur being destroyed only because Spencer was an influential man and Katie a young, attractive woman, and I wanted to slap her for her ignorance.

Katie crossed her arms and stepped back. "You're taking this way too seriously. Get real," she said. "It's a game."

"It shouldn't be," I said and walked a different direction, even though we were close to my car. I strode several blocks to a bar, the Ruby Room, where I could be assured I wouldn't run into other lawyers. At the tail edge of my college years, a group of friends used to drag me there. Ross never joined us because he was too busy working; he'd switched from teaching to a research position at the Lawrence Livermore Lab so we could afford a nanny for Tara during the hours I went to school. Though I was a couple of years older than most everyone else, I didn't look my age, and the few hours of pretending to be younger and cooler than I was had always felt satisfying. I hoped it would again.

"Martini, straight." I ordered a drink at the bar. I waved my hand to banish the smoke infused with red light that swirled around my head. "Extra olives? Thanks." I took the drink to a formica table and sat down. I slumped down in the sticky vinyl booth. The drink glowed by candlelight through the red glass candleholders. Someone needed to help me come up with a strategy for winning that didn't involve begging Spencer to dismiss us, or using my own money to pay a settlement for the lemur.

A girl with a pierced nose and dreadlocks approached me with a look of recognition. I groaned inwardly, expecting her to ask about the other Maya Ramesh. But she asked, "Are you that attorney who's representing a monkey? I saw your picture in the paper." She leaned on the table and I smelled something that reminded me of my father's kitchen, sandalwood and something more pungent.

"Why?" I asked, hunching forward because I missed that smell.

"We're rooting for your client," she said, motioning to her table. A bunch of college kids raised their glasses to me from the other table. "A monkey. That's so sick!"

I sighed. "He's a lemur."

"Can I ask you something?" she asked.

"Do you need permission to ask?"

"We'd like to make T-shirts to show our solidarity. And we want to make sure the monkey won't sue us."

"The lemur won't sue. The artist might," I said.

"Yeah, but this is an act of solidarity with the monkey. He should be free. Fuck the artist, am I right?"

I smiled to be polite, and she went away. Hours passed as I drank. On my way out, a bartender with a sleeve of dragon tattoos struck her lighter and flames skidded across the reflective surface of the bar, the only bright spot in what looked from the window like a dreary evening.

Outside, I bummed a cigarette from one of the kids in skinny jeans and studded belts smoking by the door. I lit my cigarette and began smoking. Mottled rocks jutted from the facade. Around me eddied a white-hot smell, like the world was catching fire. I didn't know what would happen if I lost the trial, and I wondered if I could smuggle the lemur out of the country, if there were some heretofore unconsidered, but adventurous way to sneak on a cargo ship and disappear. But I couldn't shake free that feeling of wanting to win, and to win, I would need to keep him here, I would need to stay here. I knew now that one copy begat another copy, and so forth, a multiplication of genes and memes so vast and viscous, it extended far beyond me. My double was somewhere out in the dark world, walking around with my stride and my expression—I wondered whether she was a copy of me, or whether I'd thought through this from the wrong direction, and she was the original Maya Ramesh.

CHAPTER 15

Along with fan mail and requests for interviews, death threats arrived in different sizes. Some typed. Others spelled out in cutout letters from books or magazines pasted to the page. They had a single thing in common: in various grotesque ways, they threatened to kill the lemur. "Humans are whack. One way or another they're going to get me," the lemur said.

"At least you're in the public spotlight now," I said.

"Don't push your luck," he said. "If it weren't for you, none of this would have happened. I'd be swinging through the branches by now, feeling the mist on my face." His words echoed something Tara had said when Ross told her that he planned to move out and that she and Mike would go with him to Berkeley. She'd turned to me at the dinner table with her fake nose ring and said in a haughty tone, "You know, Mom, if you would've paid more attention, if you would have put half the time into us you put into work, none of this would have happened."

In that moment, I wanted to point out how un-feminist what she was saying was, but knew that she wouldn't understand how hard I'd worked to have a career in the man's world of litigation at all. She had no idea of the sacrifices, the time I'd spent early in my career wishing that I could put my files down and play soccer with her at the park, or help Mike research revolution for the epic novel he was writing in red notebooks. I'd thought I was being a role model, but the way she phrased it, she thought I wasn't successful enough to imitate. I knew Ross agreed with her because he didn't say anything in my defense. We sat in silence until I said, "Who wants dessert?" In a few years, she would be moving out. I might never be close to her again, and though I hadn't been close to her at that point either, I still wanted to be careful not to say anything that would make her drift even further from me.

Inexplicably, hearing the lemur blame me for his predicament made me miss my father, too. Even though my father had never understood who I was, even though he had made me take care of Julie when I was learning to take care of myself, even though he thought I should move on from the job with Spencer, even though he reminded me that I wasn't what I pretended I was, I had a feeling that he still *knew* me. I needed somebody else on my team. I needed a sounding board. Since he dealt with patents rather than people, my father wasn't the craftiest strategist, perhaps not the most capable trial attorney for a lawsuit like this, but he was more methodical and well respected than I was. He'd help me figure out what to do to defeat Spencer, and save the lemur, whose song, once full of beauty and longing and lamentation, emanated in horrifying, ugly black waves from the downstairs bedroom. Now that Spencer had gotten to Ross, convincing him that the lemur was dangerous, my father was perhaps the one person I could trust and count on to help me win.

We were sitting in my father's large Eichler by one of the sliding glass doors, eating enormous paper thin dosas smothered in ghee, with sambar and a vendakkai poriyal. Outside, the Weimaraner, a dog he'd bought for companionship after Julie and I moved out, ran in circles, a silver space alien in the red and gold leaves that lay in thick clumps like butterfly colonies in the wet grass. She was tracking muddy paw prints across the concrete path and barking wildly at every flicker of light or odd ghostly shadow that twilight brought. I couldn't remember what the dog's name was, only assorted facts about her, like how she went running with my father every day for five miles and how she'd grown so bored back in the days when my father worked, she chewed up a hunk of drywall she retrieved after mauling a living room wall.

My father was offering me a monologue that was more of a sermon for an audience of one than a strategy session among colleagues. "And that's what I would do," he finished. Even if my father didn't respect my talent and the work I'd put into the case so far, he had a legal mind, and knew what it was to be on a team. I missed talking strategy with Spencer and Evers, eating freshly popped popcorn and drinking a double Scotch on the rocks while evening fell with the smell of hot butter in the dusty perpetual winter of office air. This discussion wasn't the same, but it was close enough.

I said, "I'm not sure that the geneticist who contacted us would be willing to serve as an expert unless we're willing to let him perform experiments on the lemur. I can find out, but we don't even know if the lemur has genetic material."

"He must have cells. It shouldn't take too much for a geneticist to analyze them and let you know if they contain genetic matter or not."

"But what if he says that they do? Is that a good thing? Wouldn't we prefer to discover he's some radical type of paint so he can't be sued at all?" I picked at the chopped okra on the side of my plate, pushing the green bits around with a fork.

"He's being sued, regardless of what he's made of. If he's paint, it's more likely they'll order him destroyed than if a geneticist says he's similar to a human," my father said, scooping into his mouth a mound of dark-brown sambar with his dosa. He drank from a cup of guava juice and wiped his mouth with the back of his hand. "Your goal should be to get him the best outcome, the outcome he thinks is best, under the circumstances. If he has living cells, the judge may find he has rights, and instruct the jury accordingly."

"What if turns out he's only paint?"

"Then maybe your sister can help you find an art appraiser."

"Julie thinks the painting is crap. She told me so back when I told her I had this case last year. Is she even in the country?"

"Does that matter? I know she'd be happy to hear from you. Her personal opinion about the art's value doesn't matter. She could connect you with art appraisers who could help you figure out a better strategy. She's your family. I wish you two would make up. It's been what, fifteen years? And all you do is spend Christmas together. She's really good with your kids, you know."

"I guess. I don't think she has the time to help me." I wanted to receive my father's advice without offending him, but the last thing I wanted was to talk to my sister. I didn't want to be judged a failure for needing her help, but also I felt like I didn't really deserve it. I hated being beholden to people. I hated the way an unpaid obligation would nag at the corners of my mind, forcing me to be more submissive in my interactions, disrupting the uneasy balance of power in a relationship.

He ran a last scrap of dosa around the plate to mop up the remaining sambar. "I think maybe she agrees with you about what happened to her. She hasn't seen a psychiatrist for years. I know she doesn't believe in the medical model as it's practiced anymore, anyway." My father stood and took both of our plates to the sink. "Call her up and ask if she could recommend an artist or appraiser you could consult with, maybe designate as an expert at trial. As I see it, you don't have much choice. You're running out of time. Here, I'll facilitate." He started clicking on the touchpad of his laptop, settled on the kitchen counter.

"No, no," I said. "Thank you, but no." He sighed loudly to indicate his irritation, and took out a dabarah and tumbler, setting them on the counter as he started to brew his filter coffee. We talked about genes for a few more minutes, and then I went home feeling exposed and anxious and unnerved that I'd asked my father for help when he'd never helped before—and still wondering what I should do.

The next morning in my own house, I whipped up the batter for lemon poppy seed waffles and started making a blueberry sauce. While the blueberries, apple juice, and sugar were simmering, a bright blue-brown against the copper pan, I checked my email from my phone.

From: julieramesh@gmail.com
To: mayaramesh@gmail.com

hi maya,
dad said you need an art expert for the case involving the lemur mural that you told me about. i suggest ben whithers at art now in San Francisco. he's served as an art expert in several art-related lawsuits. and he minored in zoology! he's a serious tastemaker and people like him immediately, which should help you at trial. and the last time we met up to talk about my work, he told me he's always wanted to go to Africa. on a safari, not to Madagascar, but otherwise so perfect, right? tell him i sent you.

autumn has come to amsterdam and it's so cold we've stopped going out on the canals on our little boat. i'm sitting by our window eating nutella straight from the jar like we used to do when we were kids. every morning, there is a thin line of smoke from the neighbor's chimney and it turns into the color of the sky and disappears. tonight, however, there was a small fire raging in that window. the police came, but nobody was hurt, not even her cats.

dad told me you lost your job. ross will come around, you'll see. sometimes what seems like a fire in the window is just a minor emergency. i hope you feel that way about these bad things happening to you. anyway, sean sends love and best wishes for the trial. we hope to see you in a few months at Christmas. xoxo j

I groaned as much for my father contacting my sister against my wishes as for her e.e. cummings style of email writing, but I also felt enormous relief at the closure of what had been a chasm of doubt and despair stretching before me. Mercifully, she didn't leave an opening that required me to apologize or talk too much about my crappy life. I typed back "thanks" and "see you soon." I left off the "xoxo" because, coming from me as I went to the mattresses, it would have seemed bitchy and sarcastic, instead of cute. Impulsively, I threw some cloves and a dash of vanilla into the sauce. I added cornstarch and a squeeze of lemon. I poured the batter into the waffle iron, shut it, and turned the handle. The batter started to seep from the space between the pans. I felt like I could conquer the world. I returned to my computer.

The lemur padded into the kitchen. He yawned, revealing all of his thin, sharp incisors, his scarlet gums. The waffle iron beeped. "Here, have a waffle," I said. I turned the iron over again and lifted the waffle out with a fork, sliding it onto a plate. I drizzled the blue sauce with its vaguely toxic shine over it. "We have a lot of work ahead of us."

"You're a little too chipper. What happened?"

"We need to contact the geneticist and tell him you'll cooperate with his research, if he agrees to serve as an expert in this matter gratis. And I'm about to call an art appraiser."

"You're joking. I told you already I'm not interested in being poked and prodded and *studied*. Why would I cooperate in this research?"

"Experts are expensive, very expensive. You want to be killed?

I thought not. So you're going to cooperate in exchange for his expert testimony. Is the situation with your song the same?"

"Worse." He opened his mouth and almost no sound came out. What had been ugly had been transformed into a hoarse wheeze, one empty of melody or rhythm or meaning. The sauce proved to be terrible, but we both drenched our waffles until their grilled faces were puddled in glossy blue.

Later that day, while the lemur sat cross-legged on the rug watching cooking shows with vacant eyes and digging chips out of the bag with his greasy black fingers, I contacted Ben Whithers, the expert Julie recommended. I'd originally planned to start preparing exhibits for trial, but instead I was preoccupied with searching online for clues. I wanted to find Evers. I wanted to find my doppelganger. Some time had passed since they'd last surfaced. Maybe they'd left the country.

More and more, I wondered if my double was really my double, though I knew that the real question was, what did that mean? From preschool onward, you're taught there is only one of you—you are a special snowflake—but from the moment teachers tried to inculcate me with that ridiculous philosophy, I fought the notion tooth and nail. It was such a blatant falsehood it made me angry—if you were truly unique in some way, other people would stamp out your uniqueness, and if you had any sense, you would let them in the interests of assimilation, in the interests of belonging, because loneliness is a black hole.

For weeks, I'd wandered past Evers's apartment building at different hours of the day to see if he'd returned, but the light was never on in his apartment and the windows stayed shadowy. I kept returning to the memory of Evers trying to convince me to run away, to escape. His belief that there was a paradise, that there were things in the natural world that were larger and brighter and more compelling than what he saw as our dreary lives in

Oakland. We hadn't been on the same page; I didn't find law firm life dreary, and I didn't feel about escape or beauty or art as he felt about it. I didn't think lofty concepts and pretty pictures would ever save anyone.

I found my double's Twitter feed and scanned it. Her last tweet had been a few days before, something about all the laoka she was eating. My online research told me that laoka was an accompaniment to rice in Madagascar; there were different kinds, some with Bambara groundnuts and pork, others with shredded cassava and peanuts. Although her biography still listed her in the Bay Area, she had to be in Madagascar. Was she part of Evers's collective? Was she hunting the lemur?

I typed "Nicholas Evers" into the search engine and found several entries about his organization, including its website. There was a web page devoted to chronicling the organization's sightings of giant lemurs. No photographs of the giant lemur were posted, only detailed descriptions of the locations and what the lemur was doing. All the notes, even the most recent ones, were signed with an "X." None were signed with an "NE" or an "MR." If Evers and my double were there, they weren't performing the online administrative tasks.

Further digging revealed that the organization's business address was a warehouse remotely situated near the outskirts of Andasibe-Mantadia National Park, the park most tourists visited to see indri. I tried to imagine Evers taking up residence in a warehouse in the middle of nowhere. He'd told me who he was. He'd told me that this escape, that conquering a new frontier, was what he wanted, but apparently I only saw what I wanted to see. I hadn't noticed he was telling me the truth.

I picked up my phone and on impulse, texted him. *Are you in Madagascar?*

Moments later, a reply came. *Why do you ask?*

Were you the one who sent me that postcard with the indri on it?

I don't know what you're talking about. I am abroad.

With my double?

Look, I don't know what you think you know, but you don't know . . .

I threw the phone down. I would never get answers from Evers, especially not about my double. Was she even a person? I'd seen her on the street but once. And there were other online sightings, but it was hard to take those as real. A shimmering flurry of wild ideas fluttered through my mind—maybe Evers had made a copy of me, a blow-up Maya doll that he carried around, or maybe I only imagined her, and all the online sightings were simply coincidences that I took to have meaning because I wanted to invest them with meaning, or maybe there was another person who looked like me, but possessed none of my interior life. There are no special snowflakes, I reminded myself. And then there was the question of whether she was simply standing in for me with Evers, or had they truly fallen in love? And if they'd fallen in love, why hadn't he fallen in love with me?

I called a private detective who I'd worked with on some of Spencer's cases; as far as I knew, he wasn't close with Spencer, and he'd always seemed professional. I didn't ask him to find the double; instead I asked him whether he could locate X, a witness in Madagascar, and convince her to come testify against Brian. It would be an expensive search and possibly dangerous, since she and Evers had made it their life's mission to capture the giant lemur, but I was pretty sure the benefits to us at trial would outweigh the risks, since one of the letters suggested that she and Evers were estranged. I gave the detective the address of the collective. He said he would start working on it once I faxed over the documents I had of hers.

After faxing the correspondence and copies of her photographs, I looked at the lemur. Why shouldn't the court find him a *person*, rather than a work of art? If he were a person, a being with his own thoughts and feelings, this copyright suit would be moot. He had committed no crime, he couldn't simply be destroyed as Spencer was advocating. His pale eyes remained blank, his hand mechanically entering the bag of chips and moving to his mouth in a kind of automation that wasn't any different from the torpor that came over Mike when he watched television. A wave of tenderness flooded me. My father was partially right: if the lemur was made of living material, if he was conscious, if he was a person, how could the state order him destroyed? The lemur's personhood was the key to the whole case. I called Stranger Laboratories to speak to the geneticist and began looking for an expert on consciousness.

Stranger Laboratories was a small campus in the foothills on the other side of the bay, several miles north of where my father lived. Shadowed by live oaks, the four buildings were an oddly bucolic setting for cloning and genetic research. I parked in the visitor lot. The lemur was reluctant to step out of the car, gripping the sides of the passenger seat with his paws, but I pulled him by the arm, and eventually he stumbled out of the car. We signed in at the front desk. Marcus Spiegelman came out to the lobby to take us into the labs, introducing himself as Dr. Spiegelman, rather than Marcus. He was a tiny, wiry man, not much taller than the lemur, with excruciatingly sharp features—a mouth like a knife, eyes that glinted, a thin nose that came to a point. I introduced them and Spiegelman held out his hand. The lemur grasped it with his paw and gave it a quick shake before letting go. After the formalities, he took us down a hall and up the elevators. We passed a couple of scientists in white lab coats in the hallway before we reached the office.

Spiegelman's office was spare and quiet with only one desk and chair. Framed photographs of a woman and children sat on the gray desk. "I've been doing a lot of research online about you. There are a lot of interesting theories out there," Spiegelman said, twirling a pen. He laughed from his belly—genuinely—and the lemur and I laughed politely. "I understand that you need an expert for your trial, so I propose that we help each other."

The lemur tensed up beside me. I put out my palm to signal him to stay quiet. "That's what I was hoping you'd say," I said. "What did you have in mind?"

"I'd be willing to run some tests on the tissue, to see about its genetic material, to determine whether it's human genetic material, if you would be willing to let me conduct further testing to determine whether cloning is possible, whether we could use your tissue to rehabilitate the indri population in Madagascar."

"Listen, I don't want to be cloned," the lemur said before I could stop him. "It's not that I'm against you helping the indri, it's that I'm probably not one, and I don't like the idea of you being able to make a copy of me."

"What if you are? What if my tests could prove that you are?"

"We're willing to consider your offer," I said. "Provided that you hold off until after the trial. It's critical that we do the tests immediately to determine whether there's any genetic material at all. We don't know what the lemur *is*. Once we know what he is, we can defend this lawsuit."

"The tests require tissue either way," Spiegelman said. "There's no need to hold off until after the trial since all we need are the samples and an authorization."

"I hate to break it to you, but you're not the only genetic lab in town," the lemur said, standing up. "Listen: I'm never going to agree to be cloned. No way, no how. No."

I thought this refusal would be a deal breaker for the scientist, but he waved his hand for the lemur to sit back down. "Okay, I understand. How about this? I take the tissue so that I can study it and testify on the topic, and use the results in future research, but we won't create a clone of you with it. Under any circumstances. We'll agree not to use it to replicate you, but we will study it and use it in other research, and you'll come in for a second visit after the trial, so that I can do some follow-up testing."

The lemur looked skeptical, but I agreed. After we filled out the forms and wrote a makeshift addendum to the release, excluding cloning as a possible use of the tissue, the scientist took the lemur into another room to have the tissue extracted. While they were gone, I walked around the sterile, windowless office. Books were crammed tightly into the shelves that lined two walls, mostly books about the environment, some with green leaves printed on their spines, and many more that were taupe and gray hardback text-books. One of the books with green leaves on the spine was called *Song of the Indri*. Curious, I pulled it out. It was full of information about indri, weaving together fact and legend in order to explain why the indri would be extinct in no time. An afterward about cryptozoology concluded the otherwise scientific book in a quirky way. I took the book back to my chair and sat down, flipping to the start of the chapter, and read the first paragraph:

> *Why have I chosen to end on a discussion of cryptozoology in a book about indri? When most hope is lost, it seems fitting to conclude a book about a critically endangered animal with the wildest of hopes. And the hope is this: there have been credible sightings of a giant indri in Andasibe Preserve. Long considered mythological—a kind of Sasquatch—the giant indri appears to be a real animal. In addition, footprints and giant bones have been found that confirm the presence of a larger creature in the rainforest. Scientists such as Dr. Marcus Spiegelman of Stranger Laboratories believe that genetic material from these larger indri are the key to preserving the ordinary indri, saving them from extinction.*

As I continued to read, I was chilled. We had signed an agreement that in the event the lemur was genetic, there would be no direct cloning, no replica made of the lemur. But the genes had a potential use outside the lines of our agreement—they could be sequenced and individually cloned to save another species. There was something noble in this endeavor, but the lemur would see it as a betrayal.

I flipped to the back of the book. Under "Acknowledgements" I found a list of ten names that the author had thanked in alphabetical order. Included among those ten to my surprise: Nick Evers and Marcus Spiegelman. Did Evers and Spiegelman know each other, too? Evers wanted to capture the lemur, while Spiegelman wanted to use his genes to save the ordinary indri. What were the chances that these two missions were not at odds, but somehow yoked together?

I needed to find the lemur right away. I needed to make sure he was okay, that Spiegelman hadn't turned him over to Evers. I took a photo of the Acknowledgements page and the cover of the book with my phone, and replaced the book back on the shelf. I left the office and began wandering around the halls.

I asked the first scientist I met where I could find Dr. Spiegelman. He told me to check with the front desk, as they could page him. The elevator didn't seem to be working. I roamed the halls, peering through the windows at the top of the doors. There was a room filled with scientists in lab coats stooped over at heat-resistant black benches that were stocked with micropipettes, beakers, and various clear test tubes. Upstairs—more offices with glass sliding doors. The lemur wasn't in any of these spaces. A rising sense of panic came up in my throat, the same sort of panic I'd had once when Tara went missing as a small child, lured by the smell of cinnamon and yeast into a chain bakery as Ross and I kept hurrying through the too-bright fluorescent mall glow to buy a last-minute birthday gift. The panic I felt now was nearly as great—something horrible had happened on my watch, and I shouldn't be responsible for another being at all. Why had I forced the lemur to come here, much less let the scientist take him off somewhere? I pictured the lemur lying on a table in a straitjacket, screaming that horrific black noise instead of the song he had come to me with, and I was ready to sob. After searching the top floor of the building, I raced down multiple flights of stairs, and ran through the first floor to the front desk.

I said something to the receptionist, who was hunched over behind the desk and bopping her head. She was listening to music on the computer with ear buds. I tapped her arm, and trying not to let my anxiety show, asked her if she could page Dr. Spiegelman because he'd disappeared for a lengthy time with the lemur. She slowly removed the ear buds and spit out her gum, and then called the different departments in the building. She shook her head at me as each person who answered the phone disclaimed knowledge.

Just when I was about to lose it, the lemur and Dr. Spiegelman emerged from the elevator. The lemur was wearing a bandage on one of his legs and limping. "Are you okay?" I asked.

"Yeah, why?" the lemur said.

"You were gone so long."

"It takes a little time to extract the cells," Dr. Spiegelman said. He put his hands in his pockets, and I noticed that his tie was covered with one of those perceptually tricky Escher prints of boxes that played with perspective. "My colleague in Santa Cruz works on extinction studies, and she may have some insights. I should have an answer for you in a week."

The lemur looked at me. I nodded and shook the scientist's hand. As we moved out of earshot, the lemur asked me why I was sweating. I didn't have the heart to tell him about the book, about the names in the acknowledgements, about the possibility that Spiegelman was somehow connected to Evers, who I also hadn't told the lemur about. We needed Spiegelman, and I'd learned the hard way that the lemur could refuse to cooperate with my strategies in a pinch. Trial loomed dangerously near. In a few weeks, we would have an answer about whether the lemur would be destroyed.

CHAPTER 16

In the weeks before trial, once I'd secured the necessary experts, all I thought about was the trial theme, the catchy single line that would capture why we should win, that would defeat whatever Spencer's theme was. Usually, the other side's motions before trial capture their theme. But since our motion work had been limited, I had to guess on a theme, based on how Spencer had reacted to the *Times* article, based on what I knew about his mind as his associate, his right hand, and I had to betray him as best as I could if I had any hope of winning. Spencer said that a good theme was like an ad slogan—"if the glove don't fit you must acquit" and all that. Picking a theme was the hardest aspect of trial prep for me, but it was made even harder by not knowing for sure what the genetic testing would reveal. I couldn't nail down the theme until I heard back from Spiegelman.

Meanwhile, the detective called and advised that it had been difficult to locate X because, although the collective maintained a warehouse in Madagascar, the building seemed to be empty during ordinary business hours. He'd posted up outside the warehouse and watched it for signs of life. I told him to watch for at least another week.

Several days after the visit to Stranger Laboratories, I met Tara for coffee at a tiny cafe by Ross's new apartment that sold chocolate. She ordered an elaborate mocha with real whipped cream and a Belgian chocolate turkey, and I ordered a shot of espresso.

"Are we going to have Thanksgiving together?" she asked, as we looked around for a place to sit. The cafe was empty except for two middle-aged women wearing wool sweaters and funky gold jewelry. I told her I didn't know.

She'd just come from soccer practice, and she had chopped her hair short—it looked like she'd cut it herself—so that it was shoulder length. It wasn't dyed, or flat ironed. It was her ordinary, wild, curly dark brown mop, a curiously '80s style against her fair skin. When you see your children every day, you forget how much time is passing, how quickly it's going. That day, I realized that even though Tara was a teenager, she looked like a grown woman. All her previous incarnations seemed to flash before me: her milk-sweet infancy, her first determined steps, the red barrettes she wore the first day of school—school is when everything changed—the way she started talking back and wearing sexualized clothing I didn't approve of. And then all the things that I regretted or hoped she would one day change. The way I said no to everything, because I didn't approve of how fast she was growing up, though I wanted to say yes because I wanted her to like me. The way she'd started running to Ross because he gave different answers, because he wasn't from a different culture—until we started disagreeing, I hadn't realized that my roots were showing, that I really was from a different culture, nor had I realized that the more conservative culture I'd been born into still pulled at me, colored my thoughts, made me feel like a bad mother. And how did Tara figure out how to get under my skin, how to make me feel like my worst self?

These thoughts flashed through my mind, but I brushed them aside so that I could hug her, and it was a real hug—we had missed each other. We sat down at the table and she bent to pull her purple leg warmers up from her ankles.

"We haven't really decided about Thanksgiving," I said. "It depends on whether the trial is over by that time. So what have you been doing? I want to know everything." Against Ross's terse advice, I was trying to pretend we could pick up where we'd left off in our telephone conversation when she'd gotten excited about me not defending "the man."

Tara scowled. The rosy cloud that had hung over our relationship, from my perspective at least, dissipated. "Everything's okay. Are you and Dad going to get divorced?" A barista brought us our drinks.

"I honestly don't know. I hope not, but everything is still up in the air until we work through things."

She perked up. "When will you know? After the trial? When is the trial?"

"If everything goes well, in a couple of weeks." I couldn't answer about when I would know, so I decided not to try to answer, and she seemed to forget, moving on to her next question.

"Is the lemur dangerous?"

"Not at all," I said. "Why do you ask?"

"The kids at school were tweeting about it. I thought maybe he was why you and Dad aren't getting back together."

"I thought you supported me representing the lemur." I downed the espresso and tried not to look too interested by the intricate feathers on her chocolate turkey. I was hoping she would offer me some, but she wiped a skinny mustache of cream from her top lip with her hand and continued to study me.

"I do," she said. "I just don't see why you and Dad have to live apart if you're only going to get back together. And I thought maybe it had to do with you representing him."

I paused. I wanted to lie. Lies always sounded so shiny, so perfect, so much better, but I worried she had gotten my bullshit detector through genetics or osmosis. "We might not get back together," I said truthfully.

"Then why aren't you getting a divorce? I mean, Mike and I have been wondering about this for a long time."

"Because we might work it out," I said. "You never know. I want to work it out. I want to know that we're going to work it out." This, I realized was true. I'd come to understand that I didn't want to be with Evers. I still wanted to know what his involvement was in the various mysteries that had collected around the lemur, but I didn't want to be with him. He was not at all who I'd thought he was, but something far more dangerous, a silver-tongued huckster, possibly even evil. Ross would have dismissed my Manichean worldview, but I was more than ever convinced that there was real evil in the world.

"Why is work more important to you than us?" she asked.

I wasn't expecting this kind of directness. I always slid between and beneath the cracks of other people's words, working out the meanings through inference. "It's not. I don't know why you and Mike would think so. Work just keeps me insanely busy." I drummed my fingers on the table for a second—the sudden flood of caffeine in my veins was making me jump—and then I stopped self-consciously.

"You got fired, but you still don't spend time with us. I think you're a workaholic."

I had no response to this accusation. All I knew was that it was easier to care whether the lemur lived or died than to deal with the incredible discomfort my family made me feel—like I was supposed to have less ego, less ambition, less of everything, and I just couldn't. Others might see me as a defective mother for not naturally wanting less for myself (and still others might think my anxiety about this ridiculous), but simply being aware of this perception didn't magically fix me. "I'm going to do better. Your dad told me you just took the PSATs. Have you talked to the school counselor about colleges that might be a good fit?"

She nodded. We talked about colleges and it soon became apparent she had no idea what she wanted to do with her life. She wanted to go to New York, she wanted to escape California, she wanted to reinvent herself in a place with seasons. Her interests weren't much different than mine or my sister's had been twenty years earlier. I'd wanted to go to New York, too, but my father, ever certain he knew what was best for us, insisted I would be too distracted by the city, so instead I'd attended Stanford, hadn't fit, dropped out, and married Ross, all before eventually going to a state school and then a good law school. "What if you don't get into a school in New York? Do you have a backup plan?"

She rolled her eyes, a disconcerting gesture under all that mascara. I suddenly flashed to her as a baby, looking at me with the same luminous, trusting brown eyes. "I'm applying to every tier of school possible in New York. Crap schools, rich-kid schools, quirky liberal arts colleges, urban, edgy schools," she said. "I'll get in someplace. And you don't have to worry. The counselor says she's pretty sure with my grades I can pick up some scholarships. Plus, there's financial aid."

"I'm not worried. You should go to the best place you can, the place that makes you most excited." Even if I were jobless, I was determined not to be like my father, scrutinizing my children's decisions from every possible angle, so that I could present reasons why they shouldn't leave me.

"Aunt Julie said you wanted to go to New York, too, but Thatha wouldn't let you because you got into Stanford and he thought it was a better school."

"She remembered that? When did you talk to her?" I was jealous that my daughter wanted to talk to my sister, but I tried not to let it show.

"Last week. She calls every month to say hello, remember?"

"I didn't know she even knew about that. She was twelve or thirteen then."

"She said she wanted to be just like you."

I restrained my laughter—Julie and I couldn't have turned out more differently. "That's news to me."

By the time she finished chugging her mocha, Tara had moved on. "Dad doesn't want me to move far away," she said, pausing and scanning my face for clues of what I was thinking. She'd turned out like me, and this didn't make me especially happy.

"You should go wherever you think is right. Sometimes he can take a while to warm up to adventure. You know that," I said. After she finished her mocha, I drove her home.

Inside the apartment, she disappeared into her room. Evidently, Mike and Ross had just gotten home, and I stood in the kitchen talking with them for a few minutes about the case. Mike wanted me to read his latest story. Ross gossiped about a bachelor in his lab. For several minutes I was filled with an ache, with a longing that surprised me. What if this feeling of wanting to be with them could last? What if the belonging I had been looking for inside the courtroom was here? It made me sad to think I'd been looking in all the wrong places, but I couldn't think about that for too long. It was unsettling and disarming, and I needed to feel strong, protected, armored—I needed to win. I needed to save the lemur from destruction.

As I strolled back to my car from Ross's apartment, I noticed I'd missed a telephone call from the detective. I listened to his nasally message. "So, great news, Maya, we have located X, or rather Xandra Jones. And you'll be pleased to know that she's more than willing to testify on your client's behalf. It may be expensive to fly her to Oakland and put her up in a hotel, but other than that, we're good to go. I'll wait for you to forward the funds."

It was all coming together. I pumped my fist with excitement before getting into the car.

The following week, Dr. Spiegelman called with the results of his testing and we planned to meet at Stranger Laboratories to discuss it. The lemur grumbled that he would have preferred to catch the next installment of a soap opera that had captured his interest. We drove across the Bay Bridge, cut across the city, and meandered through the voluptuous pale gold hills on either side of Highway 280. Particles of white autumn mist flooded the road before us like we were driving through someone's dream.

Inside, the geneticist's office smelled vaguely like lemon cleaning solution and printer ink. Spiegelman beamed as he leaned across his desk, and fluttered a report in front of me. "Good news! Great news! He's definitely made of living genes . . . There is some bad news, too, though. We couldn't figure out where he fits, in terms of taxonomy. I suppose he simply doesn't. He's something outside our classification system. We were, however, able to determine that a portion of his cells can be considered indri. And this other finding is even more surprising. Some of him—I was pleased to find that some of him—is human! My team has never seen anything quite like it."

The lemur looked pleased. I smiled. I wanted to be relieved, but the weight of our last visit still hung over me. I fumbled for a moment, trying to find the right way to bring up what had made me so anxious. "Before we continue, do you know Nick Evers?" I asked.

"Yes." Dr. Spiegelman's smile faded. The lemur looked confused. "Why do you ask?"

"Do you have a business relationship?" I didn't want to give away too much.

"No, not at all."

"But you've worked with him?"

"No. We're both interested in the plight of the indri, but that's it. I met him at a fundraiser a couple of years ago, and we have a few friends in common because he funds a group in Madagascar that's doing some interesting tracking work." He seemed to be telling the truth. There was nothing shifty in his eyes, no hesitation in responding. His clear voice didn't shake. He seemed to genuinely believe Evers performed tracking work, rather than hunting. I nodded.

"Who is Evers, again?" the lemur asked. "That name sounds familiar."

"Just another attorney I don't trust," I said.

We began strategizing about Dr. Spiegelman's trial testimony. The case was coming together, and now I was excited. I hadn't been to trial in more than a year. It was hard not to feel my whole being coming to life with the knowledge that I was about to do battle. All the fuzzy hairs on my neck stuck straight up, my blood was pumping, coursing, singing through my body. When preparing for a trial—especially one I was afraid to lose—I was reminded of what it meant to be alive.

PART III

RETURN

"There must be more to life than having everything."
Maurice Sendak

CHAPTER 17

On the morning of the first day of trial a seething mob of people with poster board signs on sticks waited for us on the courthouse steps, and although it was cold, some people were wearing only red-and-gold T-shirts screen printed with a faded black-and-white image of the lemur bearing the block letters "FREE," presumably courtesy of the group at the Ruby Room. Evidently, the T-shirts went for twelve dollars online, although a store downtown was selling them for fourteen dollars. They waved signs, some in support of the lemur, a few against.

"How do you feel about being an icon for copyright reform?" yelled someone in the crowd, a reporter, most likely.

"Go back to Africa!" someone else shouted.

"Get back in the painting where you belong!" another person yelled. I thought people generally kept their nastiness for anonymous internet chat boards where they wouldn't be spotted and shunned, where social repercussions were directed at someone they could pretend not to be, but the same sort of dark twisted anonymity existed in a mob scene.

We plowed through the dense crowd, the sticky, sweaty bodies displaying the lemur's image. People shoved me into other people wearing woolly knit caps with sports logos and synthetic puffy coats open over their T-shirts. I sneezed repeatedly, my nose itchy. The lemur wasn't doing much better; everyone wanted to touch him, mostly so that they could say they'd touched him, and he frowned, the muscles in his face tightening together like a cinched corset. If his song weren't already gone, it would have disappeared just from this maelstrom of emotion. People's fingers were reaching out, grabbing, wiggling, waving: small, square, long, stubby, paper-white, freckled, rosy, brown, black with manicured nails, nails black with dirt, nails blue with paint or marker, nails stained with nicotine, diamond rings and once, a luminous green mood ring. We pushed through the sea of grabby fingers, but made little progress.

Three quarters of the way up the steps to the heavy double doors of the courthouse, the lemur snapped and cried out with the same strange, strangled yelps he would have made in the rainforest if he were under attack there, instead of pushing up smoggy steps, rancid with the odor of bodies pressed far too close. But it was the right thing to do—alienating the crowd was probably the only way we could have made it up the glittering concrete steps. We shoved through the heavy wooden doors and made it through the metal detectors without incident.

We were out of breath by the time we took our seats at the front of the courtroom at the counsel tables. Across the way, Spencer was huddled together with Brian Turner. Brian turned and stared at me. I couldn't read his expression, whether his eyes held contempt or hatred or indifference. Spencer didn't look at us. He whispered to Brian, and then Brian stopped looking over.

The lemur waggled his butt in the chair next to me, trying to get comfortable in the hard wooden seat. His feet didn't touch the floor, and I could tell it bothered him from the way he kept trying and failing to stretch his toes to the wood planks. I'd made him shower the night before, but his fur looked droopy and his belly sagged. Under the harsh glare of the fluorescent lights, I saw silver flecks in his black fur, gray emerging from his white fur. He was, in short, falling apart, aging in the way of all living things, but also falling apart rapidly because indris couldn't live so long away from Madagascar.

Judge McCracken, a paunchy, sunburned man with beady eyes and shaggy brows, presided over the trial. I'd argued motions in front of him early in my career, and knew he was fond of imposing strange sanctions. After my first failed court appearance when I had mixed up the names of two realtors, he'd required me to write what was essentially a book report on the relationship between the defendants in a coordinated action with multiple defendants. There were rumors, too, that he wrote mean-spirited notes about the attorneys in front of him. One attorney inadvertently saw a doodle in which he'd caricatured her in pink ink. Under her likeness were little hearts and the name "Fat pig." I hadn't seen the judge in ages, but I was determined not to star in his doodles, not to screw up this time.

The judge pulled out a large sheaf of briefs and scanned the pages of the motions before him. Spencer stood up. He wanted the judge to split the trial in half, deciding on the issue of destroying the lemur first. I was terrified that he would succeed and that none of my other arguments about the lemur's personhood would be heard at all. "If that issue is determined first, Your Honor, perhaps we won't need a trial on the merits," he said.

"I've read your opposition, Ms. Ramesh. Anything to add?"

I stood, conscious of the gallery of people behind me. "Your Honor, you'll get the best sense of this case if you hear all of the evidence before making up your mind on that question. Many of the facts here are contested, so it's not simply a question of law."

"But, the facts relevant to the matter at hand are not contested, Your Honor. Ms. Ramesh and I don't disagree as to the basic scenario," Spencer said.

We argued for a few minutes. The judge ruled the trial would not be bifurcated. Relief in this one ruling gave me the confidence to continue—I'd assumed Spencer possessed an advantage in this trial not only because he'd been in front of this judge many times, but also because I'd seen his political influence behind the scenes at trials before, getting the judge he wanted for a case through his cronies in Sacramento, but perhaps not.

Most of the motions in limine were routine efforts to block evidence that each of us believed would be prejudicial. Spencer's biggest objection was to Marcus Spiegelman as an expert witness. In spite of the report, which we had forwarded to him before trial, Spencer remained firm that Spiegelman didn't have sufficient expertise to be able to offer the jury any guidance. He claimed this situation was entirely novel, and involved art, a man-made object, not genes, the interior mapping of living organisms. He resorted to name calling, claiming that Spiegelman's report was junk science. Although he'd hired a geneticist to rebut Marcus, he claimed putting a geneticist on the stand would unfairly bias the jury in the lemur's favor.

The judge overruled most of the objections, saying that if the situation involving the lemur was entirely new, who was to say it didn't have to do with biology, what life was, in which case, why not a geneticist? Spencer blustered about, but could think of no useful counter, so we moved on to the other motions in limine.

I wanted to block Spencer's art appraiser. "The plaintiff continues to present this as a copyright case, Your Honor, but the truth is, this case isn't about intellectual property at all. There's no reason to put an art expert on. This is a case about personhood, about who we allow to be a person, about whose autonomy and experiences and opinions we honor. It's absolutely inappropriate that the plaintiff continues to insist that the lemur is his property."

I had no hope of winning this argument, even before a trial. The judge wouldn't gut Spencer's case, especially after he'd alleged that the lemur was dangerous—the journalists in the gallery would have a field day. But I wanted to keep Spencer on his toes—I wanted him uncertain. I wanted to wear him out.

Spencer argued, "Your Honor, of course this is a copyright case. The lemur acknowledges he emerged from the mural. Moreover, part of our case is that we don't know what the lemur is and that he presents a danger. He gets out of that mural, and bam! The art world is thrown into chaos. Mr. Turner's life falls apart. All of civilization as we know it is threatened. The truth is, we're in uncharted territory here with this . . . beast, this chimera. We have on our hands something entirely unpredictable. We need to contain this situation. He's a potential threat to an orderly society. Even assuming for the sake of argument that he's made up of genetic material, that doesn't mean he's *not* Mr. Turner's property— just as his dog made up of genes could be his property. Surely, if you permit a geneticist to testify about a once-inanimate lemur, we can inquire into the far more relevant question of whose property the lemur is?"

I said, "The difference is that the geneticist is an expert with knowledge of the lemur. He's examined him. He's run some physical tests. The art appraiser's valuation of him as art at this point is irrelevant. It's wholly prejudicial and has nothing to do with this case."

The judge was drawing on a pad of paper. He was using a purple pen this time. I wondered if Spencer was depicted in the doodle, or if I was. And how did he see me? Without looking up, the judge said, "Mr. Clark, I'll allow the art appraiser, but no speculative testimony or documents will be allowed."

Next, the judge limited voir dire to only one hour of questioning prospective jurors. I remembered when we first started working together and I was observing my first trial, a real estate matter on which Spencer served as the plaintiff's attorney, Spencer took me out to lunch at a fancy Vietnamese restaurant during jury deliberations. Offhandedly, I'd commented on how effective his closing statement was. He swirled the thick condensed milk into his Vietnamese coffee and said that cases were often won or lost at the voir dire stage, not on direct examination, not on cross-examination, not in closing arguments, but right there at the beginning of the trial. He'd said, "That's what they don't teach you in law school, how to read people, what they want, what kinds of stories appeal to them, and how to tell those stories."

Spencer considered himself an expert at reading people, a detective deciphering the clues in someone's clothing and what his or her demeanor meant, a semiotician of human features, and more importantly, their subtle weather conditions. This was something we had in common, and maybe even the real reason he had taken such a shine to me, at first: we both read people as if they were characters in Victorian or Russian literature and immediately knew certain things about them. Like what tone of voice would be persuasive to them, rather than overpowering. Whether they were afraid of being overpowered, or whether, conversely, they were submissive people who welcomed that feeling or found it erotic. Whether they wanted to feel they'd done the "right" thing. How they felt about authority. If they believed in justice in a real sense, or only when it was convenient.

Now, looking at the group of people seated before me, I felt a certain amount of trepidation. Spencer was more naturally likeable than me. I'd been faking everything, pretty much since I'd realized it was all rigged, and not in my favor, in high school. I'd participated in newsworthy jury trials before, but always as Spencer's second chair, never against Spencer, and never in any trial where a life was at stake.

I glanced at the lemur who was sprawled out on the chair. He was trying his best to appear relaxed for the jury. Though his jaw was clenched, he looked vaguely drunk. I could sense he was thinking what I'd taught him: slow, gentle breathing, in, out, in, out, but he was still gritting his incisors. He didn't look at me.

A famous trial consultant I'd worked with on another case had schooled me about jurors who had a low need for cognition. Those were the jurors who were yawning, fidgeting, not really looking at the judge or the lawyers when they spoke. Although some of those jurors were just preoccupied with conflicts with their family or at a job, others had a low need for cognition:

they made decisions quickly and with very little need for information. Because I was presenting a less familiar concept, one I wanted the jury to learn, my goal during voir dire was to eliminate those jurors.

Spencer wasn't thinking about that issue. His supplemental questionnaire was limited; he asked the potential jurors standard questions about their occupations and families. He also asked if they were personally acquainted with any artists, which I thought a bad question, since simply knowing whether they knew artists didn't give him any sense of whether they were biased for or against artists. He wanted people acquainted with artists on the jury, but since he hadn't asked about bias, I didn't automatically strike them. He looked surprised and a little annoyed. No lawyer likes being unable to read the other side, but he should have expected it with me: the servant can always read the master better than the master can read her.

Meanwhile, I had come up with my own criteria. I was looking for tech-savvy users. Under the counsel's table during the judge's questioning, I was searching online to see if they had social media profiles, to check into matters they might deem too private to divulge during voir dire or even in casual conversation, but didn't find too private to share with the internet. You might be surprised. Spencer, as I mentioned, was old school—he frequently took cases to trial, and although he relied on insurance carriers to cave to his magnetism, he also hated them because they robbed him of his opportunities to go to trial—and he thought the suit against the lemur was a slam dunk, so he neither brought a trial consultant (at least none I was aware of) nor researched any of the jurors.

We wound up with eight jurors. Almost all had social media profiles I could examine, and though some of them knew artists, none appeared deeply invested in art.

Juror 1: Retired older woman whose large blonde swirls of

hair were tinted pink. She'd attended Cal in the sixties. She wore perfect makeup and oversized African earrings that looked mismatched, but were handmade. Uninterested in art, she was a feminist who volunteered at a civil rights organization. Although all of the privacy settings on her social media accounts were restrictive, she seemed open and forthcoming during the judge's questions. I was relying on her to be a leader in favor of freeing the lemur.

Juror 2: Heavyset black man, a civil engineer who worked in San Leandro. His Facebook profile wasn't public and his Twitter stream was similarly protected. I had no idea which way he would go, but I'd used all my peremptory challenges (challenges for which I didn't have to give a reason) and I couldn't articulate the rationale for why I didn't want him on the jury. Something in his dourness made me feel like he would see right through me and tell the others what I was arguing was nonsense.

Juror 3: Japanese-American woman who owned a small shop in the Gourmet Ghetto area of Berkeley where she sold artisanal tofu. She was unmarried and active on social media, but I was most worried about her. She sold her tofu for obscene prices. What if she felt some sort of kinship with Brian Turner? When I pressed her, she firmed up in her assurances that she could be fair, but something about the style of her website made me think she had aspirations toward artistry or at the least, an artistic temperament that might make it difficult for her to be open to my arguments.

Juror 4: White twentysomething who studied environmental sciences at Cal State East Bay. I was worried about him until his Facebook profile told me he liked *Breaking Bad* and *Dexter*, television shows featuring anti-heroes. While the lemur was not a criminal, I had the feeling Juror 4 would think he was and would secretly be rooting for us.

Juror 5: Tan, tattooed twentysomething who had never gone to college. She worked as a barista at a raw, vegan restaurant and self-published zines. She didn't watch television. She had a Twitter account where she tweeted mostly about music, enough of it punk and hardcore to make me feel secure.

Juror 6: Latino teacher who leaned toward the establishment. During voir dire, he radiated a strong authoritarianism, which I realized belatedly meant he could either sympathize with the celebrity artist whose hard work was reaping no rewards, or he could see the artist as an anti-establishment figure simply by virtue of being an artist, in which case he wouldn't be overly eager to protect him. However, from the public part of his Facebook profile, I learned to my surprise the only writer he liked publicly was the innovative writer David Markson. I knew from Tara, who read all the literary blogs and got reading recommendations from Julie's playwright husband Sean, that Markson used pastiche—I hoped that was a good sign.

Juror 7: Relatively young Indian woman with a bindi who had immigrated seven years before to live with her husband, a semiconductor engineer. We couldn't really elicit a lot of information about her from voir dire and when I went online, I found that she mostly posted pictures of her children on Facebook. Spencer didn't challenge her, apparently assuming she would have traditional Indian values in favor of authority and patriarchy. I didn't challenge her because I hoped that our shared heritage would bias her in my favor.

Juror 8: White, retired widower who could probably be best described as "jolly." He had been a cardiac surgeon in San Francisco and wasn't active on social media. But he had spent a good chunk of his retirement savings on trips to see Antarctica, an African safari, the Galapagos, and Iceland, which gave me the sense he was an adventurer: in favor of freedom.

Spencer gave the first opening statement, looping back and forth before the jury in a kind of Moebius strip. He was wearing cowboy boots, which gave him a populist edge: look I'm one of you, not someone oppressive, not someone eradicating freedoms, not someone out to kill a *person*.

"Good morning, ladies and gentlemen of the jury," he started in his folksiest voice.

"Good morning."

"I'm going to tell you a story about an artist, a man who has been building up his craft and his vision since the mid-1980s. This is a man who knew he wanted to be an artist since he was a young child finger-painting in kindergarten. While other teenagers went to football games and dances, he was painting wildlife in the creeks behind his house and sketching human portraits. He was studying his craft, practicing to 'see,' if you will, and developing a comprehensive sense of what kinds of things were worth turning into art, namely life in its many forms. He went to a famous art school in Rhode Island, studied with world-class painters, worked on crews for high-profile artists, celebrity artists like Sol LeWitt. He worked as a server at Boulevard in San Francisco while he built his painting career. He started to achieve notoriety for painting murals around the Bay Area, but his work has also appeared in Los Angeles and Barcelona. The mural that's in question today was painted in Oakland near Lake Merritt by my client, Brian Turner."

Spencer took a deep breath and gestured at Brian. Although Brian was usually pierced and wore jeans and a band shirt, for trial he wore a brown suit and a button-down shirt. I could imagine Spencer admonishing him the night before, when they were prepping for the last time, to be more conservative, but not so conservative that he didn't look like the public's image of an artist anymore. Or at least, that's what I would have done. In the moment, however, I felt nothing but revulsion for this phony, this sham artist who had somehow duped me into thinking he was original when he was not only an accomplished thief, but a pompous, entitled misogynist.

"You've probably heard of Brian Turner, famous most recently for his software applications, but also for his legendary murals and enormous paintings.

"Titled simply *Madagascar*, the mural we're talking about today was the sixth of twelve of its kind. It was well received. Critics and visitors to Oakland alike feted Mr. Turner for his rendering of an old Malagasy legend.

"Now what do I mean by 'its kind'?" Spencer gestured with both arms out, palms raised, his eyes seeking contact with the eyes of each juror to make each one think he was talking directly to him or her. "I'm talking about massively scaled paintings that you can almost walk into and that suggest they're actually breaking out of a wall and into your world. Hyperrealistic paintings placed in vastly different spaces from the ones depicted inside the four corners of the painting. Brian Turner's paintings took into account the world outside the Bay Area. In fact, his paintings expressly aimed to squeeze the enchantments of the broader world into the urban and suburban contexts of America. These were paintings intended to transform your experience of the environment, transporting you from where you think you are—downtown Oakland, for example—to where you really are: the world. These are paintings that challenge our understanding of what it means to be a global society. The mural in question was the best of the first six.

"*Madagascar* took Turner eight months to paint, but he conceived of the idea long before he set his brush to that wall. You'll hear from him how he got the idea for this image while traveling through Madagascar. Specifically, he developed a passion for the rainforests of Perinet. The kind of lemur in the painting was the indri, a rare animal, the largest kind of lemur. Turner found the indri inspiring for its call. In painting this mural, he hoped to translate the call of the indri into visual form, to jolt the viewer in the same way the real indri's call jolts a person in the rainforests of Perinet."

Spencer told them about how the mural revitalized the community and explained that it had been defaced. He claimed that the lemur was the most representative of the wildness that Brian Turner wanted to bring into Oakland. The Japanese-American juror nodded slightly under the fluorescent lights. I shifted uncomfortably in my seat.

"Mr. Turner built up his stellar reputation over a long period of time. With this defacement, he looked to the art world like merely another Sunday painter instead of the superstar he truly was. The value of all of the murals in the series went down, based on their relationship to *Madagascar*. His back catalog of oil paintings dipped in value.

"And because of these economic losses, Mr. Turner started to suffer from insomnia, stomachaches, headaches, even palpitations. He could not work. He could not paint. He could not write code for his new software-based projects. Imagine that, if you will, building up your career for more than twenty years, only to watch it go down the drain. And as you can imagine, it's worse for Mr. Turner because he is an artist. He has a sensitive temperament and this devaluation of his life's work, due to no fault of his own, has been torture for him.

"When he finally learned that the lemur had simply left the painting, thereby ruining it, Mr. Turner became distraught. This was his work of art. It was never his intention to create the mural without the lemur. The lemur you see sitting over there today was the soul of the painting, the fruit of Mr. Turner's labors. And now the soul of that painting is walking around town without crediting or compensating Mr. Turner. Mr. Turner owns the lemur, the same way you own your feet or your hands or your heart. He's entitled to keep the lemur from wreaking havoc and entitled to keep the lemur from doing whatever he pleases." The lemur sighed audibly and a musky scent rose from his fur.

"It might be tempting to think that the lemur is not art, but a living being, simply because he moves around and talks. But even if we imagine that to be true, who do we value more here, a dangerous lemur or one of America's most celebrated artists? By the end of this trial, I think you'll agree with me that we need to protect our artists and continue to give them incentives to create in order to maintain our vibrant culture. The Visual Artists Rights Act is clear that an artist of recognized stature like Mr. Turner has several rights that he never waived. Relevant to this trial are his right to claim authorship and his right to prevent distortion, mutilation, or modification that would prejudice his reputation. We also think the lemur's very existence away from the mural should be construed as a willfully infringing derivative work, and so we'll be asking you to find him in violation of the Copyright Act.

"In addition to monetary damages, we'll be asking the judge to enjoin the lemur. What does this mean? In this case, we'll be asking the judge to order him destroyed. We'll also be asking you for actual and compensatory damages in the amount of $2 million. I know we're nearing the holidays and everyone has chores to do, everybody's ready to prepare their turkeys and their pies. So thank you for serving as a jury member and giving this matter your full attention today." Spencer swiveled and sat down at his seat. He didn't look at me, but he relaxed into his chair, confident that I couldn't top him.

I looked over at the jury box and as I feared, he'd won over the Japanese-American woman. She smiled and nodded; everyone else looked receptive and relaxed. I knew they were wondering what I could possibly say that would change their minds. Every other time I'd heard Spencer speak in a courtroom—hell, every time I listened to him give me advice in the office—I'd fallen under his spell, so I knew how bewitched they were. This time, however, I saw him as a belligerent Napoleon who had spent the better part of his forty-year career glad-handing and schmoozing powerful politicos without regard to fairness.

I calmed myself by pushing hard on the muscle between my thumb and index finger, a pressure point, and took a deep breath. I rose from my seat, smoothing down the skirt of my black cashmere suit, and started speaking. "Good morning, ladies and gentlemen. This is a story about freedom. We all want to be free. Let me tell you a story that might make it clear what issues are at stake here. After I took the bar exam many years ago, two friends and I flew to Spain for a two-week vacation. Our first stop was Barcelona, next stop Seville. My goal in going to Barcelona was to decompress, to get away from dirty diapers and laundry and practice blue books. My friend's goal, however, was to see Gaudí and she wanted to spend a full five days in Barcelona.

"If you don't know his work, Gaudí is an architect who makes fantastical buildings that make the witch's house in Hansel and Gretel look tame. His buildings are weird, whimsical non-buildings made of ceramics, stained glass, and wrought iron. I didn't really take my friend's goal that seriously. What's so special about them that you skip other interesting cities just to see a bunch of buildings, right? I'd rather be eating tapas, drinking absinthe and wine, and dancing at nightclubs until five in the morning and after take the train to Seville and Granada than look at a building.

"Well, it's only when I saw one of his buildings up close and personal that I realized how brilliant Gaudí was and why my friend wanted to be in Barcelona for so many days to spend time with his work. My friend saw that Gaudí's buildings offered something that going to a foreign country usually can't offer us anymore, what with a Starbucks on every corner and a McDonald's by the bus stops. You can be truly transported, truly transformed, by Gaudí's buildings and the work of other artists, in a way that is unmatched.

"Here's the thing. I had this artistic awakening and I saw why my friend loved this building. But to this day, I don't really care about Gaudí or his personal intentions for the building. If he intended those buildings to serve as some sort of statement about nature, which maybe he did, it hardly mattered to my enjoyment of them. Apparently, he was antisocial. He was very religious. Who cares? What mattered were his creations, which have lives and meanings of their own. The meanings are those my friend and I, as the viewers or experiencers, created inside our own minds." I looked into the eyes of the vegan barista and thought I could see a spark of recognition.

"This is a story about freedom. This is secondarily a story about what art can and can't do for the human race. Do we value art because of the medium? Do we care that much about paint? Or clay? Or notes of music, for that matter? Do we value art because of what the artist is trying to say? What he intends to say? Do we value art for its power to capture our imagination, or rather for the way it sets us free? Do we value art not for what it sets out to do, but what it actually does to us?

"The lemur you see sitting here before you today did start out in a mural painted by Brian Turner. But as you can see, he's alive. Blood is running in his veins. He talks, he walks, he cracks jokes, he is conscious. And more than that, he's conscious of being conscious. The Visual Artists Rights Act protects against the mutilation or defacement of visual artwork. I'd hardly call a lemur that lives and breathes and speaks—a lemur with consciousness, who is made up of genetic material—a mutilation or defacement, would you? I'd call him a person.

"I don't think any reasonable person can see him as a piece of property rather than a person. In fact, a renowned geneticist will testify that he is a person, and that he has human cells. We have a consciousness expert who will testify that he is a person with a sense of what it's like to be himself.

"The lemur cannot be destroyed at the whim of an artist, no matter how powerful he is. It's a testament to the power of the mural that he's walking around, but does that really give the plaintiff any moral rights over him?

"The plaintiff would have you believe that he needs to be destroyed. The plaintiff would have you believe in a cult of personality, that his work is valuable because it is his, and that it is his because he put strokes of paint on a wall.

"But guess what? It doesn't work that way today. It probably didn't even work that way in the Romantic Age, from where we've derived the idea of artistic genius. You and I with our humble interpretations are what give the painting power, not him.

"And now, like any living thing, like any person, the lemur wants to return home, he wants to return to a place where he belongs. Like each of you here, he wants to live. He wants to be free. He was meant to be free. And all of you are empowered to give that freedom to him. By the end of this trial, you'll see the law requires not only that you refuse to let Brian Turner destroy him, but also that you set him free, and I know each of you, settling into this season in your warm houses and your holiday dinners, your turkeys and your tofurkeys, your cranberry sauce and mashed potatoes, your loved ones and your less-loved ones, realizes the importance of giving this lemur his liberty and freedom to live, to go home. And you'll do the right thing."

As I finished with my opening statement, I saw the tan vegan woman and the black man and the adventurer nodding at what I was saying. The Indian woman smiled at me shyly. The feminist and the Latino teacher looked more baffled than convinced by what I'd said, not a good sign, but there was a chance of repair through the testimony. I hadn't made a dent on either the Japanese-American woman or the guy who liked *Breaking Bad*. Judge McCracken was using a black pen for his doodle, and I wondered whether he was even paying attention to my statement.

As we moved into the plaintiff's presentation of evidence, I steeled myself for Brian Turner's testimony. Evers had represented Brian on a number of copyright infringement claims. In spite of a tendency to turn nasty and mean-spirited when he couldn't get his way, Brian was an excellent witness. He wasn't easily fazed during cross-examination, and he possessed an odd knack for saying what people wanted to hear. His ability to perform at deposition and, if necessary, on the stand was one reason Evers prosecuted so many of his cases. Not only did he dress appropriately for court, for the role of The Artist, he was also your dream witness, friendly, but not so friendly that he volunteered information or tried to help opposing counsel. He was clever, but he stuck with the game plan.

Spencer, for his part, hewed closely to the work I'd done to get the case ready for trial when the Eustachios were the defendants, so I could follow his thinking, too. Brian testified about his trek through the Andasibe Preserve with a famous native guide who was later murdered. He testified that he'd spotted several of these rare giant lemurs, not quite the size of humans, but not as small as most lemurs either. He said, "The moment I heard their call, I was bewitched. I've been to a lot of places and seen some pretty unusual wildlife, but this was like nothing I'd ever heard. I was inspired to paint these guys."

I breathed deeply before my cross-examination. For the first couple of minutes, Brian and I were humming along smoothly. I wanted him to feel comfortable, so that when I slammed him, he would be knocked out. It helped that he didn't see me as danger-ous, and never had.

He gave slight variations in his answers, based on the way I phrased my questions, but mostly he reiterated the theme that Spencer laid out: he was a famous artist who'd spent months working on the mural in question, and the lemur had destroyed it by leaving, resulting in his severe emotional distress.

"Did you take any photographs of these lemurs so that you'd be able to paint them?" I asked.

"Yes."

"Have you produced those?"

"The originals are lost. I've moved multiple times." I noticed Spencer blanching at his table. He couldn't tell where I was go-ing, but he knew me well enough to know I had something in my pocket.

"Mr. Turner, take a look at this photograph. Do you recognize it?" I placed one of X's photographs, which had been attached to the correspondence I gleaned from Evers's apartment, in front of him. I included the photograph in a packet of last-minute documents I'd sent Spencer shortly before trial. I knew that with no associate supporting him on the case, he wouldn't look at the packet that closely.

Brian flushed as he looked at the original photograph of the lemur. At first, he didn't respond. I could see from the cloud that passed in front of his eyes that he was trying to come up with a clever answer. I tried again.

"Have you seen this photograph before, sir?"

"Yes."

"Where did you see it?"

"I'm really not sure," he said. He stopped making eye contact and looked back and forth.

"You're under oath, so I'd really like you to think about this question and respond. Did someone give you this photograph?"

"Maybe," he said. "I couldn't say. This could be any lemur. If I appropriated it, I must have had a valid artistic mission in mind."

"This could be any lemur? Really? There's nothing distinctive about the white flame on his forehead or the flatness of his face or the size of the lemur?"

"It could be any lemur."

"Did you copy the lemur in your mural from this photograph?" I asked.

He flushed again, this time glancing at the jury to explain. "No. And anyway, appropriation isn't copying."

"I'm confused. So you're testifying that it's a coincidence how closely this lemur resembles that one?" I knew I had the attention of the jury now. The tan young woman was leaning forward in her seat, and the black man looked irritated. The judge had put his pen down.

"No."

"How about this photograph?" I placed a second photograph from X's correspondence in front of him.

"I've never seen it."

I set all the photographs from X's correspondence in front of him, one by one, and he denied ever seeing prints of her photographs.

I could feel glee rising up in my chest at his lies, my usual anger unexpectedly displaced by a kind of euphoric pleasure at being right with an audience. "You just said you didn't copy this photograph. How do you explain the fact that it's identical to the way the lemur looked in the mural? They look exactly the same, don't they?"

"Objection, Your Honor. Counsel can't testify for the witness. And it calls for speculation," said Spencer, annoyance in his voice. Whatever distress he could be experiencing, decades of practice allowed him to keep it private. *Don't be a girl,* he'd said to me after I lost my first case and thought I should quit the law because I would never be any good. I wanted to turn to see his face, to see the wonderful look of consternation that I'd outmaneuvered him, but I refrained.

"Overruled."

"But Your Honor," Spencer started.

"I've made my ruling, Counsel," said the judge. "One question at a time, Ms. Ramesh."

"Sorry. Do you have an explanation for why this photograph looks exactly like a section of your mural?"

"Yes, I must have appropriated it, but I don't remember the details. Only that it fits with my goals anyhow," Brian said. The blush had spread to his hands, which were on the podium in front of him.

"Are you aware that there have only been a couple of sightings reported of these giant indri?"

"No," he said.

I couldn't introduce the letter he'd written to Evers to impeach his credibility, because it was attorney-client privileged. "Isn't it true that you copied photographs given to you by a friend when coming up with this mural?"

"No, I don't think so." He looked shaken. I noticed his hands trembling, but I kept going. I couldn't afford to feel sympathy.

"I'll ask you again, do you have the original photographs that you used to create the mural?"

"No," said Brian, a coldness creeping back into his voice. Spencer was blushing and nervously shifting stacks of folders back and forth, an inch this way, and then an inch the other way.

"Is that because you never had the originals to begin with?"

"No, it's just that I've moved multiple times, so I don't know where all my stuff is."

We continued in the same vein for a few more minutes, Brian growing increasingly angry. I walked back to the counsel's table and found the next exhibit. "Take a look at your doctor's chart that you produced in discovery to support your claim for distress damages," I said.

In an entry marked September, Brian's doctor had written, "Severe insomnia and anxiety. Prescribed 2 mg. Lorazepam."

I don't know why they'd produced this medical record other than good old-fashioned greed. When Brian was my client, I had no intention of seeking psychological damages. When I thought about my sister's mental health history, it seemed too over the top, too risky with an artist to produce medical files and request compensation for the bills. But I guess when Spencer took over, he decided to ask for the moon, assuming that I wouldn't be able to defeat him. "Is there a question pending, Counsel?" asked the judge.

"Yes. Mr. Turner, you testified earlier that you thought the value of your paintings dropped last October, but you didn't seek help for insomnia until April, around six months later. What actually triggered your insomnia?"

"Objection, calls for speculation. Calls for an expert opinion."

"Overruled," said the judge.

"I had some personal problems," Brian said. "Nothing to do with the lawsuit."

"Didn't you have a falling out with Nicholas Evers about your plagiarism of photographs taken at his collective?"

Brian's nose turned beet red, and I felt sorry for him a moment. But in order to have the necessary killer instinct, I couldn't also have sympathy. I started asking more questions about his falling out with Evers, and he grew increasingly uncomfortable. He had no power. When I was just out of law school, I'd gone to a conference on trial techniques and seen a horde of male trial attorneys heckle a young blonde female speaker. It was like watching sharks, the enjoyment they had in questioning everything she said, making inappropriate comments about her clothing, about her style of speech, nitpicking about what they saw as errors in her speech. Afterward, I saw her in the lobby and said, "Your talk was really great. They were awful in there." And I remember she started to smile at the compliment, but as I mentioned the men, her smile faded and she gave me a curt nod, as if to say I was stupid to bring it up. I realized then, that by bringing it up, by forcing her to show it hadn't bothered her, I hadn't been sympathetic so much as an additional source of embarrassment. It would have been kinder not to say anything at all. The benefit of trial work was to be on top, like this, and never be the cause of such repulsive pity.

Spencer tried to rehabilitate Brian in front of the jury by asking about his sketches of the lemur, apparently not realizing I had a witness to impeach every word he said. According to Brian, he spent weeks constructing the perfect expression on the lemur's face, and the unusual white streak was a touch he'd added to give the lemur distinctiveness, to show he was different from other lemurs. The massive size of the lemur was not anything drawn from nature, but was only a metaphor for how the lemur was larger than life.

After the judge called a recess, the lemur and I took a victory lap around Lake Merritt, watching lilac flood the sky as the sun set, talking about the jurors and what they might be thinking. We waited for the detective to call and let us know that he was bringing Xandra Jones to her hotel, where she would stay until after she had testified. After a while the lemur and I stopped talking.

In the past Evers and I would dissect every aspect of a case over dinner. While he explained the minutiae to me, he'd seemed so smart and crafty. How devastating it had been that I was so deluded about his level of romantic engagement, nearly as deluded as I'd been about Spencer's belief in me. Yet knowing something is a delusion doesn't immediately fix feelings, beliefs being more powerful than facts. For all I knew, he and my double had run off together. Not for the first time I thought maybe my double was actually an original Maya Ramesh, and I was her copy—I certainly didn't feel bright or new: I felt run-down and exhausted with being myself.

The magnolia leaves were turning dark brown, and the ducks were wading around in the mud by the water's edge. A pair of young women smoked bidis under a sycamore tree in the violet darkness; we smelled the bidis and the scent of oranges and star jasmine floating off their hair.

After we walked through the front door of my house, the lemur started playing one of his video games on the TV. While I waited for the detective and Xandra, I texted Evers and asked whether he was in town. He sent a text back, not responding to my question, but asking how trial was going.

I sunk into the velvety cushions of the living room couch and wrote back: *Ok, I guess. Brian took the stand.*

He wrote: *Stand up to Spencer?*

I replied: *I suppose. Any chance I could call you as a witness?*

A few minutes passed, and he didn't reply. I was glad that I hadn't told him I was bringing Xandra to the States to testify. I saw two missed calls on my phone from Ross. I called him back. He said the kids were already in bed. "How's the trial going?" he asked. I could hear him puttering around the kitchen, dishes clanking and the sound of running water and Pink Floyd playing in the background. When we were first dating we used to go to laser light shows at the planetarium that were set to *Dark Side of the Moon*, so I took his nostalgia as a good sign. Hearing the mesmerizing sound effects made me recall the ginger lotion I used to wear, how the flat iron had nearly singed my hair, the clean smell of his aftershave, the taste of apples on his tongue when we kissed, and the feeling of snuggling into his warm side in the plush seats. The way we had gone home and made elaborate dinners that ended with some kind of fancy dessert I was trying to make for the first time. They were never cupcakes, though. The other Maya might have been a baker, but I had never been interested in precision. He'd always eaten the dessert, even if it had tasted like sawdust. The powerful, undeniable sensation of loss, of missing Ross and the kids, was moving through me.

"Not great, but not terrible either. How are the kids?"

"The kids are not great, but not terrible either. We're adjusting. We're getting by." I thought he might ask how I was doing, but all I heard were the kitchen noises.

"Listen, isn't that apartment kind of small for you guys?" I said, with a forced laugh.

There was a big pause as Ross considered the subtext. "If that's an overture to get back together, I have to tell you that you doing this trial isn't a good way to show us that we're more important to you than your old job was."

He was right, but I barreled forward. I felt like if I let one crack of real emotion through, it might open a floodgate and I couldn't have that in the middle of the very trial that would help me prove to my family I was not as ordinary, as much of a *nothing* as they believed I was. "I don't understand why you don't see how important this is. I want respect. More than that, I want to win. I want to belong."

"Respect and winning and belonging are three different things entirely. You've confused them all in your mind. You know, I read that piece in the *New York Times*, and like most intelligent people,

I saw what you were trying to do, spinning your little cobweb. What's important here is getting that lemur back home, but fuck the trial. Fuck proving yourself. Fuck the twelve angry men. Fuck your addiction to the thrill of it."

"Eight. Eight jurors," I said, seizing on a way to trivialize his point as much as he was trivializing mine. "This is such a typical argument from you. I try to explain how important this is to me, and you come up with why I'm dumb for thinking it's important."

"It's not that it's dumb. It's that I've known you long enough to know you're looking in the wrong places for validation. You've never really liked people. What does it matter what the jury thinks?"

In fact he was wrong, and that's when I realized maybe the problem in our marriage was not only with my permanent sense that life was always only elsewhere, but that he couldn't see me. Yes, he knew me, could even predict what I might say under certain circumstances, but maybe he didn't understand who I was at the core. I wasn't always sure of who I was either—faking it will do that to you—but as far as I knew, I'd always liked people. My acting was in order to be accepted. If I were myself, they wouldn't accept me any more than they accepted my emotionally fragile sister, which was to say not at all. Whether they'd actually liked me back was another matter entirely. Ross didn't know any of this about me, after all the years we'd spent together. Maybe he hadn't been paying as much attention as he claimed he had, or maybe nobody knew anybody. "We can't just up and leave the country, Ross. We're in the midst of a civil jury trial. His freedom is at stake."

"You can use that propaganda for the press. He wouldn't even be in this position if it weren't for you."

I hung up on Ross and decided to clear what he said out of my mind. There would be time to fix my marriage after the trial; the most important thing, the only thing that could matter now was winning and nailing Spencer to the wall. I couldn't even begin to fix my marriage unless I proved myself first, proved that all my hard work had paid off. I needed to prove it to myself, more than I needed to prove it to Ross. If I were wrong about my abilities, it meant that I had destroyed everything for nothing.

I sifted through the papers I'd left on the coffee table for tomorrow's proceedings, poring over Spencer's witness list and applying a red pen like a scalpel to fine-tune questions for cross-examination. I wandered outside. Still no stars, not even a moon. There was something in the juniper bushes, but as I approached, it skittered away. The lemur's room was dark.

The phone rang. The private detective told me that he and Xandra Fletcher were waiting in her hotel room, and I drove over to meet them. In spite of her romantic name and her association with a womanizer like Evers, Xandra was a frumpy older woman with red hair, who wore a camera on a string around her neck. She smelled like flour and sweat. We exchanged pleasantries.

I paid the detective his fee, and told him I would drive her to the airport after she testified. She sat down on the couch and gestured that I should do the same.

"So tell me, how did Evers recruit you to work for the collective?" I asked, as I sat down.

"Nicky Evers? I've known him since he was a small boy. I was a friend of his father's and we reconnected at his father's funeral many years ago. You know, I recruited him."

"You did? It was your idea?"

"Uh-huh. I've always been fascinated by lemurs. After a trip to Madagascar, I told Nicky that I wanted to start up an organization to track indri in Andasibe Preserve."

"How did you become interested in tracking cryptids?"

"I spotted one on my first trip fifty years ago. Sailing through the tops of the trees, giant and dark. It was clear to me, right away, that this was a frontier of crucial exploration that almost nobody was trying to push toward. Yadda yadda yadda. I don't want to go on too long."

"And Evers—Nick—was interested right away?"

"Oh no, dear. He was skeptical at first. But I took photographs and talked his ear off, and eventually he agreed that it could be interesting, and a decent tax shelter for him. He's always reaching into multiple pots at once. Couldn't keep still as a boy, either."

I had a hard time picturing Evers as a small boy, but Xandra's story rang true. Evers was distractible and he, too, had offered the explanation that the collective was a tax shelter. "Did you know that he was giving the photographs to his friend Brian Turner?"

Xandra's eyes darkened and her voice was severe. "I didn't. I had no idea he would try to help some hooligan steal my photos. I take my work very seriously."

She told me stories about the collective, about how she had recruited other nature photographers and scholars to lead excursions into the forests of Andasibe-Mantadia to track the cryptids she was sure were hiding there. I didn't reveal that a giant lemur was living with me, or that she would be testifying on his behalf, and it seemed she was so happy to share her stories that she had no curiosity about who my client was. I stayed for hours, riveted by her tales of life on the edge of the rainforest, how she had longed her whole life to live abroad and was only able to do so when Evers funded the collective. She wasn't speaking to him at present. "He did wrong. We talked about capturing a giant lemur together, taking him apart and studying him, not hawking my photographs. For all I know, he's given other photographs of mine to other friends. It's not right!" Her words flickered around my mind, unnerving me. I'd been performing my entire life, so when her fervor, her obsession with capturing a giant lemur made me sick and uneasy, I simply nodded and didn't even consider confronting her.

When I returned home, it was so late that it was early. I could hear the lemur stirring. He was trying to do vocal exercises and failing. The black cloud of sound hung over the house, an ugly, jangling vibration that lasted until I fell asleep in a pile of papers on the couch for the last few hours of night.

On the next day of trial, Spencer moved through the short list of his witnesses like the master of a circus, presenting witnesses who were walking spectacles, glitterati from the art world and charismatic nerds from universities and occasionally ordinary folk, just to make sure that he covered all his bases. He paraded before us an ex-Marine from the neighborhood who loved the mural and believed it added value to his apartment across the street, as well as an expert on rainforests who expressed how valuable the mural was for increasing American awareness of deforestation.

Spencer had rid himself of Vittum, the original art appraiser who believed the mural had little value, and in his place testified Angela Waldrep, a young woman from Brooklyn with a sleek bob of blue-black hair. Carrying a Kate Spade clutch to the stand, she wore crimson concentric hoop earrings, and lipstick in the same shade feathered at the corners of her lips. Unlike the other art appraisers I'd spoken to when trying to find an expert, she claimed that the mural was directly tied to Brian Turner's later successes. "If the mural hadn't connected with audiences," she said in one of her answers, "he wouldn't have succeeded with his later more risky projects. The mural was both historic and innovative, a real attempt to bring the uncanny, alien aspects of Africa to Oakland, alien yet familiar, both dark and light."

"When you say 'success,' what do you mean?" I asked, suppressing my desire to veer off track and ask her how something could be both alien and familiar, both dark and light and whether those words had any meaning to her at all or were merely some kind of art world gobbledygook of opposites that she'd put out there because she had nothing real to say.

"I mean it has value."

"Do you believe that art has value because it connects?"

"Yes, what other value is there?" said Angela.

"Just answer the question," I said. "So if the art doesn't connect, does it mean it has no value?"

"In most cases, yes, I believe that's what it means. Value is a measure of our degree of connection."

"So, Vincent van Gogh's work had no value until when?"

"Until somebody said it had value."

"So your expert opinion is that all it takes is somebody saying an artwork has value for it to have value?"

"Well, the more people that say it the better, obviously," she said, flicking something off the witness stand with her middle finger.

"Is art a democratic engagement then? A majority vote makes it art?" I asked.

"Objection, relevance," called Spencer.

"Overruled. You may answer the question, Ms. Waldrep."

"Yes."

"So you don't have any special expertise in determining art's value, just the ability to aggregate the opinions of others?"

"Well, no, I wouldn't say that. I studied art history. I know the relationship of a piece of art to the cultural conversation that's gone before."

"Is originality, at times, a marker of value?"

"Yes."

"But if something is really original, it stands apart from the cultural conversation that's gone on before, correct?"

"I don't know."

"If, as in Brian Turner's case, an artist copies a photographer's work, doesn't his work drop in value?"

"I see that as appropriation. There's a lot of literature on appropriation in contemporary art, but essentially Mr. Turner recontextualized that lemur. He put him in a mural, out on a street."

"Do you know if that was Mr. Turner's intent? Recontextualizing?" I smiled at her to make her more comfortable.

"I don't know. But it's my educated guess, based on his testimony and other statements, that he was recontextualizing an image of an endangered animal to challenge our ideas about the familiar and yet strange world around us," she said.

"And you believe that taking someone else's work and passing it off as your own is valuable?"

"Yes, if an artist calls upon other work to comment upon it and make a connection, and in fact, does make that connection, I think that was a valid appropriation."

"Mr. Turner did not testify that he called upon the other work to comment upon it. Where do you get the idea that this was his intention?"

"You can infer his intention from his actions, in my opinion."

"In other words, you're making up a motivation for him?" I asked.

"Objection. Your Honor, Ms. Ramesh obviously isn't going anywhere with this. She's harassing the witness."

"Overruled," said the judge. He had his pink pen in hand and he was looking at me. I resolved to try to sneak a peek at his desk.

"Are you making up Mr. Turner's motivation?" I asked.

"I'm constructing a motivation, but it's based on evidence. Based on my years of experience and ability to compare the mural to similar works, it is valuable. What do you want me to say?" Angela Waldrep flushed, perhaps with shame.

"You're here as an expert on art appraisal, Ms. Waldrep. And you told us that the reason the mural is valuable is because people connected with it. If people had not connected with it, would that still be your opinion?"

"Objection, speculation, lacks foundation," said Spencer.

"Overruled," said the judge.

"I'm not sure," she said, nervously intertwining the fingers of both hands.

Spencer's next witness was Rahim Ali, a young professor of zoology with expertise in African animals and sleek hair like a blue-black cap of raven's feathers. His diffidence was off-putting. He wore a pinstriped suit that looked beyond the means of the average college professor. Tara would have called him hot.

"And can you say with certainty that this lemur is an actual indri?" Spencer asked.

"No, this is not an indri. There are no indri that we are aware of that are the size of the defendant, for one thing," said Professor Ali.

"So what is this—I hesitate to label it—'creature' then?" said Spencer.

"Whatever he is, he is not a recognized species. I'm loath to even call him a 'species.' I think this is outside the realm of science, to be honest. Maybe more in the realm of *Frankenstein.*"

"Objection, Your Honor. Move to strike," I said, standing partway up.

"Overruled."

"Your Honor, it's completely inflammatory!" I couldn't keep the anger out of my voice.

"Enough with the histrionics, Ms. Ramesh," said the judge, pursing his lips. "You may continue, Mr. Clark."

"And is there any benefit to science if we allow this creature to continue outside the mural?"

"None. Honestly, it's like the white tigers that are a result of inbreeding. They're of no benefit to society and neither is an impossibly giant lemur born of someone's imagination," he said. He was grooming himself as he spoke, flicking stray bits from his suit jacket with a vacant expression.

I felt the lemur tense up beside me, his paws clenching against the chair and his breathing growing louder with an in-and-out hiss like a teakettle. When I stood to cross-examine Professor Ali, I wasn't certain how to challenge him.

"Professor Ali, you would compare the lemur to Frankenstein, is that correct?"

"Yes. For lack of better information on how to identify him, yes, I'd compare him to a monster."

"Okay. So do you realize that Frankenstein was the scientist and the monster was his invention?"

"Yes. Err, no."

"Sir, are you calling the lemur a monster?"

Professor Ali blinked at me. He didn't say anything, but there were no objections from Spencer either. The jury moved forward almost imperceptibly, waiting to see what he would say. "Yes, I guess I am."

"And your basis for this opinion is that he's original?"

"Objection," Spencer said. "Misstates prior testimony."

"Sustained," said the judge, putting on his glasses and looking down at his doodle.

"What is your basis for the opinion that the lemur is a monster?"

Professor Ali said, "Based on the earlier testimony from Mr. Turner, I'd say he's a copy, but still, there's nothing like him out there, no way of classifying him. My basis for saying he's a monster is that he exists outside my classification system, and he's man-made."

"Can you point out evidence for your position that he's man-made?"

"Isn't it self-evident?"

"You're the expert. Explain why you think he's man-made."

"He's not from nature. He's artificial, in the real sense of the word." Professor Ali looked irritated at the speed with which I was questioning him, so I pressed onward, asking questions even faster.

"You claim words have a *real* sense?"

"Er, yes."

"So you believe words are tangible then?"

"No, I guess not."

"So what's your basis for calling him artificial? An examination? A book? What? Spell it out for us."

"Just look at him!"

"So, you believe this is something a layperson can determine. You lack expertise on this matter, is that correct?"

"Yes," said Professor Ali, looking defeated. Somebody came in at that moment and whispered something to Spencer. Overhearing whatever was being said, Brian's cheeks flushed with rage. Spencer sprung to his feet, "Your Honor, may we have a sidebar?"

The judge beckoned us over. Spencer said, "Your Honor, another lemur has disappeared from the mural. Now two lemurs have disappeared from a mural that is all about lemurs. It's extremely damaging to my client's artistic integrity to have his subjects simply disappear. We again move for an immediate injunction."

The judge nodded. "Ms. Ramesh?"

"This is the first I'm hearing of it, Your Honor, but it doesn't change the fact that this particular lemur is entitled to his freedom. We request that the motion be denied." I looked at the judge's desk. He had drawn the word "monster" in about fifty different styles and a few different colors on a sheet of paper. At the bottom was a scribbled monkey with twenty arms lying on top of a bed—or was it a coffin? As my heart sank with the knowledge that the judge wasn't sympathetic to my client, he denied Spencer's motion, and we recessed for the day.

The lemur and I visited the mural before driving home, parking about a block away. Even from a distance, we could see the mural was different.

"I think, therefore I am," the lemur said, pointing to a second tagged spot. Behind the red spray paint shimmered green leaves. He looked around as if he expected that the other lemur would be standing nearby, waiting for us.

"What?" I said, as he started walking away. "Explain yourself."

"I wish I could, but I Kant. You know there are these things you can do with language. Puns. Where you use a double meaning. They're really excellent. Have you heard, 'A Freudian slip is where you say one thing—'"

"But mean your mother."

"You have heard it!" he said, looking genuinely pleased. "I don't know where he could have gone, but it's getting late and I wanted to get to the next level of my game tonight."

"You don't have any idea where he could be?" I asked.

"You think we're psychic or something?" the lemur asked.

The next day, I began presenting our case. I called Xandra. She was on time, but hiding at the back of the gallery, behind the journalists and art enthusiasts, observing the proceedings. As she shuffled up the aisle toward the stand she turned and gawked at the lemur. It struck me that perhaps it hadn't been the wisest decision to keep her in the dark about whom she was testifying for. She was sworn in, and sat down in the witness stand, but she couldn't, not even when I was speaking to her, take her eyes off the lemur. We made it through a few questions about who she was and the collective, before she said, "Forgive me, but you have one? You have one?"

"He's not mine," I said.

"But still, he's *known* now. That means the purpose of my collective is completely destroyed. Everything I worked for all these years... gone. Just like that . . . And you knew?"

The judge asked her to refrain from doing anything more than answering questions, and she nodded and apologized, but tears were welling in her eyes. I handed her tissues from a box next to the court reporter.

I showed her the photographs. "Do you recognize these?"

"Yes, I took them."

"At some point did you become aware that these photographs were being copied?"

"Yes, I found out that my partner had given the photographs to Mr. Turner for inspiration, but he copied them wholesale for his mural."

I turned and saw Brian and Spencer whispering to each other. I could see how angry Spencer was, and it gave me a little joy. On cross-examination, Spencer tried to make her admit that there were significant differences between her photograph and Brian Turner's mural, but her story, and her incrimination of Evers, never wavered. When she was done testifying, she walked past the lemur slowly, eyeing him with a mixture of marvel and distress.

Next, I called the Eustachios to testify about the negative impact of the mural on their property's value. Xandra was sitting in the back of the gallery, watching the proceedings intently, and she returned to the same seat, after the lunch recess, even though she was finished giving her testimony. I lost track of her when I put Ben Whithers on the stand.

Whithers was flamboyant, in his forties, with conservatively cut platinum hair and an all-black dress shirt and tie and suit. As Julie had promised, he was brilliant and while the jurors didn't appear to be particularly taken with his appearance at first, there was still time for them to be taken by his testimony.

"What is representational art?" I asked.

"Representational art is any kind of art where you know what it is when you see it. A forest is a forest. If a lemur is painted on a wall, a lemur is what's meant by that image of the lemur, for example."

"Does the mural we've been talking about have any value as representational art?" I asked, putting a hand on the witness stand.

"If we're treating it as representational art, as this lawsuit suggests, the mural is without value. It wasn't particularly artful in its original presentation. The brush marks don't possess any great beauty. The paint is muddy in sections, and it feels like a mistake. This kind of muddiness isn't the same as the brownness in Rembrandt's paintings, for example. It's like two kinds of paint were used that don't belong together. You might see this effect in Abstract Expressionism, but this is clearly not a work of Abstract Expressionism. It's naïve in certain respects, but other parts are too hyperrealistic to consider it in the camp of Naïve or Primitive Art. The trompe l'oeil is certainly skillful in a kitschy way, but not outstanding. What it comes down to is that you can find this kind of mural anywhere, but it doesn't speak to other art or culture, the way it would if it had real value. It's all craft and no art if you look at it as representational. On top of that, the mural wasn't kept up. From my examination of the surface of the mural, no care has been taken to ensure that it would retain even a little bit of what made it appealing from the perspective of the viewing public."

"Is the mural valuable from any perspective?" I asked.

"Yes, the mural becomes valuable to the extent we reevaluate it as process art."

"What is process art?"

"Art in which the effects of nature remaking the mural are more important than the fixed image that was originally put in place. Viewed as process art, we can see that Mr. Turner's initiation of the mural, putting it in place, triggering a public response, and then, of course, the lemur leaving it, are what make it an interesting or valuable piece, one that's noteworthy. But in that case, the lemur's act in leaving is not a mutilation, but a part of the art itself."

"So the lemur leaving is what adds value to the piece?" I asked.

"Yes."

"And it doesn't subtract from any inherent value?"

"Correct. When viewed as a process taking place over a period of years, there is some small value to the plaintiff's mural."

"Do you disagree then with the plaintiff's expert who claims that the painting is worth $1 million?"

"Yes, I disagree completely. It bears not even a loose connection to the work that made Mr. Turner a household name. To the extent he wants it to be viewed as a work of significant representational art, I'm afraid it's not even worth remarking upon as above-average juvenilia."

During his cross-examination of Whithers, Spencer looked somber. "You've made your name as an appraiser of installations and more conceptual pieces, correct?"

"Yes, that's true."

"How many traditional paintings have you appraised?"

"Probably in the hundreds, if you count all the work I did at Sotheby's."

"But that's not your specialty?"

"No."

"And did you write at one point that all representational art was dead?" Spencer asked. My jaw clenched. I couldn't remember reading any articles by him about this topic.

"I don't remember. Sure sounds like me."

Spencer showed him a clipping from *Artforum*. "Did you write this article?"

"Yes."

"Can you read the first line from the top of the page for me, Mr. Whithers?"

"And so we must conclude that representational art is dead because reality is no longer operant," said Whithers, scanning the rest of the page.

"Reality is no longer operant. Do you disagree then that there is such a thing as reality, Mr. Whithers?"

"Objection. Relevance," I said. Was I about to be fucked?

"It goes toward the question of Mr. Whithers' credibility as an expert, Your Honor."

"I'll allow. Overruled," said Judge McCracken.

"Your Honor, it's an absurd question," I said.

"Not at all," said the judge. He was once again drawing something, his pen making large loops on the page.

"Your Honor, let the record reflect that you have been writing the word 'monster' on your legal pad," I said. I only realized that I'd made a grave error when the judge put his pen down and stared at me with beady eyes. He scowled. I could almost feel Spencer smiling, and when I looked over, he had a smug look on his face.

"Ms. Ramesh, I suggest you focus more on the substance of the testimony and less on what I may or may not be doing," the judge said. "For the record, I have not been drawing the word 'monster' on this pad."

"Your Honor, I saw you," I protested, even though I knew I was crossing further and further over the line, and even though the lemur's cold furry hand was seizing at my hand—I could feel the pressure of his grip on my ring finger, where my wedding band was.

The judge smiled at me, but I saw more of a grimace of pale eyes and yellow teeth. "You must have been mistaken," he said.

"Your Honor," I started.

"Counsel, I expect you to be prepared and respectful when you're in my courtroom. I'm afraid I'll have to sanction you. Since you seem confused by the subject, I'd like a one-hundred-word brief on what "relevance" is by tomorrow morning. You may fax it into chambers."

"Yes, Your Honor," I said.

"Madam Court Reporter, would you read the question back?" the judge asked.

The court reporter read the question about whether the expert believed in reality. I dropped down in my wooden chair, my cheeks burning hot with humiliation. I took a sip of water and scooted forward, the chair scraping against the floor. I felt like everyone was looking at me. At least if I'd been found in contempt, I would have been significant. Instead the judge had treated me like an insubordinate child (or a first-year associate). I could feel the lemur's eyes fixed on me, watching as I adjusted my expression to appear more aloof and cold than I felt.

"No, I believe there is a reality," Whithers said.

"So you lied in this article?" Spencer asked. He looked positively cheerful.

"No."

"In the article you say reality is no longer operant," said Spencer.

"Yes, reality is no longer what we function on, not that it doesn't exist."

"If we don't function on reality, what do we function on?" asked Spencer. Short and trim, he had tilted his head as he asked the question, which made him look inquisitive in the manner of a velociraptor eyeing its prey.

"Objection, calls for speculation," I said, my voice shaking despite my best efforts. To his credit, Whithers looked unfazed, slightly bored, but not snarky, like he was trying to be respectful even though Spencer was wasting his time.

"Counsel, where are you going with this?" asked the judge. He was no longer doodling, but he looked decidedly bored.

"Your Honor, if he doesn't believe in reality, how real can we assume his expert opinions are?"

"I'll allow, but get to your point quickly," the judge said, rubbing his nose.

"Do you believe in reality?"

"Yes," repeated Whithers.

"Then why would you write this line?"

"I was working from the premise that in our postmodern world, the images we see on screens, whether they're televisions or movies or screens, are more real to us than what surrounds us on a daily basis. So, just for example, we're more interested in what our screen friends are doing, than in what our flesh-and-blood best friend is up to. If you read on, you'll see that I mostly disagree with that idea. I think art as process or gesture, interactive art that inspires dialogue and response, is the most real thing of all."

Spencer nodded, but after years of being his associate, I could tell from his expression that he'd already gotten lost in what Whithers was saying and he'd only skimmed the article. "Keep it simple," he'd always advised me. "Jurors don't have the attention span for complicated arguments."

There had been no way to take his advice in this trial. When I looked at the jury, I could tell that they wanted to sympathize with the lemur. Perhaps they would forgive how hard the expert testimony was.

Late that afternoon, the lemur and I left the courthouse, and were stopped on the courthouse steps by Xandra. "Why didn't you tell me you had one?" she asked me. Her tone was confrontational, and she looked as if she had been crying. The sky, narrowed by the line of tall marble and concrete buildings, was gray with the threat of rain.

"Look, lady, she doesn't 'have' me. I'm not her possession," the lemur said.

"I didn't think it was relevant," I said, taking a step away, and pulling the lemur with me. I was concerned at her lack of inhibition, remembering how she and Evers had plotted to capture the giant lemur and dissect it.

"I've built my entire life around these creatures, around catching them and studying them. And all this time, you'd already done it." Her voice grew louder. "I deserved to know that. Does Evers know about him, too?"

"I think Evers is aware of him," I said.

"He is?" the lemur asked.

"He was watching the house and saw you in the kitchen back when this began," I said, speaking low to try to avoid any further inquiry by Xandra.

"And he didn't tell me? Instead, I've been going along, all these months, trying to figure out a capture plan, how to break through what seemed impenetrable, the barrier between us and the deep forest," Xandra said.

"He hasn't been in touch with me. I assumed he'd been in contact with you," I said.

"I certainly have a few words for him."

"Sure. I'll call you later about giving you a ride back to the airport." I tried to seem amiable. I took the lemur firmly by the arm and we hurried down the steps. After we walked about a block, my hand still on the lemur's arm, I glanced over my shoulder. Xandra followed at a distance.

The following morning, Marcus Spiegelman, the geneticist, took the stand as my next expert witness. He explained to the jury that he'd contacted me because he wanted to clone the lemur, that cloning could be used for good, specifically to prevent the eradication of endangered or rare species like indri.

"And did you examine the lemur before coming to your conclusions?"

"Yes," he said. "Or rather I examined his tissue."

"Is this your report on what you found?" I entered his report as an exhibit. It was a report I liked, that I found credible on its own, even though Marcus Spiegelman was proving to be an odd duck, the kind of witness who wore red-striped socks and suspenders to court, evidently not realizing the impression they made. The jurors wore expressions I couldn't decipher, eyebrows raised, but most lips tilting slightly upward. Were they bored? Disbelieving? Did they not understand genetics? Most likely.

I'd forced myself to understand enough to ask questions, but science was about as comprehensible to me as religion. I didn't know all that much about it, but since I also didn't have traditional religious beliefs, I'd pinned all our hopes and dreams and values on science instead. Isn't that what most of us are like today? Which is all to say, I put on the genetics expert more for purposes of credibility than science. Spiegelman was not charismatic enough to sell genetics as the answer to everything, maybe because he really was a scientist and not a salesman. But at least he gave the proceedings the aura of rational thought.

We proceeded through the details of his examination, before diving into the nature of the report, which boiled down to the question of whether the lemur was biological. The answer, Spiegelman believed, was yes, the lemur was biological. Even though the test results came back with somewhat unusual findings with respect to the DNA, which showed the lemur was a mixture of indri cells, human cells, and some unknown material, not animal or human in nature.

Spencer's cross-examination was rooted in the idea that genetics was irrelevant, but I could tell his faith was shaken by the finding that the lemur had some human genetic DNA. Nonetheless, he forged onward. "Interesting choice of words: material not animal or human in nature. After hearing all the evidence over the past few days, in your expert opinion would it be fair to say that it's clearly artistic?" asked Spencer, with a smirk.

I stood up almost reflexively, the floor suddenly wobbly beneath my feet. "Objection, Your Honor, speculation. It's completely outside the scope of this expert's expertise. I want that stricken and the jury to be instructed to disregard the question."

The judge called us into a sidebar at the bench. He gestured at Spencer to indicate he could speak. "Your Honor, I question whether we can call the lemur biological if he's made up of an element that's not DNA. He's art. Therefore, he's owned. I have to be able to show the fallacy in this 'expert's' thinking."

"Your Honor," I said, trying to forget my humiliation. "The expert has detailed that the lemur is physical, is real, is biological, in fact. He doesn't have the expertise to answer a question about whether the lemur is also art. His focus is on the biological aspect. Asking whether it's art is what the art experts are for. Emphasizing that art is property, whereas nature may not be, is something that Mr. Clark should have addressed during his principal case if he thought it was relevant." I glanced at the judge's bench. The top page of his yellow legal pad was empty. He wasn't doodling anything, nor even writing any notes.

"Overruled, Ms. Ramesh. Fair is fair. You opened up this line of questioning by asking if the lemur was biological and introducing a geneticist into the lineup of experts. Mr. Clark is simply trying to rebut that claim. Mr. Clark, lay a foundation."

The lemur tensed beside me as I sat back down. Spencer resumed his questioning of Spiegelman. "In your expert opinion, does the lemur have animal or human DNA?"

"Both and not exactly either. You see—"

"And so what is your basis for calling the lemur biological?"

"If you read the report, you'll see that I explain he has living cells. He's made up of living physical matter that fits with indri as well as humans. He's very much alive."

"Are plants also living?"

"Yes. But structurally—"

"Is your opinion that he's biological based on his ability to speak, rather than any hard, genetic evidence?"

"No."

"Is whether or not something is *living* typically within the province of geneticists?"

Spiegelman sighed. "No, but geneticists study genes, which are molecular units of heredity in living organisms. And if you look at my report, you'll see that he is made up of molecular units of heredity. He has some genetic matter that is recognizable and other matter we're not accustomed to seeing."

I breathed a little more easily. Okay, he was sticking with the program. There were some holes in his testimony, but none of the jurors looked particularly offended by it.

"And can you exclude the possibility that the lemur is simply art?"

"I can't exclude that, no," said Spiegelman. "But based on my examination, it's unlikely. And I'm not entirely sure he can't be both, both living and art. Doesn't the best art live, after all?"

Spencer looked confused and changed the subject. "Are you being paid to be here today?" I pushed forward in my chair, straining to anticipate an objectionable question.

"No," Spiegelman said.

"You offered to testify for free?" Spencer asked, swiveling, the top of his brown cowboy boots burnished by the light.

"Not exactly."

"What are you getting in exchange for your testimony today?"

"I was given the opportunity to take some of his cells for scientific study." Spiegelman crossed his arms.

"A scientific study you're conducting at Stranger Labs?"

"Yes."

"So, it advances your career to call the lemur living?" Spencer asked.

"No, I wouldn't say that."

"You believe, don't you, that you could acquire a certain degree of fame and fortune by studying the defendant further?"

"Not at all. I want to study him further because I wanted to see whether we could use him to clone certain cells to protect endangered indri," Spiegelman said.

"You plan to clone a dangerous animal?" Spencer turned so the jury could see his expression of faux-horror.

"No, I'm not allowed to clone him."

Spencer paused for a beat. He was not expecting that. "In any event, you are getting compensated for testimony that supports the lemur's freedom?"

"No, I wouldn't call further investigation of cells already in my possession, or even further examination of the lemur, compensation for testimony," the geneticist said, cringing at the thought.

"But you have an invested interest in his freedom?" Spencer asked.

"I wouldn't say so."

They danced around the issue of compensation for a few more minutes. Spencer looked certain the geneticist's credibility had been shredded when he sat back down.

"Mr. Spiegelman, you're trained as a scientist, correct?" I asked on my re-cross.

"Yes."

"And as a scientist, you're trained to look at an issue without bias, correct?"

"Yes," he said.

"In this case, do you have any bias toward the lemur?"

"No."

"Is it in any way necessary for purposes of your career to study the lemur?" I asked.

"It would be nice to be the one to research him if this court determines he can be free, but it's not strictly necessary. I do have his cells to work with," Speigelman said.

"Do you have an art background?" I asked.

"No."

"Are you qualified to call the lemur art?"

"No, but I can say he's living, and that is based on the fact that he has the building blocks of a living being," Spiegelman said.

My final witness was a cognitive science professor from UC Berkeley, an expert on consciousness: Lia Goldstein, a middle-aged Korean woman who'd been adopted by a family of Jewish people in Washington D.C., when she was a baby. *Too murky*, said my father when I'd run by him the idea of providing testimony on consciousness. *Nobody will understand that this is even a debatable area.* I'd decided to use her anyway.

"There's a paper about this very issue by philosopher Thomas Nagel," Goldstein testified. "According to him, and I agree, a creature has consciousness if and only if there's something that it is like to be that organism, something it is like for the organism to be itself."

"Do you think the lemur has ideas about what it's like to be himself?" I asked.

"Yes. It's clear that the lemur has ideas about what it's like to be him."

"And you're basing that opinion on what?"

"Partially his deposition testimony, but also my conversations with him and the raw unedited footage of his interview with the *New York Times*. All of them evince strong opinions about what he believes his place in the world is. I should say that any conscious creature only knows what it's like to be him or herself."

"And is consciousness the one thing that separates persons from other animals?"

"Yes, it's probably the one necessary condition for personhood," Goldstein testified.

When it came time for Spencer to cross-examine, he looked annoyed. He hadn't retained a consciousness expert of his own, and I was pretty sure it was because he didn't believe anyone could take seriously that the lemur was conscious. His first few questions were lulling and pedestrian, and then he launched into his effort to undermine my expert's opinions. "Isn't it true that fetuses aren't conscious?"

"It depends on the standard being used and the age of the fetus," Goldstein testified.

"An eight-week-old fetus. Is that conscious?" Spencer's face was calm, but he swaggered back and forth in front of the witness stand with a false bravado that meant he was nervous.

"Probably not."

"Fifteen weeks?"

"Probably not."

"Twenty-four weeks?"

"Yes, I think it might be by that point," she said.

This claim flustered Spencer. He scuffled around the witness stand for a moment, clearly trying to collect his thoughts. In an ordinary trial, he would have found out this opinion during deposition, and found a way to counter it before trial, but presumably because he'd assumed that I wouldn't be able to pull competent expert witnesses together in such a short period, he hadn't looked into the expert's opinions as closely as he should have. "But a fetus can't live outside its mother independently at twenty-four weeks," he said.

"Whether it can survive on its own is irrelevant to whether it's conscious," Goldstein said. "There's some evidence—not all evidence, mind you—to suggest he can feel pain. Reflex actions and such."

"Are you saying that the lemur is a person if it can feel pain?"

"Yes, he's not only a person who can feel pain, but we can observe the pain on his face and in what he says. He has the understanding and language to articulate his experience of being alive."

As Goldstein said this, I looked over and the lemur had his hands under his chin propping himself up, looking both wise and ridiculous.

"But you can't prove that he actually experiences what he says he experiences, can you?" Spencer asked.

"He's conscious," Goldstein testified. "I'm willing to stake my reputation on it."

When I finished presenting my case, I moved for a directed verdict on the grounds that the lemur had human cells and couldn't be destroyed. The judge pretended to think about it, before he denied my motion. We presented our closing arguments. Spencer paced in front of the jury, explaining he'd proven that the lemur as painted in the original mural was original and had also proven that the lemur leaving the painting was a defacement, the act of a monster leaving his master. "In a desperate last-ditch defense, defense counsel has argued that my client 'stole' the photograph of a mentally unstable woman who lives in the rainforest." Spencer threw up air quotes around "stole." "Perhaps the two images are substantially similar. They depict the same species and really, how many variations on this type of lemur can there be? But substantial similarity is not the same thing as plagiarism. As you can see, the lemur in that itty-bitty photograph is smaller than the one from the mural. All art arises out of varying degrees of appropriation. If Mr. Turner appropriated that photograph, if he recontextualized it in order to make the alien familiar and the familiar alien, you must find in his favor." He wasn't making much sense, but he was a better speaker than I was. Some of the jurors were nodding. The lemur was breathing heavily beside me.

I stood by the black man at the far end, clasping my hands in front of me through my closing and making eye contact with each juror to avoid appearing nervous. In my closing remarks, I noted that Turner had stolen Xandra's photograph and copied it without ever paying her, and that in spite of his oppressive surroundings, the lemur had escaped the copycat mural and in so doing had radically improved the artistry of the piece, a piece that possessed no real value as a tangible fixed product with a copied lemur on it, but had plenty of value as process art that brought the lemur to life.

"And if you disagree with plaintiff's counsel and you agree that what the geneticist said is more likely true than not, then you must also believe that the lemur you see before you with your own eyes is alive. He is original and living. The fact of his being alive, moving among you, will serve as the greatest proof that he is a person. He must be allowed to continue to live and given the same rights as you and I." By the end of my closing, I was still uncertain about the Japanese-American woman who made artisanal tofu, but I thought I saw nods among the other jury members.

The men and women in the jury box shuffled out of the courtroom to deliberate for a few hours before being sequestered in a hotel downtown. The lemur and I beat through the crush of press to go to Luka's for an early dinner. The photographers on the courthouse steps outside were using flash because the late afternoon light was dim. I rubbed my eyes. The lemur wobbled as he walked. He was as clean as possible, but he was certainly larger in girth than he had been when I met him. I looked over my shoulder a few times, but Xandra wasn't following us this time. She was nowhere to be seen. Her plane ticket was for a midnight flight and I resolved to contact her that night after dinner.

At the restaurant, we split mac and cheese fritters with buttermilk sauce. I ate tender Prince Edward Island mussels with harissa, washed down with two glasses of champagne, and still hungry, ordered the next thing on the menu, seared yellow tuna fin. The lemur ordered a pear-and-persimmon salad and a vegetable tagine. Before digging into the salad, he picked out the spiced walnuts one by one with the small fork and placed them on my plate. "Don't do that," I said, revolted. The nuts looked like droppings.

"Why not? They'll go to waste," he said, continuing to dig for walnuts. "So. You could've been a little clearer in there."

"You didn't buy my argument?" I put down my fork.

"I bought it, but I don't know if those dunderheads will understand the half of it. You were maybe over their heads. That art appraiser was good. It was good he had a kind of bored look. Unlike their art appraiser, he didn't crack under pressure. Tell your sister thank you for referring us."

"Okay."

"Even if I get out, I don't want to cooperate with the geneticist. I don't want my genes to be copied, even individually."

"Cloned."

"Whatever. You think it's necessary?"

"Maybe we'll worry about that fork in the road when we get to it?"

After we finished dinner, we returned to the house, and I texted Xandra, asking when I should pick her up to take her to the airport. Inside, I had the vague sensation that we were being watched and kept looking out the window, expecting to see a face pressed up against the glass. When no face appeared, I did my best to ignore the creeping sense of dread. I typed my brief about relevance for the judge, and the same old sense of shame filled me. I faxed it to chambers and settled into the living room couch with a glass of red wine. The lemur was playing video games, and the pow pow pow sounds muffled the knock on the door at first. It was a soft knock, like a child would make. I went to the door to answer. I looked through the peephole. On the front step a bottle was quivering, and I opened the door out of curiosity. For a moment, I was going to pick it up.

The explosion blew the front door inward, divorcing it from its hinges. The door flew toward me, but I turned and it slammed the side of my body, knocking me to the floor. A cloud of smoke rushed into the room, bringing with it the stench of burning chemicals. The lemur and I lay on the living room floor for a minute. I couldn't move at all, and then my lips parted. "You okay?" I said. I turned my head sideways on the carpet to look at him a few feet away. His fur was sooty, the black fur tipped in gray, and the white fur almost black. His eyes were closed.

I saw someone wearing a black ski mask reach down and drag the lemur by the arm toward the gaping hole where the door had been. The lemur pulled back, evidently trying to resist the person in the black ski mask. The person wasn't very tall, and only moderately muscular; I couldn't tell if it was a man or a woman, though from the bulge at the back of the ski mask, I thought it might be a woman with her hair pushed up under the fabric.

"Help me!" he said.

I stood up woozily and went after them, grabbing the lemur's furry arm and holding tight.

"Stop, you can't take him," I said. Some neighbors had come out of their houses and were standing in the street, watching, looking utterly confused. We heard sirens wailing on Keller Avenue, winding up the hill, growing louder and louder as they approached. One of my neighbors had heard the blast and called the police.

The lemur's captor released his arm and took off down the street. Nobody tried to stop him or her. I brought the lemur back into the house, his black-and-white fur bedraggled, and his eyes weary. Firefighters, police, and EMTs showed up, and the night in front of my house was streaked with blinking red lights. One cop ran down the street, pursuing the mystery attacker who had tried to capture the lemur. The other one stayed and took our statements, which were meager, since neither of us knew the mystery person's identity, nor the purpose of the bomb.

"Do you know who might want to harm you?" the policewoman asked.

The lemur looked at me. "I don't know," I said. "I doubt it was meant for me. It was probably somebody that wants to harm him."

After the policewoman recorded our statements, and photographs had been taken, and the idle firefighters milling about had created a makeshift duct-tape hinge for the door, and the cop that had chased the mystery person returned empty-handed, I looked at the clock on the kitchen microwave. It was 9:45 pm—I should have called Xandra and taken her to the airport by now. I looked at the blank screen of my cell phone—no missed calls. As the police continued to pick up the shards of the bottle bomb for evidence, I called Xandra's cell phone. No answer. I tried the phone in her hotel room. I called the front desk of her hotel, and the clerk who answered told me she'd checked out late that afternoon.

"Was anyone with her?"

"A man came to pick her up," the clerk told me.

"Blonde hair under a Kangol? Tall?

"That sounds about right, though I'm not sure."

I hung up, knowing that the lemur and I needed to stay elsewhere. My house was no longer safe, and it was possible—even likely—that Evers and Xandra had been behind the bomb. I told the policewoman my theory, explaining that they were interested in capturing and examining the lemur. I said we would need to stay elsewhere. The policewoman who had taken my statement agreed. "We can try to find the culprit, but sometimes a wrongdoer tries again, and it's better to be safe than sorry."

I made a call to Ross and packed swiftly, while the police continued working and the lemur perched on the edge of the bed and observed me in stoic silence. I asked the policewoman to board up the door before leaving. We locked the other doors and windows. The police were still packing evidence into plastic bags as we hurried out to my car, climbed in, and sped down the hill, following the fire trucks for a time, and then veering out on our own toward

Berkeley. We arrived at Ross's apartment. The lemur still hadn't said anything by the time I parked. "Well?" I asked.

"Got nothing to say. There are some truly demented humans out there."

"Yes. But they don't know we're with Ross or where Ross lives, so we should be okay here."

I lugged my two duffel bags up the stairs and to Ross's door, the lemur keeping pace. From the green strip in front of the apartment, I could see that all the lights but one were off in the apartment. Upstairs, the air remained musty, the fresh paint smell having worn off. The door opened.

Ross, with a concerned expression, beckoned us in. "Who would want to bomb you?"

"Somebody that wants him," I said gesturing at the lemur. "But it's just for tonight. We'll check into a hotel while we wait for the verdict to come in, starting tomorrow."

The lemur nodded at Ross who clapped him on the back. "You're welcome to stay here," Ross said.

"We don't want to put your kids at risk," the lemur said.

"There is that," Ross said.

He set us up in the living room—the lemur on the floor, and me on the couch. Tara appeared in her pajamas while we were unrolling sleeping bags. "You're the one my mom is defending?" she said to the lemur.

"Yep."

Tara didn't say anything, but she wore a pleased expression as she went back down the hall to her room. Ross followed her shortly after that, and the lemur fell asleep on the floor while I did an online scan to see whether I could find any sign of Xandra or Evers. There was none. I fell asleep with the laptop open on my lap.

The next morning, the kids woke us early while getting ready for school. The familiar clatter of dishes and pans. The easy banter and the sound of cereal rustling into ceramic bowls. The smell of a pot of coffee brewing. Mike's warm arms around my neck. Tara's quick wave before running out the door. After they left, we rolled up our sleeping bags, packing them back into the closet. Despite the unfamiliar environment, I was overcome by nostalgia. The apartment smelled more like home—that faint heaviness of roasted cumin and onion—than our house did, no doubt because of Ross's cooking. The lemur lay down on the couch and clicked through morning talk shows. I chugged coffee and called the courthouse. The jury still hadn't reached a verdict.

My cell phone emitted the cheerful ping of an email. I clicked the mail icon and read.

> maya,
> has the jury reached its decision? ben whithers
> contacted me and said that you were very gifted
> compared to the other attorneys he's worked with.
> he said that you "got it." so proud of you! it reminds
> me of how you used to stand up for me when we
> were little. you were always meant to be a lawyer
> defending the vulnerable. xoxo j

I tried not to smile. It was nice of my sister to congratulate me, but what I really wanted was the glory and public acknowledgement that came with winning a major, spectacular trial. Afraid of embarrassing myself, I decided to put off answering the email until I learned the verdict.

The lemur looked melancholy, staring out the window and probably not listening to the prattle of the talk show hosts. We decided it would be better for the kids' safety if we checked into a modest hotel near the courthouse, even if we still spent time at Ross's place. At the hotel, they charged me an extra fee for the lemur, who they considered a pet. A bellboy brought up our bags. From the window, we had a view of a dirty stucco wall.

After we settled into the room, I called the police to find out the status of our case. The policewoman who had taken our statements said it appeared that Xandra Jones and Nick Evers had taken a flight out of the country early in the morning. The policewoman couldn't tell me where they'd gone. "We weren't able to confirm it was them, but it does look bad that they fled," the policewoman said. "We plan to continue to investigate. The bomb was somewhat advanced, and you were lucky it didn't do more damage. You need to be more wary of suspicious objects, ma'am." I agreed, to be polite, and hung up.

"Of course it was them," the lemur said, when I told him what the policewoman said. "You said it yourself, that they want to dissect me, study me. And that woman was shady as all hell, outside the courthouse. What do we have to worry about with this Evers character?"

"I used to work with him," I said.

"And?"

"And he's resourceful. But if he's not even in the country, I'm not sure he can harm you."

"Maybe he's got henchmen."

"Doubtful." I said this firmly, without any extraneous words to undermine my authority, but the lemur didn't appear satisfied. He stood by the window examining the stucco with an intent expression for hours. Meanwhile, I tooled around online trying to see if Konakoffee had commented on any other articles or appeared elsewhere. I found a few comments by him here and there, the last made about two weeks before. They were all in relation to the lawsuit, and followed with comments by Cornflake Girl. I studied them, trying to see what they were designed to do. For the most part, they were planting negative opinions about the lemur, suggesting that he needed to be locked up or destroyed.

That night we went over to see Tara, Mike, and Ross, at their invitation, but I could barely focus on them. Ross and the lemur were formal with each other. After we sat down, Ross handed me a glass of Bordeaux so that I could relax. Mike brought out the Scrabble board. While they spelled words like podcast (Tara) and zither (Ross) and strange (Mike), building them up in boxes that gave them triple the points, the lemur and I spelled three-letter words like awe in the boxes that had no exponential value. I couldn't think strategically anymore, and the lemur looked defeated and haggard. The three of them seemed to pity us, but it wasn't as bad a feeling as I thought it would be; in fact, I felt relieved they still cared.

A sensation crept over me, a mixture of guilt and gratitude. For twenty years, I'd wandered around feeling like a puzzle with certain irregular shapes missing. I blamed it on getting married so young—that was how I'd justified my affair with Evers, too—but maybe I was wrong, and what was missing was my own care for the muted ordinary moments, the moments nobody would bother to record or congratulate me for. I stiffened and dismissed the thought. I had to go back into court, hear the verdict, and reveal zero weakness. Right then, I couldn't care about the feeling that something inside me was changing, expanding, breaking.

After I tucked Mike in, Ross walked us to the car. The lemur got in. "This will be over soon," Ross said kindly, instead of reminding me for the fifteenth time that I should have taken the lemur back to Madagascar in the first place. He hugged me, and I could smell the clean laundry smell. For years, that smell had failed to arouse me, but now, knowing there was another version of me out there somewhere, hunting with Evers, this shoulder felt like home, and that was weirdly, unexpectedly exciting, so much so, I almost started crying. As we drove back to the hotel, the lemur patted my arm awkwardly. "You'll be back with them soon," he said. "But damn, Scrabble is some boring shit."

CHAPTER 18

When the jury returned with a verdict the next afternoon, we pushed back into the courtroom and took our seat at the table in the front. I didn't dare speculate about the faces of the jury members—some of them were visibly tense. I focused instead on what I knew was likely true: the trial had been won or lost during voir dire. I pushed my seat forward as Judge McCracken read the materials. He pursed his lips before handing the forms back to the bailiff, who handed the papers to the clerk who read the case information. Eyes cast down, the clerk read, "We the jury of the above entitled action find the following. Question number one: Is the lemur a person? Answer yes. Question number two: Is the mural an original work of art subject to the protections of the Visual Artists Rights Act? Answer no. Question number three: Did the lemur deface the mural? Answer no."

The jury found in our favor. When the jury was polled, the artisanal tofu maker was the only one who found against us, as I'd suspected. Noise erupted from behind us as the audience started expressing dismay and glee. The lemur and I looked at each other, and started to jump up and down. The judge pounded his gavel, and in a few moments everyone quieted down.

The lemur said, "So we're done. Finally. Just like that?"

I tried to put my laptop away with an air of casualness, but the excitement made me giddy.

I won. I won. I won. My whole body was one enormous perfect flame.

But a few moments after the judge pronounced the verdict, I realized that what I felt was not so much the euphoria of victory that I had expected to feel as an excitable despair—the challenge had passed.

I had done it, I had beaten Spencer, and I had done so mostly on my own, and yes, I was relieved that the lemur would live, but it was only in winning that I also saw there was no camaraderie, no belonging, no feeling of contentment in being a winner for me, only the feeling of wanting still more. And was this the only place in America where such a verdict could be reached? Here on the Left Coast? This was the best that it could get for those of us that didn't fit the scripts society told us to live by, and yet it still wasn't quite enough.

I glanced over at Spencer, but he was talking to Brian and putting away his papers. He didn't look at me. He'd called me bright as he fired me, and I wondered if anyone with that kind of authority would think I was bright again, even with this win. How badly I'd needed affirmation, and now that I had it, I realized that what I'd wanted more than that was Spencer's friendship, his recognition of me as his equal. I closed my eyes and swallowed.

The door to the courtroom burst open and the sound of the press waiting, the clicks of digital cameras, and the sounds of reporters chattering outside hit the room like a tsunami. Spencer came over to the desk before leaving. "Congratulations," he said, switching his briefcase to the other hand to shake my hand. I had clung to the idea that if this day of victory came, he would invite me back to work at his firm again. He would smile and say in his old friendly way that I'd done a good job and that he'd been wrong about me and my potential, that I'd made him proud. Even though I already had a father, if Spencer had approved of me, it would have meant I'd arrived, it would have meant everything, and although I secretly bore a sense of shame about how desperately I wanted his approval, the embarrassment never turned into not wanting it anymore, in the usual sour grapes way. His approval would mean that I was, from an objective, distanced perspective, an accomplished trial attorney. We would go get turkey sandwiches on whole wheat. A root beer. Dill pickles on the side. My kids would be back at Spencer's house playing on the Wii. I would be back on the partnership track, and someday rule that firm. Everything I'd lost, I would regain. Things would return to their normal state.

"Thanks, Spencer," I said, trying to keep the panic out of my voice as he turned and simply kept walking toward the door at the back of the courtroom, the increasing physical distance serving only to aggravate my sense that, in spite of winning, I had not won at all. I waited for the lemur to say, "I told you so," but he was silent. As we were about to leave the courtroom, someone tapped my shoulder.

"Brilliant job, Maya," Marcus Spiegelman said.

"Oh, thank you. We couldn't have done it without you." I glanced at the lemur, who looked more annoyed than grateful, and shot him a warning glance. He glowered.

"I hate to disrupt what I'm sure will be a celebratory day for you both, but I wonder if we can get the lemur in for that second follow-up examination we talked about?"

"Of course," I said, taking out my calendar. "How about next week?" We scheduled a date for further testing, and then disappeared into the crowd outside the courtroom.

"Can we get a statement?" somebody called.

"Yes," I said, holding a hand up to silence the lemur. He would wreck the public image I had so carefully crafted if he so much as said a word. "This has been a truly trying time for us, but the support so many of you have given has been remarkable. You've welcomed the lemur into your hearts, and for that, we are truly grateful. Justice was done here today. Thank you." A crowd of photographers snapped photos and the white flashes blinded us. The journalists parted for us this time. We could see a mob through the glass in the front doors and decided to sneak out the back way, taking an alley route to the car.

"I want to go home," the lemur said, sounding short of breath. He climbed into my car and sighed. "I have no desire to be the further subject of research, no matter how helpful that guy's testimony was."

"I know. I was just making the appointment because we were in the courtroom and I didn't want to upset him."

"Seriously? I was certain you'd sold me out to win that case. You know it's partly because of him we won, right?"

"Thanks a lot. We won because of me. Not because of that guy," I said.

"You know, it doesn't diminish you to give credit to somebody else," the lemur said.

"I know that."

"Do you? Because sometimes I hear you say bullshit and realize that maybe this isn't an act and you actually think it's A-OK to be the most selfish and difficult person ever."

"You sound like Ross."

"That poor sucker."

We stopped by my boarded-up house on the way to the hotel. The door appeared to be secure, the duct-tape hinge doing its work. We picked up the mail. Back at the hotel room, I sorted through it and found another postcard of an indri, hanging upside down from a branch. It reminded me of a tarot card of The Hanged Man that a friend in high school used to write poetry about. Where the other postcards had depicted two or more lemurs, this was a solitary lemur with his eyes closed to the photographer. There was something defeated about his face haloed in fur. I turned it over.

On the back was an ink pen illustration of a structure that looked like a barn in the countryside with tiny animals, cattle perhaps, in front of it. A small curved arrow pointed to the entrance of the barn and the word "PERINET" was written in block letters below. I went into my bedroom and pulled out the three letters I had stolen from Evers, comparing the stamps and the handwriting, looking at the illustration. I'd been in bed with Evers one afternoon and telling him about my teenage years. About how I had loved a small bay mare at the stables in the hills near my father's house, and how, after much begging on my part, my father agreed to lease her for me. We had ridden for two years all around the hillside, past the fields of mud-slow cows and through the forest of live oaks, splashing through the dank creeks alive with the sound of frogs croaking. I told him how my horse had bitten off my riding teacher's finger one summer day, and I had never been able to climb on her and ride again without feeling precarious and threatened, even though she had always been absolutely gentle with me. I gave up riding, from fear, shortly afterward, and then high school started, and I didn't think about horses so much as I thought about boys and getting away from the place where I'd started. Then Evers had mentioned that he'd grown up in a forest and he missed his connection to the land. His perfect life would be in a forest somewhere. Like his fantasy about running away to Madagascar, I'd paid little attention to the details of his forest fantasy, because I was focused on my epiphany and a little put off that, as my lover, he wasn't as enraptured by my revelation about myself as I was.

This had to be him, I thought. I wondered if he and Xandra had taken a flight back to Madagascar, back to the collective, and how they could possibly repurpose the collective now that the giant lemur would no longer be considered their discovery. The lemur was eating chips and watching television, and I was overcome with tenderness as I looked at him. I put the postcard next to the other postcard in my duffel bag and opened a room service menu to order champagne to celebrate.

The next day, my voicemail box was full of messages from newspapers, bloggers, and radio shows, all hoping that the lemur could give them an exclusive, or at least a comment. "I wouldn't mind," he said. He drummed his paw on the table. There was a text from Ross asking if the lemur and I wanted to get pizza with the kids before we headed back to Madagascar. I texted back "yes, let's plan on Saturday" and jumped online to find airfares for the following week.

After I purchased our airfare to Madagascar, I noticed an image of the lemur started circulating online, a gif of his face with the question *To Free or Not to Free?* printed in block letters over the top of his head. It was everywhere. "Nobody asked me for my permission," the lemur complained.

We began scheduling a few live appearances for that week. I was reluctant, but it seemed a shame not to cash in on the attention, if only so I could get another job. "You got to let me do the talking," said the lemur. "This is *my* story."

"Isn't it really *our* story? I'm the one who won the trial."

"Nobody likes a braggart."

We appeared on the *Today* show, *The Daily Show*, and *The View*. The audience was crazy about the lemur and he hammered it up— to give them what they wanted, I thought. Later, watching the tapes of these appearances, I would realize it was to give them what *he* wanted. Before I went on one of those shows, I thought the producers made generous use of laugh tracks, or at least that some of the audience was composed of plants in order to trigger a mass laugh response: so few of the things that guests said were funny in that belly-laugh way. But the real crowd laughed spontaneously at the silly stuff the lemur threw out there, and some of his charisma seemed to rub off on me.

It was intoxicating to be on stage with those celebrities—an expansive high that made me feel like I'd binged on sugar, or like my brain was bursting out of my skull. I knew the hosts weren't interested in me. They threw me a bone now and then by asking what it was like to litigate such a high profile case, but as soon as I answered, they shifted back to the lemur, who was making up responses to their questions, talking about "the energy" and "the power" that called him off the wall. Nobody can resist explanations of empowerment these days.

The attention was at least partly mine because I'd fed him the stories he was now telling. His answers were answers that we had rehearsed. His anecdotes about the trial were stories I'd pulled out of him and helped reshape. I'd made him, so I couldn't help but see it as a victory for both of us, even if he was the figurehead, the one everyone wanted to see. It certainly couldn't hurt my legal career to be on television, to be so recognizable as the person who had won *that* trial, and I was right, because as it would turn out even years later, people wanted to be represented by me for the novelty if nothing else.

One of the hosts on *The View* asked what we planned on doing next.

"I'm heading back to Madagascar. It's been fun, but—"

"Oh, really? I understood you had agreed to working with Stranger Laboratories on cloning."

"Naw. I'm on a plane at the end of the week," said the lemur.

I nudged him, but the damage was done.

We stopped by the house to pick up the mail. As we pulled into the driveway, rolling over the newspaper in the driveway, I heard the landline phone ringing inside. I'd missed five calls on my cell, all of them from Marcus Spiegelman or someone from his labs. I played them on speakerphone.

> *Maya, I was shocked to hear that you won't be holding up your end of the bargain. We agreed that if I testified, you and the lemur would cooperate with a second examination. I put my career and my professional judgment on the line for you. You've left me no choice but to ask the courts for an injunction to bring the lemur in for testing.*

"Holy shit," said the lemur. Based on his testimony at trial, I thought that Spiegelman had sampled enough to study the lemur even without our cooperation, but apparently it still wasn't enough.

"We have to leave now," I said. I couldn't open the front door with the duct tape in place. We went to the backyard, and I jimmied a window that I knew was loose. We crawled through and I went upstairs to my room. I stuffed a pile of clothes into a carry-on suitcase with wheels, and gathered my cosmetics into a plastic bag. I searched the nightstand and found my passport. I called Ross and the kids, but since it was the middle of the day, I wasn't surprised when nobody answered. I left a message on Ross's machine: "I'm really sorry that we didn't get to meet and grab a pizza, but I absolutely have to take him now. I'll be back after I take him home, and I hope we can catch up then."

As we were loading a suitcase into the car, a person in a baseball cap came up to me. "Maya Ramesh?" he asked.

"Yes?" He handed me an envelope. "You've been served."

I took the envelope. He eyed the suitcases and took a cell phone out of his pocket. I could hear him say, "Yeah, looks like they're headed to the airport. You might want to tell the client."

We drove to Palo Alto first. The lemur opened the envelope and I glanced at another summons and complaint while we waited at a stop sign. Marcus Spiegelman was suing us for breach of contract and asking the court to ensure we not leave the country. My father drove us to the airport in his BMW. The air-conditioning was on and a gamelan CD played. "You have everything? Your passport? Your e-tickets?" he asked.

"Oh my god, of *course* we have that stuff," I said. He popped open the glove compartment and handed me an envelope packed with traveler's checks. The sweet, strange tinkling of the gamelan felt like we were floating on water somewhere instead of inside a car speeding down a California freeway. "Dad, you didn't need to do this. We're set for money. We're fine."

"Can't hurt to be prepared. Separate it out in case you get pickpocketed." Sighing, I put a few traveler's checks into my carry-on. Sitting in the front seat, the lemur stayed quiet.

"Go, go! We need to get a flight now, or we'll be stopped."
As we drove north on the freeway, the lemur tapped me on the
shoulder and pointed. On a billboard was the gif, the image of
him that had been circulating on the internet, perhaps one million times larger than he was in real life, looking out over the
smog. At that size, his expression looked more dangerous than
alluring and he was holding a cell phone to his ear.

"I'm an ad," he said. I couldn't tell from his face if he was
thrilled or disgusted; perhaps he was both.

At the airport, we were waiting in line to exchange our ticket
when a teenager spotted the lemur and screamed, "It's him!" A
crowd surrounded us. They called for autographs, waving their
pens and smartphones around to take pictures. He was bathed in
the furious camera flashes, his black fur shiny in the rapid onset
of lights. I broke away and bought the ticket. When I returned,
the lemur was buried in a dense mob, and for a moment as I
pushed through the bodies, I thought I would be unable to pull
him out in time for our flight. "Get in line," one woman snarled at
me as she shoved a pen at the lemur for his autograph.

"He's with me, you dingbat," I said in irritation, trying to drag
him out of the mob, which darkened within seconds. I couldn't
breathe and I imagined that the lemur couldn't either. Suddenly,
someone in the group started pulling back on his other arm. Another person grabbed his legs. They yanked so fiercely, so ada-
mantly I thought they would pull his limbs out of their sockets.
Somebody started hitting a person who was pulling at his legs.
We were all pulling, and I wanted to let go, but I also didn't want
to let go, because I was certain that if I did, they would kill him
in their enthusiasm.

"Let go!" he screamed as a pencil stabbed into his arm. His
scream was primal, a call of self-defense against the attackers, a
cry so pure and frightened there was nothing in it to deify.

Everyone, all the humans including me, let go with an expression of fear and revulsion. "OMG. Get over yourself. You're just a monkey, for fucksakes," one boy said as he walked away. "A fat, dirty monkey."

The mob dispersed. The lemur's limb was disjointed from his shoulder and his fur was mussed, his face cut, and there was a deep puncture wound from the pencil, a pinkish mouth in his flesh from which ruby-red blood was oozing. We hurried to our gate, but they weren't boarding yet. I took him to the restroom and washed his wound. It wasn't as deep as it had looked initially, and I created a makeshift bandage with a strip of a T-shirt in my suitcase. When I'd tied the cotton cloth around the wound, I told the lemur to go wait for me by the gate while I finished up in the bathroom.

When I exited, I could see the lemur on my smartphone, talking and gesturing animatedly. "So there is another one of me. You don't really need me," he explained.

I seized the phone from him and looked at the caller ID. It was Spiegelman, so I hung up on him. "Did you tell him where we were?" I asked.

"Never. I just told him he could get the same biological information from the other lemur, if he could find him."

"You sold out the other lemur?" My body went cold.

"Spiegelman wasn't in court the day we found out. I thought you'd be pleased I figured out a way to make him lose interest in me."

"You didn't have to do that to the other lemur. You put him at risk. We already won, and we're going to board in half an hour."

The lemur shrugged and scratched his fat distended belly. As we waited, I had nothing to do for the first time since Spencer had let me go. I'd forgotten my laptop. I kept expecting Spiegelman or the police to pick us up, but nobody came, and finally, they boarded our row.

CHAPTER 19

The lemur and I arrived at the Tana airport on a smoky-orange afternoon, hovering over a range of eroded brownish mountains and a patchwork of unevenly stitched fields before touching down. After braving the baggage claim, we stumbled into the humid smog. We stood on the side of the roundabout and tried to flag down a driver in the line of clean, cream-colored Renault 4s outside the airport.

Finally a car stopped. The driver, leaning over the passenger side to unlock the door, grinned at me, a kind of insulting leer without any reason I could discern. Was I dressed wrong? Too Western? I couldn't say. The heavy traffic flowed slowly past ramshackle houses, stacked on the crimson hillside like hatboxes. The driver turned on the air-conditioning. I glanced through the back window at the shimmer of lights as the airport receded.

The driver spoke to the lemur in French. "He wants to know if we want to stay in town," the lemur said. "I think we should just head out to the Perinet Reserve."

We sped past women draping snowy lace from a line that stretched across a backdrop of a chocolate-brown lake reflecting mountains, and wound our way through mountains scrubby with low, stout trees, and avoided men herding zebu down the red road. "How are you feeling?" I asked the lemur, who looked, quite frankly, sick. In this new environment, I could see even more clearly what he was supposed to look like, instead of the gradual mess he had become during the trial. He was supposed to be spry, perched on the edge of the cab seat, ready to be in among the trees. Instead, he was slouched and slumped, his furry belly oozing over the top of the seatbelt and obscuring the strap from view.

I lowered the window and stuck my head out. The wind whipped through my hair. I'd been waiting for this wild, unbridled space.

Along the roadside walked a lithe woman cradling her baby in her arms. Up ahead, cattle were being herded through the sun-dappled field. Hours later, the land ripened into rainforests, the flurry of leaves sometimes so thick that no sunlight made it through the leaves, and then cleared to reveal sky the intense hue of a strawberry daiquiri. Eventually, the sun slipped behind the palms looming over the road, and a crescent moon sailed into view.

We drove and drove until darkness clotted around us, arriving at the Perinet Reserve at eight. We didn't talk much. I could tell the lemur was tired. Our driver left us at a lodge, but because it was so dark and the flight had been so taxing, the lemur decided to wait until morning to hike into the rainforest. "One last dinner?" he asked. His once-beautiful voice was merely a croak. We dropped our suitcases off in our cabin. I changed his bandage.

We decided to dine at a hotel in the railroad station, where tourists speaking French and English congregated around the teak bar. Enormous, stout-necked jars of different kinds of rum—gnarled vanilla pods floating in alcohol, chunks of ginger sloughing off thin strings of spiciness while settled at the bottom of another—were stored at the back of the bar. I wolfed down a dinner of rice, vegetables, and zebu meat. The lemur picked at his vegetables.

Our waiter placed another tumbler of vanilla rum in front of me. He smiled and said with an air of familiarity, "How have you been?"

"Do you know me?" I asked.

"Yes?" he answered. I couldn't tell if he really recognized me, or didn't quite understand the question, but drinking this particularly potent form of alcohol cleared some of the fog that had set in from jet lag. I overheard some British and German tourists at the next table, talking in English about a collective tucked into a vanilla farm down the road. According to these people, the collective was run by cynical expatriate Americans who used the farming and export of vanilla as a front for other less wholesome activities, including the hunting of indri. Was this Xandra Jones's collective? It had to be. How many of them could there be?

I was startled when I heard one of them say the name "Evers," or were they just using it as a word, as in *I don't ever want to go there again?* They mentioned a rave.

"Don't get any ideas," the lemur said to me in a gravelly rasp.

"But it won't take long. We'll stop in for a minute and see what it's all about," I pleaded. I noticed the British tourists were closing out their tab.

"You don't care about a collective," the lemur said. "What is this really about?"

I pulled out the postcard and put it on the table. "Okay, don't overreact, but I want to see what's going on with this." I had to know, I had to solve this mystery—I had to see Evers one last time.

"No. We're not gonna follow that rabbit hole any further, not after that bomb incident."

"But aren't you the least bit curious?"

"No. We are not going to god-knows-where so that you can chase whoever or whatever you now think will bring you recognition this time. Haven't we walked down that road before? Have you learned nothing?"

"I don't know what you're getting so worked up over. We're here, after all. Tomorrow morning we'll be hiking into the preserve and just like that," I said, snapping my fingers, "it will all be over. Quick, quick! They're leaving. Excuse me, but we heard you mention a rave. Do you mind if we join you?" I grabbed my bag and the lemur's arm.

The woman smiled at me, pulling her hair into a green scrunchie as she placed some traveler's checks on the waiter's bill. "The more the merrier."

The lemur sighed, but didn't walk away. We joined the group as they moved down the road into a blackness so thick and cold that when I saw my breath in front of me, it looked like a cloud of cigarette smoke, thick and pulsing, lit by just a few flashlights on the tourists' smartphones. They spoke about the rave, but they also talked about somebody named Eddie, about a corrupt politician back home, about how inefficient they found the world outside of England. One of them turned to me and asked where I was from. When I said America, he said, "No, but like India? Or Bangladesh? Or Sri Lanka?" So I said "America" again, and then he didn't talk to me anymore.

Alongside the road, small eyes of nocturnal animals gleamed. There was a rustling, a constant rustling that suggested some parallel world was operating in the grass, with its own kingdoms and crimes and sorrows. "I don't like this," the lemur said again. He was breathing heavily, as if he was exhausted. In about twenty minutes, we saw the enormous farmhouse, faintly illuminated by the lights inside, as if a spaceship had landed in the field there. I thought a vanilla plantation would reek of vanilla, but the air was a muddle of grassy notes, the coldness it imparted more apparent than any fragrance from the land.

"Should we go to the door?" I heard someone in the group ask as we approached the farmhouse. Nobody answered, but in a few moments, we found ourselves standing at the front door, which looked remarkably like the one in the postcard. Sound was trying to grind its way out of the building, the *whump! whump!* of an acid house beat squeezed out of whatever cracks existed in the structure. The woman wearing the green scrunchie knocked and then knocked again.

"Why don't you just try the door?" one man said.

The heavy door was pushed open and we trailed in after the group into the red-and-blue flashing lights. A deejay was spinning vinyl with a dissonant bass line in the corner of an enormous room in what looked from the inside like a warehouse, rather than a farm. Loads of younger people of all different ethnicities, most wearing sweaters and stocking caps and ragged jeans, were dancing, or moving in a way that pantomimed club dancing, in the center of the room. The crowd was hypnotic. It was a little like watching a jellyfish pulse back and forth, first migrating across the room this way, then stepping back in the other direction.

Some of the people around me were sucking on pacifiers, some were waving glowing light sticks in time to the music. A black man wearing a lamba handed me a bouquet of pee-colored lollipops and disappeared. I wondered for a moment if it was the same man I'd seen at Evers's penthouse, but pushed past that thought. The lemur frowned.

"Okay, you see? Are you getting it yet?" he said. I could tell he was trying to yell, but I could barely hear him over the sound. "There's nothing here for us. Let's go."

"We just got here. Let's look around and see what's going on," I said. Carrying the lollipops, I pulled him with me into the throng of people toward one of the walls. The bruising shoulders of various ravers banged into me here and there no less than they had back in my mosh pit days in late high school. Everyone was friendly, so much so that anyone who touched me left their hands too long on my arm or the top of my head. There was a vacancy, and yet there was also a euphoria that was unmistakable and intoxicating, even experienced secondhand.

I was dragging the lemur along with me through the crowd. Someone tried to grab my free hand to pull me into the dance, but I yanked away, focusing instead on the concrete walls, which were dimly lit with candles lodged in wall sconces. At another point in our path through the crowd, I noticed a familiar head, a familiar bald spot bobbing through the dancing mob. Convinced it was Evers, I said, "Come on." We followed that balding head toward the center of the mob before the person turned so that I could see his profile, his Roman nose and sparse, pale eyebrows; it was someone much younger than Evers. We were stuck for a few moments, watching not-Evers dance, and then the lemur moved toward a different wall and I followed.

We traversed the long wall before encountering a door that would have escaped our notice from across the room, so closely did it blend with the wall, so fine were the four lines between it and its frame and the floor. The knob was a nondescript brass. "Should we go in?" asked the lemur.

"I guess." We opened the door and stepped into a dark room lit only by oil lamps on small tables that circled the room. The floor was covered in straw, like a barn. But the strangest thing of all was the sound: a recording of the indri's song was playing in the background, its mournful calls accentuating the darkness. I looked at the lemur, but he was advancing toward the center of the room. I placed my purse on the table by the door.

We moved forward for a closer look. Four stark white columns rested in the middle of the room, none of them very tall, none of them ornamented in any way. They stood far enough from the door that we could see all four in their entirety, almost architectural in their simplicity and solidity, their sense that they were giving shelter to something undefined—surely the effect that the person who had built them intended. "Paper?" asked the lemur, coughing as we moved closer to the columns. Too late, I noticed that the door had thudded shut behind us. The sounds of the rave were muffled behind the door and all we heard was the recorded indri song.

The columns were indeed made of paper. Sheafs of paper of varying textures stacked to desk-height. At the bottom of the stacks were packs of paper in olive-green file folders, similar to those that we had used in the cabinets at Spencer's office. At the top were various newspaper clippings. I tried to read them. By the dim lamplight, we deciphered a few lines from those pages.

Donate money today to show your support of this glorious mural symbolizing Oakland's capacity to grow. (Indrilove.tumblr.com)

Both alienating and familiar, Brian Turner's mural represented the dark, yet light forces of the wilderness as they took over a dense city. (San Francisco Chronicle)

Why should you care? Because this lemur is a monstrosity, said a zoologist in the courtroom today. (All Things Great and Small blog)

"What is this?" the lemur said, scanning the headlines. "Were you sending clippings to someone?"

I shook my head and circled the columns, looking at the top pages. The top pages of the other columns were on legal pleading paper with the original caption of the lawsuit: *Brian Turner v. Peter Eustachio et al.* A mediation brief. The first amended complaint. A page of interrogatory answers.

"I don't get it," said the lemur. "Is this supposed to be art?" He started coughing hard.

Behind me, I heard the door to the room opening in the darkness and the sound of acid house washed around us, drowned out the indri song. A dark figure was silhouetted in the doorway. For a moment, I smelled a familiar cologne, an exotic smell of Old Spice and decay. I couldn't see the man's features, but I knew and mistrusted the smell of him, which I'd smelled any number of afternoons.

"Evers?" I said. At the sound of my voice, the man bumped into the oil lamp on the side table. He turned abruptly and hurried back out the way he came, letting the door slam behind. "Evers, wait!"

We ran to the door, knocking into each other at the entrance. It wouldn't open. I kept tugging. We both started screaming, but we knew nobody could hear us over the acid house. The song of the indri sounded increasingly menacing, like an army of them were descending upon us.

Oil from the overturned lamp soaked into the straw on the floor, followed by the reach of a pale, blue-hearted flame that shot toward the ceiling. And then another. The intensity of the heat, the smoke. After looking at all those clippings, I had the hysterical thought of tabloid headlines the day after: *Burned Alive!*

I looked around for a window, but saw only outlines of forms in the dark beyond the flames. The lemur kept tugging at the door. "Help me," he said, making small gasping sounds.

Somehow, we managed to tug the door open. Perhaps Evers had been trying to trap us, but had done a bad job. There was no way of knowing. I grabbed the lemur's arm and pulled him with me out into the party.

"Fire!" we shouted. "Fire!"

The music was too loud and the red-and-blue-tinted partygoers were entirely absorbed with their pacifiers, their glow sticks, and their lollipops. They hopped around in a trance, circling each other. From inside the larger room, the only sound you could hear was the acid house. A few people were talking but who knew what they were saying. A couple of people looked up and smiled lazily, evidently thinking we were offering some kind of entertainment, rather than a warning. The lemur got up in one woman's face and yelled, "There's a fire! You have to evacuate!"

"Yeah, man. I mean, monkey," said the woman. "Hey, you're soft. So soft. You look like that monkey that's been in the newspapers!" The lemur gave up. We pushed through the crowd of dancers toward the front door. I scanned the partygoers. Far away, by the other wall, I saw her standing there. My double with her long curly hair and scarlet lipstick, wearing her trench coat and a feline expression. She was me and not me. She was standing at the periphery of a group of men wearing lambas and was watching me try to exit the warehouse.

I raised a hand to greet her and gestured back at the room shouting, "Fire!" But the sound of the music was so loud, I couldn't hear my own voice. Perhaps I'd thought a man had tried to trap us and it had actually been my double? Perhaps they were working together? But if they were really trying to trap us, we wouldn't have gotten out, would we?

The lemur grabbed my arm with his chilly, rough paw. We pushed out of the room into the cold night. I looked back one last time, but my double was gone.

We walked back through the short stretch of field to the dark road. "It was this direction." I stumbled after him up the hill to the dark road where the only sounds were of frogs, insects, the wind in the trees, and the only smell I could identify was cow patties. I wondered if I'd gotten some on my boots, but it was too dark to see. I rubbed the bottom of my boot against the grass.

We were far more vulnerable than we had been at the bar at the hotel, dizzy with hot smoke and still panicking over how easily Evers and my double, or someone else, had trapped us. After a few steps, I heard a loud rustle and the intense sound of bursting. We looked back. A conflagration was starting to swallow part of the structure from the inside, and people were pouring out of the front door yelling in various languages and dispersing in all directions, some toward us, but most running pell-mell out into the field. If Evers was among those people, I would never know. The fire behind them rose high enough that it cast long shadows in front of them as they ran through the grass.

"Run!" said the lemur, bounding forward. I could barely see him in the dark, but I followed the road, not much caring whether he was with me. Behind me other people were running and screaming and swearing. I stopped and I heard him stop, too.

"What do you think all that meant?" I asked.

"Fuck if I know. I'm just glad we made it out alive." His voice had grown terribly hoarse. It was almost gone. His eyes were dull. On a dark night like this, they usually glowed with a supernatural intensity, but tonight the color was damped down.

"Are you okay?"

"Not really," he said.

"Just hang in there. You'll be back in the woods tomorrow morning. I promise."

"When have I heard that before?" he asked.

We had already gone up the driveway to the lodge and crossed the bridge over the lake that the lodge was built over when I said, "Shit. Oh, shit! I left my purse with my passport and money on the table back in the room with the sculpture." The lemur looked at me.

"Say something! Oh my god," I said.

"Anyone back home have a photocopy?" he asked.

"Yeah, my dad can get the copy that Ross has. But there's no bank near us, the stuff in the purse was everything." I took the hotel key from my pocket and opened the front door of our cabin. We went inside the small room. I grabbed one of the twin beds and crawled in with my clothes still on. The lemur decided to take a shower before turning in for the night. He'd given up trying to sing, and the only sound that emanated from the bathroom was the sound of running water. When he emerged, I was already half-asleep. He went to his bed and pulled the beaded metal string attached to the desk lamp and the room went dark.

The next morning, we hiked up a narrow trail into the rainforest, not sure where we were going. We climbed up an embankment where the trees cleared and we could see the forested mountains in the distance and the vast vista with its ashen fields of cassava, maize, rice paddies, the graphite mines, lumber yards, and the arecas blowing in the cool, damp wind. Enormous butterflies floated up from the grass and scattered like flame-colored rose petals shaken from stems. Every once in a while, I spotted an enormous chameleon or a brilliant, giant beetle, an odd treasure in the grass.

The lemur trailed behind me. I sounded like a high school gym teacher as I urged him up the hillside. I heard the sounds of other indri calling from faraway and the sound, at once familiar and yet perpetually foreign, chilled me to the bone. The lemur lay down on the floor of the rainforest. He looked up at me and I rubbed his stomach, the way I used to do for Tara and Mike when they were sick. His eyes were so weak, he had to shade them from the cool, faint morning light as it drizzled through the leaves.

"You just have to make it through for a few more minutes. I'm sure you'll feel better."

"Not gonna happen," said the lemur.

"It is. You have to believe," I said, even though I didn't know what sort of belief might revive him, what sort of story I could tell in order to get him back on his feet. "We didn't come this far just for you to miss your homecoming."

He mumbled something. I was sitting on my knees, my knee-caps touching his side, leaning over his face, but I could barely hear his words, whether they were wise or banal or tender. I closed my eyes. It was a freefall, a feeling of rapid descent through space and time. A sinking, lucid, controlled realization that, in moments, I was about to be utterly alone here in the forest, and it was the worst feeling I'd ever had.

He exhaled. The knowing brightness slipped out of his eyes, a shadow passing before them. I touched him lightly at first, but even before my fingers felt his cold, dull, black fur and the un-moving flesh beneath that, I knew he was gone.

It was only after his death that I lay down next to him in the long, papery leaves, wanting to bridge the distance between us, the living and the dead. I lay there for a long while and the sounds of the indri faded as the morning sun burned hotter. The after-noon was long and stark. I examined the jigsaw blue of the sky through trees, smelled the dark wet ground. I closed my eyes for a while. As dusk approached, the sounds of the other indri rose in volume, and perhaps I was imagining it, but they seemed to be singing dirges, songs of mourning at a higher pitch than usual, more haunting and lovely. I opened my eyes, and I was surrounded by indri, ordinary indri. Perhaps a hundred of them. They were huddled around the giant lemur, staring at his dead body, staring at me.

I knew they wouldn't hurt me, but I stood and moved away from his stiffening body because they were claiming him as one of their own. I didn't look back at the body that wasn't him anymore. I walked down the trail to the lodge, avoiding eye contact as I crossed the bridges of the lake that the lodge rested on, past the large plots of garden, and up a path to the cabin where my room was.

I called my father straightaway from the disposable phone in my bag and he answered on the third ring. "So you arrived. Is the lemur back in the forest?" he asked.

"No, he's gone. He's—" I knew there was anger inside me somewhere still, if only I could pinpoint a lightning rod with which to channel it. But there was nobody here to see me, nobody to judge me but myself. I explained that I didn't have my passport anymore, without going into truthful detail about why. I was blubbering, the sort of crying where syllables seem switched and mangled or run through a shredder before coming out, but I could tell that my father understood what I was saying, which seemed a minor miracle.

"Stay there," my father said, taking down the details of my location. "It may take a couple of days to get a flight out there, but we'll get you home."

I crawled into the bed, a low, hard affair with tough pillows, stiff sheets, and a bright orange coverlet. And from that location, curled up into a kidney bean shape, I could see myself still lying in the same place years into the future, aware that there was nothing for me at home, if home was what you'd call that elaborate boarded-up house in Oakland, empty of Ross and the kids and the numerous objects that somehow symbolized our souls, objects collected over many years. Everything I'd poured myself into had been empty. And worse than them being empty, something that some people seemed to realize, was me believing so hard in the value of having them. What killed me was the hours I'd spent to make all this happen, the many years that were now lost to Spencer and his idea that there was any redemption in the law. Yes, it was a privilege to represent someone, to help them, a privilege at least to represent some of them, but the glowing, glistering ocean of time, always endlessly vanishing both in front of me and behind me, was irretrievable. That was the lie, wasn't it, of those vampiric billable hours? That you could mark time with tasks meant to push ahead the wheels of commerce and capitalism, and feel productive and happening and up, fueled by caffeine and cocktails and all manner of things with pretty, varnished surfaces, when really your soul was being ravaged.

I heard tourists pass by the window, talking in a mix of German and British English. The orange shades were drawn and the room stayed so dark, I didn't know if it was day or night. With the doors closed, the perfume of ylang-ylang, embedded somewhere in the room, grew more powerful, but I didn't have the energy to locate the smell and rid myself of it. I was here and yet I wasn't here. I was shoveling through my regrets like regret was going out of style. I believe days passed.

I took the lodge phone off the hook and sat in the darkness, thinking about the time Ross and I were on a boat in South America for our tenth anniversary, the twinkling in the water like shooting stars, and how I told him I was cold, that we should leave that moment because I was so sure there would be more of those moments. And that was the last time I could remember being happy. It's easy to celebrate firsts because their novelty calls attention to them: my first kiss, Ross and I going on our first date to a Bharatanatyam recital he enjoyed more than I did, our shabby first apartment with a broken furnace, Tara's first birthday, Mike's first birthday. But what about lasts? There were just as many lasts that I'd never mourned because I didn't know enough in the moment to know something important and irreplaceable was ending. Most of those last moments were entirely forgotten and it could be months or even years before I started to notice the absence of what was lost.

Finally, I dragged my body into the shower. I turned on the water, waiting for it to get hot, and pulled the curtain away from a tiny open window. The water turned only lukewarm, but I stepped into the small enclosure and rinsed away the dirt and grime from the fire, the hike, and the flight before that. I'd like to say I felt purified after the shower, that it made me feel I'd cleansed my immortal soul, but my skin felt pruney and sensitive, scrubbed raw, and when even the concentrated blast of rain from a showerhead couldn't make me feel right, I wondered if I would ever feel a sense of equilibrium again.

I left my cabin and went to see the person at the welcome desk in the lobby. I asked if she could arrange to squeeze me into the next group of visitors on a horseback ride through Perinet. I hadn't ridden a horse in twenty years, but I had a vague recollection of the wind, the warmth, the feeling of being held aloft.

After she made the arrangements, I sat down to breakfast at the lodge restaurant. After a couple of days of not eating, I hadn't the stomach for anything on the menu. I drank coffee boiled with sugarcane and watched other people on their vacations eating and talking and laughing.

A man at the table next to me was sitting with his laptop closed. "Excuse me," I said. "Could I use your laptop to send an important email? I forgot mine at home." He nodded.

Inside my inbox, there were many new emails, mostly interview requests for the lemur, but a few asking to speak with me, too. I deleted all of them. There was no email from Evers. The more I thought about it, I wondered about whether my double had been the sender of those messages, whether my double had been Konakoffee. Those odd answers. How she had known I would receive the postcard and when. How she always seemed a step ahead of me, almost as if she was me. When I thought of Evers, the way he would drive into me as we had sex or pull his shirt on afterward, I used to feel a tingling sensation. Now, there was nothing. There was relief in this. I began typing an email.

To: julieramesh@gmail.com
From: mayaramesh@gmail.com

Julie - I just wanted to say thank you for your help, for securing Ben Whithers and also for, strangely, continuing to believe in me. I also want to say I'm sorry. Sixteen years ago, I thought that telling the truth meant white-knuckling it and accepting the worst things people thought about you. I thought there was a right answer and I was somehow privy to it. I thought that you had to give other people what they wanted, instead of finding a balance, and I resented you for marching to a different drummer. I was wrong on all counts.

Love,
Maya

A few people huddled by the front desk and I guessed that they were the group slated to take the horses. Our guide showed up shortly and we hurried out along a path to the stables. The guide gave me a bay horse, who stomped the sand of the stables repeatedly. After a couple of unsuccessful tries, I heaved myself into the saddle.

We followed our guide up one of the trails through puddles

and grass that looked electric, standing straight up in the light. As we ascended the hill in the shade of the forest, we passed a woman with voluptuous hips and a small child carrying baskets. The guide motioned to the west at a lake glittering like a billion sapphire stones. I could hear tweeting, scurrying, and rustling as we pushed past leaves, and the clopping of many hooves wearing away at the damp, packed earth. The forest was so lustrously green that the air itself seemed a living, writhing mass. The other tourists spoke loudly to each other, spying countless marvels along the way, bugs as big as my hand, clouds of butterflies, plump birds wearing saffron feathers, coiled, sleeping chameleons that looked like extensions of the ferns, frogs as luminous and orange as jalebis. I fell behind, taking it all in.

I heard somebody behind me, trying to catch up on horseback, but out of breath. There was no point in turning, so I pulled my horse over to the side to let whoever it was pass.

"Hey," said Ross's familiar voice.

"What are you doing here?" He was riding a gray mare. Although I was more relieved than I felt I had a right to be, I also didn't know what to make of his sudden appearance. I'd thought my father would come get me.

"They told me where to find you. I brought a copy of your passport," he said. "And money. You need those, right? Or maybe not. This seems like some kind of paradise."

"Thanks." I was trying to figure out what to say. It seemed an apology was in order, but anything I could say would be meager in comparison to what I owed. We rode along in silence for the whole day. We rode along the top of the hill as an evening pink blossomed on the horizon. Although we were riding at a decent pace, we fell further and further behind the group and the guide. The only sounds were those of our two horses, the little creatures around us and our breathing, which together constituted a different kind of conversation. I broke first. "So . . ." I said.

"So . . . I have some time off work. What are your plans? When do you go back to work?" Ross tilted his head. No shaving for a couple of days had left his jaw shadowy. His eyes were hooded, the smile lines even more pronounced than usual, I supposed with a lack of sleep, or maybe it had been years since I had really looked at him. Though we were here on horseback in a foreign country and approaching middle age (if not already there), if I wanted to, I could conjure up the oak-studded hills by my father's house, at the community college where we met when I was nineteen, the large, thickset black-and-white cows with nostrils like soup tureens, the sound of skateboards against the glittering concrete parking lot, and the talk, all of the talk, and therefore all of the world opening up in front of us, a blinding kind of optimism about the future. *I think I like you.*

"Do you really want to know?" I said, patting my horse on the rear.

"Certainly."

"I'm going to start my own practice. I'm going to do things my way."

"That's going to be a lot of work," he said. Seeing my surprise that he had pulled back from a critical comment, he laughed. "What? I'm trying."

"I know," I said.

"Should we try again?" he asked.

Attention spans were so short that by the time we returned to America the lemur billboard had already been taken down. Evidently people weren't interested in buying phones associated with an endangered animal. And my passion, the trial, was endangered, too, going the way of legends, a victim of insurance companies and their settlements.

A few years after the billboard was removed, the fading mural by the lake—now empty of lemurs—was torn down with the building, and the physical copies of its photographs were destroyed or lost, replaced in some instances by a retro technology similar to the hologram. People weren't interested in the lemur lawsuit anymore. The memes and news articles about it were still accessible on the government's new data communications network, but everyone knew that the government had doctored our histories, had prepared copies of everything and everyone—clones—in the event of a nuclear holocaust, and the indri could very well be made up, could easily be another piece of propaganda.

Years later, however, our grandchildren would ask me to tell them the story of the lemur and we would gather around, toasting s'mores over a virtual fire, while I told them about the trial. Ross, white-haired and adjusting the hearing chip implanted in his failing ear, would stay quiet through the retelling, maintaining a skeptical silence.

Sometimes, I still thought about my double. Was she the original version of me, living a kind of dark happily-ever-after with Evers, or had they perished? I searched my name online, but there were no new entries to the search results. The blog entry in which my double had been mentioned had fallen by several pages, and my solo practice and news clippings about my trial wins were at the top of the search results; nobody but me was searching for that other Maya Ramesh. There were no obituaries for her or Evers.

On that day when Ross arrived to take me home, we turned the horses around and retraced our steps back down the darkening trail. Rain fell, pinging softly at first and then hard and true. From somewhere in the back of the forest, an indri called, and then another, and another, and although the melancholy symphony of song made my heart constrict, knowing what had been lost and